INVASION!
"THE TALES ARE ALL TRUE. THE DEMONS HAVE RETURNED."

General Kellen of the Klingon Empire spoke to his crew, his normally calm voice brimming with terror and anger. "They have come back and they are on that ship out there.

"It will take all of us to defeat them," the general continued. "Call the Empire for reinforcements. Track that ship, but do not go near it. I will go for help."

"For help?" his first officer asked. "From where? From whom?"

"We need a demon to fight demons," the general said at last. "I will will get one. I will get Captain James T. Kirk."

Look for STAR TREK Fiction from Pocket Books

Star Trek: The Original Series

The Return
The Ashes of Eden
Federation
Sarek
Best Destiny
Shadows on the Sun
Probe
Prime Directive
The Lost Years
Star Trek VI: The Undiscovered Country
Star Trek V: The Final Frontier
Star Trek IV: The Voyage Home
Spock's World
Enterprise
Strangers from the Sky
Final Frontier

#1 Star Trek: The Motion Picture
#2 The Entropy Effect
#3 The Klingon Gambit
#4 The Covenant of the Crown
#5 The Prometheus Design
#6 The Abode of Life
#7 Star Trek II: The Wrath of Khan
#8 Black Fire
#9 Triangle
#10 Web of the Romulans
#11 Yesterday's Son
#12 Mutiny on the Enterprise
#13 The Wounded Sky
#14 The Trellisane Confrontation
#15 Corona
#16 The Final Reflection
#17 Star Trek III: The Search for Spock
#18 My Enemy, My Ally
#19 The Tears of the Singers
#20 The Vulcan Academy Murders
#21 Uhura's Song
#22 Shadow Lord
#23 Ishmael
#24 Killing Time
#25 Dwellers in the Crucible
#26 Pawns and Symbols
#27 Mindshadow
#28 Crisis on Centaurus
#29 Dreadnought!
#30 Demons
#31 Battlestations!
#32 Chain of Attack
#33 Deep Domain
#34 Dreams of the Raven
#35 The Romulan Way
#36 How Much for Just the Planet?
#37 Bloodthirst
#38 The IDIC Epidemic
#39 Time for Yesterday
#40 Timetrap
#41 The Three-Minute Universe
#42 Memory Prime
#43 The Final Nexus
#44 Vulcan's Glory
#45 Double, Double
#46 The Cry of the Onlies
#47 The Kobayashi Maru
#48 Rules of Engagement
#49 The Pandora Principle
#50 Doctor's Orders
#51 Enemy Unseen
#52 Home Is the Hunter
#53 Ghost Walker
#54 A Flag Full of Stars
#55 Renegade
#56 Legacy
#57 The Rift
#58 Face of Fire
#59 The Disinherited
#60 Ice Trap
#61 Sanctuary
#62 Death Count
#63 Shell Game
#64 The Starship Trap
#65 Windows on a Lost World
#66 From the Depths
#67 The Great Starship Race
#68 Firestorm
#69 The Patrian Transgression
#70 Traitor Winds
#71 Crossroad
#72 The Better Man
#73 Recovery
#74 The Fearful Summons
#75 First Frontier
#76 The Captain's Daughter
#77 Twilight's End
#78 The Rings of Tautee
#78 Invasion 1: First Strike

Star Trek: The Next Generation

Kahless
Star Trek Generations
All Good Things
Q-Squared
Dark Mirror
Descent
The Devil's Heart
Imzadi
Relics
Reunion
Unification
Metamorphosis
Vendetta
Encounter at Farpoint

#1 Ghost Ship
#2 The Peacekeepers
#3 The Children of Hamlin
#4 Survivors
#5 Strike Zone
#6 Power Hungry
#7 Masks
#8 The Captains' Honor
#9 A Call to Darkness
#10 A Rock and a Hard Place
#11 Gulliver's Fugitives
#12 Doomsday World
#13 The Eyes of the Beholders
#14 Exiles
#15 Fortune's Light
#16 Contamination
#17 Boogeymen
#18 Q-in-Law
#19 Perchance to Dream
#20 Spartacus
#21 Chains of Command
#22 Imbalance
#23 War Drums
#24 Nightshade
#25 Grounded
#26 The Romulan Prize
#27 Guises of the Mind
#28 Here There Be Dragons
#29 Sins of Commission
#30 Debtors' Planet
#31 Foreign Foes
#32 Requiem
#33 Balance of Power
#34 Blaze of Glory
#35 Romulan Stratagem
#36 Into the Nebula
#37 The Last Stand
#38 Dragon's Honor
#39 Rogue Saucer
#40 Possession
#41 Invasion 2: The Soldiers of Fear

Star Trek: Deep Space Nine

Warped
The Search

#1 Emissary
#2 The Siege
#3 Bloodletter
#4 The Big Game
#5 Fallen Heroes
#6 Betrayal
#7 Warchild
#8 Antimatter
#9 Proud Helios
#10 Valhalla
#11 Devil in the Sky
#12 The Laertian Gamble
#13 Station Rage
#14 The Long Night
#15 Objective: Bajor

Star Trek: Voyager

#1 Caretaker
#2 The Escape
#3 Ragnarok
#4 Violations
#5 Incident at Arbuk
#6 The Murdered Sun
#7 Ghost of a Chance
#8 Cybersong

For orders other than by individual consumers, Pocket Books grants a discount on the purchase of **10 or more** copies of single titles for special markets or premium use. For further details, please write to the Vice-President of Special Markets, Pocket Books, 1633 Broadway, New York, NY 10019-6785, 8th Floor.

For information on how individual consumers can place orders, please write to Mail Order Department, Simon & Schuster Inc., 200 Old Tappan Road, Old Tappan, NJ 07675.

FIRST STRIKE

DIANE CAREY

INVASION! concept by John J. Ordover and Diane Carey

POCKET BOOKS
New York London Toronto Sydney Tokyo Singapore

An *Original* Publication of POCKET BOOKS

POCKET BOOKS, a division of Simon & Schuster Inc.
1230 Avenue of the Americas, New York, NY 10020

This book is published by Pocket Books, a division of Simon & Schuster Inc., under exclusive license from Paramount Pictures.

ISBN: 0-671-54002-5

First Pocket Books printing July 1996

10 9 8 7 6 5 4 3 2

Printed in the U.S.A.

SPACEQUAKE

Danger is never the barometer of an officer's conduct.

—Joseph Conrad
Lord Jim

Chapter One

"THE SUN IS GROWING!"

"Impossible. Is it an illusion?"

"No! No! Also reading a reduction in mass! Seventy-one percent and dropping!"

A relatively small star system—only five planets. Two livable, one worth conquering.

Now, through some unimagined power, the sun was engaging in a practice heretofore reserved for balloons.

It was expanding. Dilating. It was growing.

"General, the planets! Same effect!"

"I'm standing next to you. Calm down when you speak. Is the speed of orbit increasing with reduction in mass?"

"Yes! And they're spinning faster and faster!"

"Stop shouting. No one else shout anymore. We will look at this and decide."

The crew of the Klingon patrol cruiser *Jada* swung to look at the rows of auxiliary monitors showing views of the five planets. Two of the planets, the two nearest the sun, were dilating too—blowing outward from their cores as if puffed up by breath. A second later, the other three puffed also. And all solar-system bodies and debris were racing faster around the sun with every passing second.

But the first two planets were not only blowing apart—they were charging out of their orbits like balls swung on strings that had been suddenly released. No longer held in a curve around the sun, they were launched on elongated orbits. The arc was widening—distorting.

In horror and shock, the crew and their general measured the impossible occurring around them. The sun, minutes ago as normal as any other, now had swollen to fill their main viewscreen. The screen mechanisms whirred to compensate for the blinding light that had flared too fast and set the crew to shielding their eyes.

It could not happen, but it was happening. Their general swung his squat, broad-chested body to the main screen when the light finally dimmed. The light still hurt his eyes but this was something he had to see for himself.

His voice was very quiet. "Are we falling toward it?"

"No!" the tactical officer punctuated, then remembered what the general had said about shouting. "Position stationary. But the ship—it—we . . . we . . ."

"Speak, man."

"Reading a reduction in registered mass for us as well! All other ships reporting the same!"

Suddenly the helmsman said, "Ship's speed is increasing, sir! But I have not done it!"

To their left, the tactical officer turned to the center of the bridge, stared at Captain Ruhl, and confirmed, "All five other ships reporting the same thing happening to them."

"Compensate." Ruhl was the newly assigned captain of this ship, a narrow-bodied individual with a missing tooth in front. When the general did not stop him, he gained confidence and snapped his fingers at his officers. "Keep the speed down."

"Trying," the helmsman uttered, but he was involved

in a struggle. "Point four five of sublight . . . point five zero . . . still increasing . . ."

"Everything is speeding up," the tactical officer abridged, gasping as an animal does on the run.

Lack of inhibition about his own ignorance was Ruhl's only good trait, and in fact was the qualification that had gotten him this command. He had no ego at all. No problem turning to their elder and asking, "General Kellen, what should we do?"

Sensing the panic about to erupt around him, the general held out one hand for silence. Five ships to protect, a vaporizing solar system . . . they wanted answers from him. Solutions. He had none.

He would do as he always did in wild situations—he would become calmer than anything or anyone around him. He would lower his voice, contain his stance, raise his chin, and deliver a glacial demeanor. He had long ago discovered the best key to winning: When the situation becomes tense, become correspondingly calm. He could win over anyone that way. Being a Vulcan among Klingons, controlled and contemplative, would supersede any Klingon. Most Klingons despised Vulcans. That made his advantage even greater.

Now he was a general of the highest mark. Unexcitability had served him so well that it had become the mantle of his reputation. He rather enjoyed that.

Except in situations like this, when there was a panic but no thinking enemy to outthink. He could not outcalm a natural disaster. He found himself irritated by that, and by the blustering fear demonstrated around him.

Critical seconds ticked off as Kellen maneuvered his wide body toward the science officer.

"What is your name?" he asked.

"My—I—"

"His name is Karn," the helmsman blurted, anxious enough to interfere.

"Karn," Kellen repeated, "explain what you think is happening."

Pressing both hands to his head as if to hold in the flurry of details, Karn looked at his instruments, then back at the general. His mouth opened and closed several times before he found his voice.

"Mass," he began, "is failing to register on my instruments. Not the *matter* . . . just the mass!"

"The sky is falling and we seem also to be falling," Kellen said evenly. "Keep talking."

Frantic, Karn battled to control himself. He put his hands out between himself and his commanding officers and made shapes as if sculpting his words.

"Every moving thing possesses a certain amount of energy. How quickly it moves depends upon how much energy and how much mass. Velocity is mass versus energy. If the mass drops away but energy doesn't, velocity must increase. If one or the other is taken away or added, the nature makes it balance. Mass is slipping away, but the energy is still there. So everything is speeding up!"

His eyes were wild with confusion. The anchors of his life, the precepts of concrete science, were slipping their hold.

"How can mass be taken away?" Kellen asked him.

"I do not know that! But you see it happening!"

"I feel it happening. And when one of my girth becomes lighter, one notices."

Karn nodded, breathing as if he'd just come up through water. "If it reaches zero . . . if it reaches zero . . . Once the mass of all those planets and the sun hits zero—if there is only energy and *no* mass—everything will go to light speed! Every particle!"

"Like photons," Kellen considered. "Are you sure this will happen?"

Seeming frustrated that his general was content to discuss this theory—which was quickly manifesting itself as much more than theory—the sad scientist continued to lose color from his bronze face. "I am sure of nothing! This has never happened before! But I *think* it will happen!"

"Nothing in nature can go to light speed," the helmsman argued. "It makes no sense."

Karn cranked around. "Neither does the mass dropping!"

"So the planets explode," the helmsman said. "So what?"

"Idiot!" Karn slashed a hand toward him. "Don't you understand? We are all part of the existing universe!" He pointed frantically at the internal readouts. "Our mass is going away too. The moment it hits zero, every one of our molecules will move away from each other at the speed of light! The energy *has* to go somewhere!"

Ruhl squinted at him. "We explode too?"

Karn nodded so hard that his hair bounced up and down at the back of his neck. "At the speed of light!"

After a lifetime in space, Kellen understood immediately and paused as comprehension dawned on each of the others, blanching their faces one by one.

"Read out the mass falloff," he requested quietly.

Karn's gnarled face was chalky with fear as he stared into his instruments, but he took his general's example and tried to rein in his panic. "Forty percent now and still dropping, sir."

Ruhl glared at him. "Is it a weapon?"

Pressing a lock of neatly clipped hair away from the side of his face, Kellen ignored the question and snapped instead, "Go to battle mode. Deflectors up."

Ruhl pulled himself to the helm, rather than bothering to shift the responsibility to anyone else, and with one finger punched in the shields-up.

All at once a hand of nausea swept down upon them all, and they were released from their own weight. The deck slid away from their boots.

Loss of mass—loss of gravity!

As he grabbed clumsily for a handhold, Kellen called out over the noise, "Compensate. Compensate, you clumsy amateurs!"

"Trying, sir!"

"Trying, sir!"

"Compensating, sir!"

They were trying, he could see that. The helmsman fought with his controls while holding himself to his seat with his knotted legs. The ship raced through open space on a nonsensical course around the solar system, leading the other five ships in the fleet as they all struggled for control.

Planets blew to bits, no longer possessing mass enough, therefore gravity enough, to hold themselves together. Moons dislodged from their orbits, then also expanded as if inflated from inside. Asteroids bloated to dust, and the dust scattered.

Now only thick clouds of ejecta rushing far faster than ever nature intended, the freewheeling satellites continued to distend, continents shattering, oceans spraying out into space to become ice clouds. Like the pulsebeat of a superbeing, the sun dilated more and more, sending its incendiary kiss out to the rubble of planets it had moments ago nurtured. No longer bonded to each other, the sun's burning particles ballooned outward. The gassy inflation consumed the rubble of the first planet. Life on the planets was already destroyed. Millions of years to evolve, seconds to suffocate.

A sun—a huge thermonuclear fusion bomb held together by the natural magic of gravity. When the gravity goes, the bomb starts to explode.

From where he hovered over the helm, Kellen stared at the viewscreen and monitors, one after the other, slightly less familiar than those on his flagship, and he imagined what those life-forms must have felt just now. Terrible things. This nausea, the loss of weight. The ground falling from beneath their feet, the air gushing out of their lungs as the atmosphere flew outward as if torn away in a great sheet. The land around them crumbling, trees launching toward space, no longer rooted, for there was no more soil.

How advanced had they been? There hadn't been time to investigate. Had intelligence come to them yet? Did they have the sense to be afraid? To understand the last glimpses of each other as they vaulted toward open space, into a sky no longer blue?

Instruments on the bridge chattered and screamed for attention, reading out the disaster on molecular levels and striving to compensate for the changes pouring in through the sensors.

He heard the sound of his men's panic throbbing in his head, calling for him—*Kellen! Kellen! Kellen!*—but he couldn't respond or turn from the hypnotic destruction on the screens. Certainly what he heard was only his sanity calling to him in the midst of madness. For the first time in his life he honestly did not know what to do.

He wasn't even on his own ship, with his own science officer.

"Hail the *Qul,*" he said steadily. "I want to speak to my own science officer."

"Yes, General!" the shuddering helm officer choked. Abruptly he looked at Ruhl, frightened that he might have overstepped his post by not waiting for the ship's commander to relay the order, but Ruhl nodded and the contact was made. "Go ahead, sir."

Kellen drew himself closer to the communications link. "This is Kellen. I wish to speak to Aragor."

"We can't find him, sir."

"You can't *find* him?"

"Not . . . presently."

"Find him anyway."

"Yes, Commander. Stand by."

"Give me a view of the fleet," Kellen ordered as he waited.

The tactical officer jumped to the necessary monitor. The screen flickered, but came on, showing all five other ships, greenish white hulls drenched in solar flush. Their bottle-shaped forms jerked unevenly through space on *Qul*'s beam, and clearly they too were having problems keeping their speed from increasing out of control. None of them knew how to fight against this.

"General Kellen, this is Aragor! Are you there?"

Kellen twisted back toward the comm unit, and almost made another full twist around—he was losing his grip on the deck. Losing mass. "Of course I am here. What's happening to us?"

"Our instruments are reading a reduction in mass! It seems to be continuing—I cannot explain it. Artificial gravity is—!"

"I want a way to protect ourselves from it. Think of something."

"We must keep our mass!" Karn shouted from behind him. "Some part of it—a fraction of it! We must not go to zero!"

"He is right, General. We might be able to shield ourselves from the effect." Aragor's voice bubbled through the communications system, stressed and gaspy.

"With what?" Kellen asked.

"With . . . shields. If we divert all possible power, we might be able to stall the effect—"

"Do it. All fleet science stations and helms tie in with Karn and Aragor. Match what they do. Aragor, do it."

"Yes, General."

Karn flinched, then said, "Yes, General."

The tactical officer panted, "Mass at twenty percent and dropping!"

"Triple shields." Aragor's voice funneled through the communications system, no longer directed at Kellen, but at the science stations on all six ships. *"Sending the deflector formula through now. All systems accept and confirm."*

Karn and the tactical officer worked frantically at the controls while bracing themselves in place against seat backs and other crewmen.

"Ten percent and dropping . . ."

"Outside mass reading is separating from inner reading." Karn's voice shuddered with a ring of success.

"All stations report inner mass reading. . . ."

Solar matter continued to fly outward through the system, cooking the planetary refuse, bombarding the fleet's shields and tormenting the crews with the garish noises of primitive assault.

Kellen hadn't been weightless since his first training missions, yet the sensation was familiar, one of those things the physical body never quite forgets. He recognized the bizarre release of his internal organs from their own weight, the light-headedness, the loss of equilibrium, and fought to ignore those distractions. No control over gravity—without it they dared not go to warp speed. That meant they were trapped fighting to stay at sublight against an effect that would ultimately drive them to light speed, in the midst of a slaughtered solar system about to go nova down to the last particle.

"Outer reading, five percent . . . inner reading, five point one percent . . ."

As he listened to Karn's voice, Kellen paused to think. Decrease in mass causing increase in velocity . . . mass shrinking, but with the same amount of propellant energy. As they fell apart the outer planets were moving faster and faster, whipping around their expanding sun. Such a sight! If he died seeing this, certainly there were worse deaths.

"Outer reading, two percent . . . inner reading, two point zero four . . . zero three . . . zero two . . ."

Rubble from the decimated planets and space debris rattled against the hull of the ship and caused an awful percussion from bulkhead to bulkhead. The bridge crew clamped their hands over their ears, and so let go of their handholds and free-floated, bumping into each other in midair.

Soon they were all tumbling.

"Outer mass at one percent!"

"Inner, one point zero five!"

"Divert impulse power to the shields!"

"Outer at one point zero one percent—"

The drone of numbers began to buzz in Kellen's mind. How long had it been? The effect of gravity suspension couldn't travel faster than light . . . that would affect things. The pull of the sun had been suspended long enough to release the inner planets from their orbits, but it would take four or five light-hours for that effect to reach the decimated outer planets. For now they were just clogs of shattered ejecta crashing along in their regular orbits. When the suspension of the sun's gravitational pull reached them, they would free-fall out of orbit as the inner planets had. If the effect lasted more than a few minutes—if the mass reached zero—the sun would never recover. The system would be gone forever, just dust particles racing through space in all directions.

If it did stop, the velocity would drop and there would be a primordial system again, as there was five billion years ago. The whole configuration of this area of space would be forever changed.

"Inner mass at one-sixtieth of one percent!" Karn was hovering near the port auxiliary monitors and tipped entirely onto his head in order to read the mass change. "Mass outside of our shields is zero, sir! Zero!"

Between the "zz" and the "o" of his last word, the planets of this solar system, now hardly more than loosely grouped areas of rocky debris, seemed to vaporize before them, molecules flashing in a million directions. All but the sun was decimated. The sun itself, too big to move far, expanded to unthinkable size now at the speed of light, well off their scales and engulfing all their screens. The shapes of the other five ships on the auxiliary monitors were only glazed silhouettes—

And suddenly there were only four other ships.

"The *Shukar!*" Ruhl shouted. "General!"

Kellen stared at the brightening screens until his eyes watered. The *Shukar,* blown into warp in a billion bits. An explosion so fast as to be virtual vaporization. Molecules suddenly radiating away from each other at the speed of light. They had failed to hold mass.

"Inner mass, one one-hundredth of one percent!" Karn whimpered, shielding his eyes with both hands as he hovered upside down. "One one-hundred-twentieth—we can't hold it!"

"Feed all weapons power to the shields."

Aragor was fighting to keep control, but Kellen knew him and heard the tremors in his voice. They barely had any mass at all, in practical terms it was nothing, but in physics the difference between *something* and *nothing* was a universe of difference. They were managing to remain intact while everything exploded around them, but the power drain was fabulous. Seconds were slipping away.

The planets were gone. The sun was still expanding. In a few more minutes—

Suddenly a great hand swatted Kellen toward the deck. His arms and legs flew upward, and he hit the deck on his considerable stomach. Ruhl landed on top of him, stunning them both. Confused by the sensation of their own weight, the bridge crewmen rolled about momentarily, searching for equilibrium. Was down once again down?

Kellen put his palms on the deck and heaved upward, pressing with his shoulder blades. For a moment he felt like a bird-of-prey in battle poise, wings down, shoulders tensed, knuckles in.

Ruhl rolled off and was dumped to the deck at Kellen's heels. Kellen pressed down his need to vomit and clawed toward the helm. "Status of gravitational forces system-wide!"

The crew shuffled dizzily to the shelf of readouts on the starboard side. Ruhl's reddish hair had come loose and was hanging in his face like a ragged mop. He was still trying to do too much himself. Promoted too quickly, it seemed. Not used to delegating responsibility. Sometimes promotions happened that way when a family was too well connected. He would learn.

"All readings returning to normal, sir!" Karn called. He swung around to look at the forward monitor.

Kellen did the same, as did everyone. The sun would tell.

Before their eyes the swollen, overextended mass of solar matter was drawing inward toward its core again, shrinking with a terrible violence to its normal size—but some of the solar matter flung off during the loss of mass was too far away to be pulled back and spun outward in all directions.

Now shorn of any life or growth, with the bits of living bodies crushed amid the rubble, the planetary material was bashed to primordial rubbish, thrown away at light speed, and all bets were off. The sun would have to gather itself, then slowly begin once again nipping at deep space to draw bodies to orbit it. The eons had begun again.

"Aragor," he said. "Aragor, are you there?"

The long silence was unfriendly. Had the same tragedy happened to *Qul* as to *Shukar?* He began to look from screen to screen.

"Aragor, sir," the comm system rasped. *"The . . . sun has moved several millions of miles . . . recoalesced because of its size once gravity and mass returned . . . It is no longer actually a sun, but a hot cloud of gas beginning to act again as nature intended. . . . The planets are gone. . . ."*

Random observations, coming as Aragor thought of them. He was deeply shaken.

"Everything has stopped," the science officer continued before Kellen has a chance to encourage him on. "The velocity must have been reduced to its previous levels somehow as the mass returned. . . . It must have something to do with natural conservation of energy. . . . Energy has to come from somewhere . . . it cannot just appear. . . . As long as we maintained the slightest mass, we remained . . . intact . . ."

He was searching for words. Saying what they were all thinking—that these things cannot happen, but they just had. Where had the energy come from that had caused this?

"What stopped the effect, Aragor?" Kellen prodded.

More silence came back at him. He glanced at Karn, who stared at him, waiting for Aragor to bear the weight.

"Nature stopped it."

Another stretch of silence.

Kellen could sense Aragor thinking and thinking.

"Mass . . . energy . . . and velocity are all related. When mass was taken away, nature balanced with more velocity, all the way to light speed. When the mass suddenly returned, velocity of the matter substantially decreased."

"But velocity is only measured relative to other things," Kellen broke in. "It decreased relative to what?"

They were all staring at him now. He felt the tense stares of men on the other ships too. They were all waiting for him and his science officer to find the answer.

"I do not know." Aragor sounded whipped. He hadn't wanted to say that. *"I could be completely wrong. I see it, I can describe it . . . but I cannot explain it."*

"Sir!" Ruhl gasped, moving on shaky legs back toward his own command chair to where Kellen stood near the helm. "Could it have been a weapon?"

"If it was theirs," Kellen said, "they have destroyed themselves with it. If it was someone else's, then we have a new war on our hands."

Ruhl came to hunch beside him over the shuddering helm. "Starfleet?"

Kellen did not respond. There were some things even a Klingon preferred not to guess.

Starfleet. Their old enemy. His oldest. Certainly those people were capable of developing a mass-blanking weapon, but he wondered if Starfleet would use such a thing. Yes, but not without provocation, and there had been none lately.

Kellen knew that, because he had asked to do some provoking and been turned down.

The solar system remained in chaos. As the sun broiled fiercely during its reintegration, alone in space now.

Nothing left to conquer. Had the predator been starved by the prey's self-immolation?

If not a weapon, then what?

He turned to Ruhl, and found himself about to speak to a shag of reddish hair, and it threw him off for a moment. He shook his own combed locks as if in example.

"Ruhl, at least get your hair out of your face when I speak to you."

Pawing his hair out of his face, Ruhl caught part of his long mustache on a fingernail and ended up with one hand caught near his ear. He shook it loose, embarrassed, wondering if he had just been given an order or only a suggestion, and muttered, "Yes . . . yes, sir."

Rather than appease him with acknowledgment, Kellen said "Assess damage in the fleet and make a full sensor scan of the area."

Ruhl's small eyes grew wide. "What shall we scan for?"

"Whatever you find."

"Yes, Commander. . . ."

"Karn," Kellen began, and turned to face the startled science officer of this ship, so Karn would not look bad in the eyes of his own crewmates. "Was the suspension limited to this solar system? How far did it reach?"

Karn struggled to avoid thanking the general for his attention, and poured himself into the readouts. "Long-range sensors suggest it reached at least sixteen light-days."

"Dispatch immediate reports of all this to the Empire."

"Yes, General."

"General," Ruhl interrupted, "we should tell them the Uri Taug star system is now devoid of life. Otherwise they'll wonder why we failed to conquer."

Kellen held a hand toward the godlike ruin on the screens. "We'll tell them we did conquer. After all, the system is ours now. What's left of it."

"Sir!"

Both Kellen and Ruhl turned toward Karn. "Yes?"

"Sir . . . sir!"

Kellen swatted the young man's arm. "We are both here. Say something!"

"A . . . a . . . change!"

The baffled science officer stepped aside with forgivable gratitude as Kellen pressed toward the science station and Ruhl pushed in after him.

In the middle distance, reading only a light-year away, a core of turbulence had opened up on their screens. On each screen it looked different, for each screen picked up different elements—spectra, energy, spatial disruption. Not a swirl, but not a crack, yet still it moved. Like a piece of woman's fabric strung in space and waved by a giant hand, it taunted them.

Squinting, Kellen wondered aloud, "What is that?"

"Some kind of . . . storm?" Ruhl sounded compelled to invent an answer.

"A storm with good timing? I doubt that."

"Then what do you think?"

"I think we're seeing the cause of what he have just felt." Kellen straightened and reacted briefly to a sharp pain in his left shoulder from their experience. "I should be on my own flagship for whatever is coming. Continue to monitor that phenomenon. Remain at battle configuration."

"Yes, sir," Ruhl said.

"Aragor, are you still standing by?"

"Yes, General!"

"Are you reading this phenomenon?"

"I . . . see it, sir."

That was Aragor's way of admitting to Kellen that he hadn't a clue what the waving veil was.

Using the confusion of the moment to shade the fact that he didn't feel like walking all the way to the transporter room, Kellen plucked his handheld communicator from its holster and snapped it open.

"Pick up my coordinates and beam me back directly to the bridge immediately. We will find out what did this. If it is an accident, we will explain it. If it is a weapon, we will own it. Activate transporter beams now."

"Transporter officer, energize beams. Bring the general directly to the bridge."

Aboard the Border Fleet flagship *Qul,* Science Officer Aragor drew a long breath of relief that soon General Kellen would be back aboard and would take command during this strange time. Though he tried to appear supremely Klingon in front of the bridge crew, Aragor was frightened. The impossible had just happened before his eyes, and his whole body was still quaking. Had the mass drop continued a few more seconds, they would have become part of an uncontrolled whirl of hyperlight.

A drop in mass! Unthinkable! It couldn't possibly happen naturally.

The general would figure it out. He would find the answers. The two of them would piece together the data, and Kellen would decide what happened. Kellen was the smartest warrior in the universe.

The whine of transporter energy chewed at Aragor's ears, and he turned toward the open area of the bridge to which Kellen was being beamed. Seconds now.

A pillar of expanding lights appeared, many bands, bringing the disassembled atoms of their commander across the emptiness of space, to be reconstructed here. The pillar coalesced into shoulders draped with fabric, a broad torso clad in stiff metallic fiber. For a moment there was a short clean-cut beard and bronze hair trimmed above the shoulder. A thin mustache, as if stenciled on.

Then, the wide pillar of light began to fade. The whine rose to a scream. The lights thinned out.

"What is this!" Aragor struck the communications pad. "Transporter officer! What are you doing?"

There was no response. Before him, General Kellen's partially formed face frowned as if sensing the transportation going wrong. His right hand turned slightly outward from his robe, toward Aragor, and the fingers opened in beckoning.

"Transporter!" Aragor called. "Bring him in!"

"Trying," the comm buzzed. "There is interference, sir!"

"Fight for him!" Aragor waved the other bridge personnel back, away from the pillar of sparkling light, so no one else's physical presence would attract any of the particles trying so desperately to reassemble.

What was happening? The transporter should easily be able to do this. Ship-to-ship transportation at this distance was nothing. Nothing!

The pillar of lights surged once as if succeeding, but then suddenly sizzled completely away. The dim bridge lighting seemed somehow much dimmer now.

Aragor swung around to glare at the main screen, which showed a picture of the fleet ships. "Ruhl! Do you have him?"

"Not here," the other captain's voice came back, high with tension. *"We do not have him!"*

"Where is he? Where is he?" With the heel of his hand Aragor struck the intraship unit. "Transporter! Where is he!"

His transporter officer's voice was thready, shocked. "Sir, the beams . . . they went into that twisting form out there. I do not understand how it could happen—he was drawn in, as if magnetized!"

Aragor jumped to his science station, where he was met by the tactical officer, and together they stared into the science readout screen.

More of the impossible—the transporter beams, presented in an image of chittering energy, looped like the tail of a running animal, then were swallowed by the phenomenon out there.

As they stood together and watched the screen, a form began to take shape, emerge from the gash in open space. A solid form. A vessel . . . a ship . . .

"Taken," the tactical officer murmured. "Absorbed!"

With both hands Aragor gripped the rubber rim of the monitor. "I want him back, Vagh. . . ."

He plunged to the helm, hammered the controls until the main viewer switched to a sheet of black space incised by the waving valence of new energy.

He stared into the vision. His wail rattled the bones of his crewmates.

"I want my general back!"

Chapter Two

VOLCANIC WIND . . . perfumed, reeking atmosphere . . . and a sound of engines.

Kellen materialized gagging.

As soon as the transporter beams released him, he stumbled back against a hard surface, and choked. The air here was heavy, vaporous; the surface against which he leaned was mossy. He huddled against it until his eyes adjusted to the dimness.

The ceiling was only an arm's length over his head. Higher in some places. A tunnel of some sort? A cave?

Hard ground beneath his feet. Skin itching. Plant life—sedge, burrs and creepers, algae, spotted cabbage, puffballs, adder's tongue . . . He recognized some of them; others were familiar but had the wrong color, the wrong shape, or the wrong smell. He was no botanist.

Pungent odors . . . If he could only get a whole breath. Then he could think.

Think, think. Cling to self-control.

He had been transporting from Ruhl's ship to his own. Now he was on some planet, in a cave.

"But there were no planets left," he rasped. The sound of his own voice anchored him. "Especially none with life. . . ."

He pressed his hand to the wall. Parasites jumped from the moss onto his hand and skittered in confusion. Life.

Small life, but company was company.

At least he could eat.

He pushed off the cave wall. He took one step, then stopped as he thought of something else. Kneeling, he peered at the ground. There was growth here too, but vetchy, flattened growth. Flattened by other footsteps? Where he could walk, so could others.

Others . . .

He brushed the ground with the side of his hand, to tidy it a little, then stood up. That sound—he remembered it now, and in remembering heard it again. After so many years in spaceships he had come to ignore the necessary thrum of power generation.

"Engines," he validated.

His experienced ears knew the sound of a power source, but he could see none, nor discover any specific direction from which the dim thrumming came. He must be near a factory of some kind. A power generator.

If there was power, he could use it to get back to his fleet, or at least to send a signal.

So the mass drop must have been some kind of weapon or distraction, and now he, the fleet leader, was kidnapped.

Speculating made him uneasy. He would deal only with the facts. Footmarks and power, on a planet with caves.

And light? Where was the light coming from? Another power source? The sun they had watched blow up and shrink back?

He paused to see whether the light changed at all. It remained hazy, but steady. No way to judge whether it was natural or not. No draft, no wind, yet the air was tolerable now that he was breathing more slowly.

Where was he? A planet with atmosphere.

A momentary panic struck him that he could be on a distant outer planet, waiting for the second wave of gravity gap to wash outward from the sun for a second apocalypse, yet he had seen those planets shatter, and even if they were balled up again there could be no life, no moss or insects left.

No. We reached zero mass. There is no planet left here.

Dismissing the possibility that he could still be in that mutilated solar system, he selected a branch of the cave at random and moved through it. The tunnel was narrow, but roomy above his head. Within twenty steps he found himself in another open area. Here the sound of the power source was stronger and he became more sure that he recognized the tenor of it. In fact, he noted the pitch was higher than normal . . . normal for what?

There was nothing here but another tunnel. He went through it into a darkness that nearly turned him back. As the blackness closed in, he paused to let his eyes adjust and to shore up his courage to move forward and not back into what he already knew. The fleet would be looking for him. He had to contrive a way to let them find him.

The darkness became blackness. The blackness pressed inward against his shoulders, down across the crest of his brow. He pressed back with his will, blinking his eyes as if they were the problem. The tunnel closed tighter at his sides—he could feel the change. He saw nothing, yet he sensed much.

A throbbing glow—with a regular pulse. Red . . . blue . . . red . . . blue . . . He moved toward it. Only a few steps now. He must control himself.

He came out into a wider area, greatly to his relief, and all but ran forward, chased by the narrow dark section. Stumbling out into a broader area, he sucked air as if surging up out of a pool in which he had nearly drowned and only then realized he had been holding his breath. Taking it again nearly set him on his backside. He stumbled against the cave wall.

At his side his dagger thumped against the rock—the sound was strange. Metallic. On moss?

With one hand on his dagger and the other on the moss, he pushed himself from the wall and took further steps into the chamber, where suddenly his heart recoiled within his chest and he stared to the point of pain.

Draped with shrouds of green witch's hair, the walls stared back. Within the spongy, foul moss, churning with what must be insect life, lichen wept from dozens of niches, each the size of a half-grown Terran pumpkin. His favorite food rode into his mind on this irrational bolt of fear, but gave him no comfort nor any anchor. Fear held on, for in most of these dark punch-outs, perhaps two-thirds of them, were perched bleached and staring skulls.

Though all had eye sockets and peeled-back grinning mouths, those were the only common elements. Some had stumps of horns, others a dozen small holes over the gaping eye sockets, others were of such shape and description that churned the ugly bowels of Klingons lore in Kellen's head. Constructed to terrorize, tales of imminent evil rushed forward out of his childhood, beasts of prey infused by the wills of demons, who then had the abilities of both.

Blood-chilled, Kellen's body convulsed and he staggered sideways, catching his heel upon the ragged floor and staggering further. Shivering, he struck the wall again and felt his dagger bang the wall again. Again, that metallic noise—and this time a faint red-then-blue glow coming on and off, on and off, under the moss.

He yanked his dagger from its sheath and sliced into the moss, a long gash as if taking an enemy from throat to belt. The moss pulled apart and the lips of the gash quivered. Kellen dug his fingernails into it and ripped the moss away in sheet.

Through a cloud of spoory dust, two panels of variegated lights blinked at him, casting red, yellow, and amber haze. Below the panels, a pulsebeat of technical readouts blipped up and down on a screen.

Kellen tore the sheet of moss further all the way to the floor. It came away cleanly, but for its own green cloud, and there was a manufactured metal wall, a right-angled corner, and part of a tiled floor.

He stared at the wall, kicked it, then looked up into the skull niches and the eyes of the catacomb corridor. All at once, the sound he had been hearing made sense to him. He knew what he was hearing.

"A ship . . . a spaceship."

His voice startled even himself, and he flinched, but even more horribly it startled someone else.

The wall was looking at him. A pair of eyes—real ones, live ones—opened in among the tenleaf and creepers on what he had thought was a cave tomb. White-ringed and wide, the eyes were yellow as the middles of eggs, each pinpointed in the center with a black dot focused like a drill on Kellen.

The eyes came forward slowly from the witch's hair, bringing strands of it stretching along.

Suffused with horror, unable to call upon his tremendous discipline this time, Kellen watched as a creature's form took shape and pulled out of the growth. The top of its head was being eaten by a mass of moving white tendrils, each alive and fingering the green wall hungrily as the creature drew farther and farther out into the corridor.

No, not eaten—the tendrils were *part* of the creature's head! Growing out of it like things he had seen in the sea! Grotesque, poison-tipped things.

Instantly he looked up at the skull niches and searched until he found the one nearest him with the holes in the top. It was the skull of that—*that!*

The creature peeled out of the wall and with measured movements shed itself of the gluey membranes pulling at it from the wall. Each as long as Kellen's forearm, the anemone-tendrils on the beast's head swirled to one side and back to the other, seeking the open air as if driven by currents. Some of them still reached and snipped at the fungusy wall, plucking at it with tiny suckers.

A ship, specter-crewed!

As his renowned sobriety crumbled, Kellen raised his thick arms and warned the creature back with a senseless shout, but had no effect.

He scoured his earliest memories, and called the thing by name.

"Iraga!" he shrieked.

"Approach pattern *SochDIch* on my mark!"

"Yes, Science Officer!"

"Forward vessels, disruptors on full double-front! Target engines! Repeat—engines only until we have made our pass!"

"All are ready, sir. Three ships in forward configuration, two behind us!"

"Tell all the others to put their shields on priority. For us, I want scanners on priority, set to seek out Klingon physiology. Transporter, stand by."

Science Officer Aragor gripped the command chair with both hands until his fingernails made impressions on the simulated animal hide. The sudden silence on the bridge made him realize that he and the bridge crew had been so excited they'd been yelling at each other. In each echo he heard the ghost of Kellen's voice—*Be quiet. Speak softly. Calm down.*

He battled to contain himself. He wanted his general back and he would get him back. Now he had a target.

A ship had come out of that crack or hole or blur in space. There had been a great shaking, not as great as the mass drop, but enough to send the fleet spinning for a few seconds. When they gathered themselves, there was a ship there.

Configured like no ship Aragor had ever seen, this alien vessel was the length of their entire fleet—six ships laid beak to tail—and shaped like a corkscrew. Great fans of black and purple hull material fanned out and overlapped each other in a spiral against each other, arching forward like welded petals into a point. There was no top or bottom, no visible bridge or command center. Seeming almost to flex its way through space, it was constructed perfectly to screw through that opening out there. The more he stared at the hornlike ship, the more Aragor became sure these last moments were no accidents. The mass falloff had something to do with these newcomers.

Interlopers, he charged. *Unlawful entry into Klingon space. Kidnappers. Invaders!*

Thought after thought, he built himself into a mode of attack. This wasn't his job, but he would accept it. Never in his life had he seen an effect such as that ship's entry into this sector from wherever it had come, and no power of that magnitude could be taken lightly. He would have to get Kellen back, and Kellen would agree. Together they would conquer before they were themselves taken. It was the Klingon way.

Or at least, it would be today.

"All is ready for the run, sir," Tactical Officer Mursha reported, and looked at Aragor as if to confirm.

"Handle the scanners yourself, Mursha," Aragor said in a last-minute change. "Find him."

Mursha looked afraid for an instant, then straightened so sharply that it seemed to hurt his shoulders. "I will! I'll find him!"

Aragor felt an urge to chide him for his hesitation, but Mursha had just taken the tactical position two days ago. Aragor left him alone.

"Attack configuration. Flank speed. Keep full speed until we get within transporter range. No veering off until my order, do you understand?"

"I understand, sir," the helmsman said.

"Fleet . . . advance!"

With three ships forming a point before it and one other ship riding behind its starboard beam, the *Qul* surged to full impulse. The five ships rocketed through open space toward the massive arrangement of curves, targeting the deep pulsing mauve glow of the conical ship's engines. Aragor recognized the surge of matter-antimatter propulsion and was reassured by it, but the color was unexpected. The color of Klingon blood.

The fleet ships arched in, keeping formation tight and maneuvering for position as they reached the invasion ship. The outer ships opened fire. Phaser energy blanketed the other ship and brightened a veil of otherwise unnotable particles of dust in space. Suddenly the whole area was shimmering.

At once the unfamiliar ship declared itself an enemy ship—it fired back. Globular bolts were launched from the inner folds of the huge purple-and-black fans, striking the first three Klingon ships without wasting a shot. Energy foamed over the Klingon ships' deflector shields and skittered into space to wash across the *Qul* and its flanking ship.

The *Qul* shuddered under Aragor's chair. Phaser wash broke between her hull plates and shriveled the outer mechanics in their trunks.

"Some systems overloading, sir," the helmsman called over a sudden braying alarm.

"Lock down," Aragor said. "Never mind trying to repair now. And cut off that cursed noise!"

The alarm growled down to a sorry *woooo,* then broke off. Closer and closer the Klingon fleet raced, skating the length of the enemy vessel as if measuring it.

"Keep firing," he said, too softly to be heard.

The other ships had their orders—they fired relentlessly and took the incoming blue foam of return fire on their forward shields, maneuvering to protect the *Qul,* whose power was concentrated on sensors. *Qul* had some shields, but not enough to take direct hits of that magnitude. And if Mursha found the commander's physical blip, *Qul* would have to hammer a hole in the enemy's shields, then drop her own shields completely to beam him up.

"The phaser fire is bouncing off the invader ship!" the helmsman blurted. "But I don't see any conventional broadcast deflectors at all!"

Aragor squinted and watched. That could make his task easier. The enemy ship was taking the direct fire on its many fan-shaped hull sculptures.

"This must be their manner of defense," he said. "There must be another ship, the real ship, hidden inside the outer fan arrangement. That makes it almost impossible for a moving vessel to hit. In order to incise that inner ship, an attacking vessel would have to hover over it and fire down between the fans."

"That would be suicide," the helmsman said, and gripped his controls tighter, as if afraid he'd made a suggestion that might be taken.

"Well?" Aragor roared at Mursha when his nerves took control and thoughts of a second run began to form. He didn't want to make a second run. The lead ships were being pulverized. Their shields wouldn't take a second bombardment.

"Scanning . . ." Mursha had his mustache to the readouts, both hands on the curved adjustments, looking for Klingon life signs.

The bridge erupted in sparks and smoke puffs as damaged systems began to overload. More hits broke through the formation and began to pry it apart. If the forward ships couldn't hold their position, *Qul* would have to bear off.

Tense silence gripped the bridge. No voices. Only the sounds of the ship straining around them as they maneuvered their deadly tight course.

On the main screen, huge hull fans blew past beneath them, like a petals of a massive orchid.

"Sir!" Mursha gulped. "I believe—"

Aragor shoved out of the command chair. "Activate the beams immediately! Beam him up! Transporter room, do you hear me? Activate beams!"

"Vergozen!"

"Speak softly, Morien. Your voice is hurting me."

"Many of us were resting or eating in the Barrow when a strange creature came there!"

"We are all strange creatures, Morien. You mean you did not recognize this one?"

"Or his kind. Not at all."

"Describe him."

"He had a helmet for a head, black hair around it, a skeleton on the outside of his chest, and long sleeves almost to the ground. He shouted at me and danced!"

"He danced?"

"Then he churned into lights and disappeared. What does it mean? Have we done something wrong?"

"No. The others have already reported an intruder aboard. We were sending the guards when those ships came and somehow he was plucked away. Now we have alterations to make on our equipment. We must be sure this cannot happen again. And send a message back along the wrinkle. Tell them we seem to have betrayed our arrival and now there are ships following us. There is apparently a destructive effect involved in the process of transferring. Suggest it be corrected before the fissure is opened again."

"Yes, Vergozen."

"Morien, tell me . . . how many eyes did this creature have?"

"Two that I could see. Unless there were others hiding."

"Two eyes . . . well, it's a beginning."

"Why did you bother with me! Why didn't you beam an antimatter explosive into that ship while you had the chance! They had no shields! At terrible damage to the fleet you came in to rescue me, and now we have lost the chance to destroy them!"

The booming voice was glorious anger to Aragor as he stood without moving while General Kellen shouted at him. Aragor didn't care that he had made a mistake, because he had his commander back and he would walk fire for Kellen.

The crew stood before the general in utter numb shock. They had never heard him yell before. Never.

The general's clothing was coated with fine green dust, his usually neat hair disturbed by burrs and bits of mold, and he was consumed with shuddering in terror, but he wasn't hurt. He vented his terror by shouting at Aragor and glaring wide-eyed at the enemy ship as it slowly moved away on their main viewscreen. Its purple fans were reflected softly in the lenses of his eyeglasses.

At last he gave up on Aragor and swung on the tactical position.

"Mursha! Analyze the enemy ship. Can we still beam in?"

"No, sir. They have made some kind of energy web around their ship that resists transporter beams. Not deflectors as we know them, but—"

"But our chance is lost!"

Aragor continued staring. That voice—so loud, so completely uncharacteristic.

"Sir . . . sir," Aragor began, "we had no salvo prepared for penetration. We thought we should take the opportunity to rescue you before we—"

Kellen rounded on him again. "You had one chance! You will not have that chance again! Next time the choice is to save my life or take an enemy life, take the enemy life!"

Nobly said, but Aragor remained confused. He lowered his voice to compensate for the boom of Kellen's.

"Sir, *why* do you want to destroy them? What did you see there?"

Breathing heavily, Kellen fell suddenly still and his eyes fogged with fearful memory. He gazed again at the enemy ship. His voice changed. The skin around his eyes tightened.

"All these things we tell our children to scare them . . . things we pretend to have conquered in our own minds . . . they're all true, Aragor. There are demons. Real demons."

"Demons? Which demons, sir?"

Two strong shudders washed through Kellen's large

body, but he valiantly controlled himself and spoke with steady confidence.

"I saw the Iraga first," he told them, and paused.

A chill washed through the bridge. Aragor's heart began pounding. The other crewmen were looking at him as if to wonder whether to be afraid of their general's sudden insanity or afraid of what he was saying.

They didn't really think he was insane. They knew he was not.

That meant he had seen . . . it.

Kellen's frazzled condition and overheated excitement ran like a virus through them all.

"Then there were others," he added.

Aragor's hands were clenched. He could barely find his voice to speak. "More . . . Iraga?"

"No, other kinds. After the Iraga came out of the wall, others came too. Demons with vestigial membranes expanding from their shoulders . . . they spread their arms and the membranes opened and filled the space before me . . ."

"Shushara!" the helmsman gasped.

"Others had fingers that reached to the ground . . . and with fangs protruding from their foreheads . . ."

"Hullam'gar!" Mursha whispered, his face blanched. He looked at the helmsman, and together they were terrified.

Watching realization dawn in his crewmen's faces, Kellen nodded slowly. As he transferred his excitement to the crew, he seemed to grow more like his usual self, recapturing the restraint that had brought him ultimately to power.

"The tales are all true," he said. "They have come back as they promised they would . . . and they are on that ship out there."

His knees barely steady enough to support him, Aragor moved toward Kellen. "What should we do? What can we do?"

"I know what to do," the general said. "It will take us

all to defeat them. Aragor, you beam onto Ruhl's ship and take command of the fleet. Call the Empire for reinforcements. Track that ship, but do not go near it. Do *not.* I will go for help."

"For help? From where?"

"I said it would take us *all,"* Kellen repeated.

Once more he turned to the viper's tongue of a ship on the main screen. He began distractedly plucking the bits of moss and dust from his hair.

"We need a demon to fight demons," he said. "I am going to get one."

I begin to like you, Earthman. And I saw fear in the Klingon's eyes.

—Maab of Capella IV
"Friday's Child"

Chapter Three

"LEFT FLANK, secure position and open fire!"

Ah, life in space. Weeks of tedium broken by moments of terror.

For centuries they'd said that about being at sea. It was dead true about both.

Dust rolled off the ridge from photon salvo bombardment and turned into a shimmering heat in the valley below.

Two hundred enemy troops. Maybe more. Almost the whole crew of a large battleship. That meant there must be more than one ship up there now, and probably a conflict going on in space.

The captain's dirty hands and torn uniform tunic attested to a stressful morning. Barely noon, and there had been four major skirmishes already.

Through the shaggy hair of his attacker he had shouted to his own men, while chiding himself for having been surprised, for concentrating so much on the movements of the troops that he'd let himself be jumped. His face cracked into a grimace as he took a numbing blow to the side of his head and had to damn away the dizziness in order to keep fighting. If he had to be close to a Klingon, this was at least the way. Punching.

Beneath his soles the dry earth drummed with the thudding boots of men fighting all around on the jagged, jutting terrain. He sensed a shift in the attack pattern. Saw nothing, but he knew what he would do in this terrain, with these objectives, and made a bet with himself that the enemy would do it too. The chips were the lives of his men, the pot this planet and its sixty million tribesmen, some of whom had no idea the others existed.

The sky here was unforgiving, cloudless. His opponent twisted sideways and forced the captain's face into the sun, blinding him, and he staggered. The Klingon's shoulder crashed into his cheek. He felt his own teeth cut the inside of his lip, and the sudden warm salty taste of blood filled his mouth. It made him mad.

He spat the blood into the Klingon's glossy bronze face.

The Klingon arched backward and took the captain by both arms. They sawed at each other for a terrible instant before the grip was broken and the captain managed to land a knot of knuckles where they did some good. The Klingon spun and slashed downward with his hard wristband.

The captain raised his own arm to block the blow. Bracing his shoulder for the impact, he took it full force but managed to deflect it to the side and keep his skull from being cracked open, though the force drove him facedown to the ground. He sprawled. His skin shriveled in anticipation of a hit, but luck was with him. The Klingon stumbled.

Bracing his palms on the ground, the captain shoved upward, balling his fists in a single surge into the Klingon's solar plexus. He felt his hands go into the soft organs beneath the Klingon's rib cage, slamming the air out of the big alien's lungs.

The Klingon gagged, staggered, and went down, suffering. The captain scraped to his feet, knotted his rocky right fist, and delivered it like a piledriver into the soft spot at the base of the Klingon's skull. The attacker went down and didn't get up.

One down, two hundred to go.

Chest heaving, he straightened and looked around. Disruptor fire glazed the air and raised a crackle of burning ground cover and scrub brush. Hacking, shouting, and shooting, the Klingon wave was attempting another surge over the grade to the captain's left, their disruptor fire hampered by the rock formations, but creating dangerous shrapnel out of the stone.

He drew a breath and shouted.

"Spread out! Separate!" If his men weren't close together, there was less chance of having them mown down. "Go right! Move! Move, move!"

They swerved and scrambled in the direction he waved, the knuckle of rocks bearded with dry growth that would provide cover long enough for them to take a breath, reorganize. Motion diluted the terror with the twisted passion of combat.

"Take cover!" he shouted.

Not retreat, and they didn't.

Below, on this side of the narrow gravelly ramp leading between two towers of rock, his battered men lined the gully. Their red and gold backs created a necklace of ruby and amber jewels across the bright throat of the ridge as disruptor fire cracked over their heads. Among them were the native Capellans, taller than the humans by a head, and flamboyant with bright blocks of color on their long-sleeved suits and snug hoods that imitated helmets.

Hand-to-hand fighting had broken out in four places that he could see—make that five. Anxious to be in five places at once, he forced himself to keep low. The valley was dotted with solid patches of color—the Starfleet red and gold, the native purple, black, blue, green, and even pink now and then. They looked like giant Ninjas in goon boots and windbreaking capes, with fur stitched across their chests and hanging in long stoles over their shoulders.

He didn't care if the natives wore fishnet stockings as long as they backed up his troops, and they were doing that. He brought his palm-sized communicator to his lips and flipped open the antenna grid.

"Kirk to *Enterprise.*"

The ship didn't answer. Why not? Where were they?

In his mind Jim Kirk saw the giant cruiser looping the planet in orbit, emptied of a third of her crew because he needed them down here, and he gritted his teeth. Why wasn't the bridge crew answering? What was wrong?

At dawn, when he ordered his ship piloted away from the planet, everything had been peace, quiet, mission accomplished. He'd secured mining rights and turned the leaders of this province away from dealing with the oppressive Klingons. Now look.

Unfortunately the Klingons hadn't gone away pouting. They weren't satisfied at having been legitimately edged out. If they couldn't have this planet by trickery or bribery, they would take it by force. They'd come in with the sunrise over this region.

Leaning his communicator hand on his bruised knee, Kirk paused to catch his breath and scan the battlefield. It figured. Just when he got complacent, easy in his place as a spacelanes wagoneer, the universe snapped his axle.

This was nonaligned space, and that was the problem. Having made the treaty, Kirk was obliged to veer back in and protect the Capellans against the insulted Klingons. It was a good thing he was obliged to come in, because he was mad and would've come in anyway.

He had ninety-four men on the ground, plus sixty Capellans from the nearest tribe. Others had been summoned in the night from far-distant tribes, but they wouldn't make it in time. The battle was here and now. The next few minutes would tell.

The line of Starfleet crewmen was jagged because of the terrain of bulging rocks. Above them, in the taller and deeper rocks, native Capellans bombarded the on-coming enemies with stones and sling-pellets. Not deadly, but confusing. Soon the enemy would be fun-neled into withering fire from the Starfleet hand phasers.

The enemy surge was a litter of silver tunics and black sleeves, dark beards and sweaty bronze complexions, faces furious as if their land were being snatched instead of the other way around.

"Kirk to *Enterprise,*" he said again, then again. With bloody fingers he tried to adjust the gain. "*Enterprise,* come in. Mr. Scott, come in."

The instrument only crackled back at him. No answer.

He readjusted it for local communication.

"Kirk to Spock. Kirk to Spock . . ."

Nothing.

He looked up, scanned the bright rocks for the form of his first officer.

There was no other slash of color like Spock in this battlescape. All other Starfleet forces were command or security troops, wearing gold or red tunics. Commander Spock's lone blue shirt stood out. Among the hundreds of Terrans, Capellans, and Klingons, he was the only Vulcan.

He had been the only Vulcan for a long time, the first in Starfleet, and bore his solitude with grace. Kirk watched with appreciation, but also annoyance. Why wasn't Spock pulling out his communicator and an-swering?

The Dakota-like terrain, baked by midday sun a few shades brighter than Earth's, was hot and dry as baked clay. His men maneuvered in companies of twenty, each under a lieutenant. If he couldn't talk to them, how could they be effective?

The captain slid to one knee, barely realizing his own flash of weakness, and shook the communicator.

"Kirk to Spock, come in!"

Neutralized somehow. He couldn't reach the ship, but also couldn't reach his own men down here. Without communicators, he was back in the 1800s, orchestrating ground assault with hand signals, smoke, and mirrors.

He looked around, picked a huddle of his own troops down the incline, and skidded toward them.

"Jim! Where'd you come from?"

Kirk waved at the dust he'd raised and looked toward the voice.

Ship's surgeon Leonard McCoy's face was almost unrecognizable, his squarish features coated with sand, brown hair caked with sweaty dust until it was the same color as his face. His tunic, the only other blue one on the terrain, wasn't very blue anymore.

"What happened to you?" Kirk asked.

"What d'you mean, what happened to me? Klingons all over the place, Capellans knocking me down left and right, and Spock doing his Wellington imitation in my face!"

"Give me your communicator." Without waiting he snatched the doctor's communicator from his belt and snapped it open. "Kirk to *Enterprise.*"

The empty crackle aggravated him.

"Kirk to Spock. Kirk to anybody."

"What's wrong, sir?" A skinny lieutenant named Bannon sagged back against a rock for a moment's rest and knuckled his dust-reddened eyes.

"Instrument failure. Try yours."

The red-haired lieutenant tried, then looked up guiltily when he failed. "Sir . . ."

"You too," Kirk said to the three others, all ensigns, huddled in this clutch of rocks.

"How can they all be broken down?" McCoy asked as Kirk tossed him his communicator. He rattled it at his ear.

"They can't."

Lieutenant Bannon rubbed his bruised jaw. "Can't we reach the ship, sir? They could break through the communications trouble from Lieutenant Uhura's console, couldn't they?"

Nettled, Kirk frowned until his face hurt and didn't meet Bannon's questioning eyes. "Probably."

One of the ensigns glanced at Bannon, then asked, "Does that mean they're in trouble up there? They can't come after us?"

"Don't worry," McCoy supplied, sparing Kirk having to answer. "Mr. Scott's a no-guff man. He'd step over anybody's line. I wouldn't get in his way. If the Klingons do, it's their own bad luck."

Kirk looked out between two knuckles of rock at the Starfleet company nearest to the ramp. "That's Lieutenant Doyle's group. Phasers up . . . they're looking for a target. Awfully quiet down there all of a sudden . . ."

"Maybe the Klingons are retreating," McCoy suggested with hope in his blue eyes.

"Not likely." Kirk leaned forward with both hands on the rocks. "The local Klingon commander's in trouble. He lost his mining deal with this planet when we showed up. If he goes back a loser, his career's in the dumper."

"Jim, keep your head down! They can take aim on you from up there!"

Dropping only a couple of inches in response, Kirk glanced up, up, up to the highest crags, where Klingon lookouts had taken position.

Below that, Lieutenant Doyle's bright blond hair shone in the hot sun, but he was behind cover, huddled with about fifteen other Starfleeters and a handful of Capellans. Kirk saw the lieutenant's arm move as he gestured weapons up.

A dozen hand phasers came nose up, then leveled and took aim.

"He sees something we can't see." Kirk made silent bets with himself about what Doyle saw. "They're taking aim . . . I see the Klingons."

"Where?"

"Over the top of the incline."

"How many?"

"Not enough for a dozen phasers, that's for sure. And they're not charging. They're moving back and forth up there, trying to get attention."

"You think it's a trap, sir?" Bannon asked.

"I think it's something. Trick of some kind . . . Doyle's being enticed to fire. I need communications!"

"I'll go, sir!" Bannon thrust to his full height, almost as tall as the native Capellans but about half as thick.

McCoy grabbed him and forced him back down, out of the line of fire from the upper rocks. "Down, boy!"

Bannon's red hair was plastered across his pale forehead and he seemed exhausted, but there was determination in his eyes. He was willing to go.

"All right, go," Kirk said. "But keep low. Don't get any closer than you absolutely have to. I don't want all my people bunched up."

"Aye, sir!" The young officer took his own phaser in his hand and scraped away on the slanted slabs.

Klingon activity on the top of the incline was increasing. Still no advancement, just more figures moving this way and that, taking potshots with disruptors at the hidden Starfleet forces. Rocks splattered and splintered with every miss, but they kept shooting, even without clear targets.

Bannon made a red and black streak of color as he moved across the lower landscape, picking his way toward Doyle's company. Slow going. As Kirk watched he felt bad about the terrain. Down on the plain the ground was nearly level. Large groups could move more freely, attack more openly, but there would be death by the hundreds. Here, the ground was ungiving, stony, and damned, but there was cover.

Before Bannon came within earshot, Kirk saw Doyle's men stretching out their phaser arms. In his mind he heard the order—*Ready . . . aim . . .*

"Not yet," he uttered, feeling the sweaty tension of McCoy at his side. "Not yet—"

Ducking blue disruptor shots from above, Bannon was moving slowly, but he was nearly there.

Fire!

A globular burst of red-pink phaser fire launched from the huddled Starfleet group and struck out at the incline. The up there Klingons ducked out of sight. Not one was hit.

Instead, an answer came from overhead—a gulp of bright bluish energy sprayed from the cloudless sky and landed squarely on Doyle's men as if a giant flyswatter had just come down. The sheer whine of sound drove Kirk, McCoy, and the three ensigns plunging for the ground, cuffing their ears.

Kirk forced himself up instantly and looked down into the valley.

The bodies of his crewmen and several tribesmen streaked the dusty flats. Two hundred yards short of his goal, Bannon lay knocked flat. Fury roiled in Kirk's chest. He'd been outthought by the enemy.

"What the blazes was *that?*" McCoy gasped, peering at the sky, then back down at the draped bodies.

"Some sort of response to the phasers," Kirk muttered.

"From where? A ship?"

"Maybe a shuttlecraft."

"Let me go down there!" the doctor asked. "I can treat those men."

"You stay put." Kirk heard the anger in his voice and valiantly tried to keep it from lopping over from his own self-recriminations and onto McCoy. He didn't bother pointing out that those men were probably beyond treatment.

"Captain!"

The familiar baritone call caught him fast and he turned and headed toward it.

"Here!" he called. "Spock, over here!"

From among the whey-colored rocks, First Officer Spock kept low but hurried to them, carrying a bow in one hand and an arrow in the other. He'd holstered his own phaser, and that meant something.

"Did you see the flash?" the Vulcan asked without amenity. "Disruptor backwash came from the sky."

Kirk nodded. "What do you think it is? A ship?"

Spock shook his head, squinting. "Too low. More likely a satellite keyed to Starfleet phaser energy. You will recall that Klingon disruptor fire did not set it off."

"Could it be affecting our communicators?"

"I have no facts to corroborate that, but the theoretical conclusion bears some logic." Spock's dark eyes scanned Kirk's blood-splattered gold shirt. He was assessing his captain for injuries, but he said nothing about it. He too was breathing hard, despite this hot weather's being more natural for him than shipboard climate.

Kirk looked up, scanning the sky. "If Scotty could get in close with the ship, he could knock any orbiter out with one shot."

"We must assume he is occupied." The Vulcan's words were laced with portent. He offered nothing more specific, but there was concern in his dust-grooved expression.

"We're on our own. McCoy, corral those three ensigns. We're going to need runners to communicate with the field positions."

"Yes, sir," McCoy responded, with fear clutching his sudden sense of purpose. At least he didn't argue.

"All right, if that's the way it is," Kirk huffed to his first officer as they watched they doctor pick his way back to the grotto. "They neutralize our weapons, then I want theirs."

Spock nodded, scanning the enemy lines. They hung together in silence for a few seconds, and Kirk listened to the sound of his own heart pound in his ears.

His left middle finger was hurting. Probably a sliver. Felt like it might be under the fingernail. He glanced down, but didn't see anything through the dirt plastered to his fingers, and thought the sight of their captain picking at a fingernail might not do his crew any good.

He shook his head. Out of all the bruises and cuts, a sliver was distracting him. Battle could be a fun-house mirror sometimes.

As the ground cover crackled behind him he spun around and almost lashed out, but Spock pressed him back somehow, subtly, only raising one arm a little. Kirk glared at what had startled him—McCoy and the three ensigns slipping into the cover of the rock with them.

Steadying himself, he tilted a silent thanks to Spock and motioned the others toward him, then gestured them to huddle.

Crouching behind the big flat slab, Kirk looked at his men one by one. "We think the Klingons have deployed a satellite or shuttle that blankets the immediate area with destructive power when it detects Federation phaser fire. Your job is to get to our commanding officers and relay information. Standing order is phasers down, indigenous weapons only. Consider the phasers neutralized. Draw the enemy into hand fighting if possible. It'll give us a more equal chance than letting them have wide berth. New goal—capture Klingon disruptors."

"Sir, I don't see how we can fight disruptors without phasers," Ensign Dunton said, a gaunt scrapper with a gap between his front teeth.

"Phasers can target thousands in open ground," Spock said calmly, "but at close proximity, it may not be any better than a sword or knife, Ensign."

"It's awful," Dunton uttered, glancing out at the collapsed forms of his shipmates. "They shouldn't have to die in the dirt like that."

"We're here to knock the Klingons back," Kirk said firmly. "That's the bet all spacefarers make. Our lives might come down to this."

He saw in their faces that they suddenly understood something they'd never thought of before—that this might be the real fate they'd signed up for. No stars nor bright nebulae, but the dust of some distant alien planet between blood-crusted teeth, and the taste of foreign soil on a dying breath.

Beside Dunton, Ensign Fulciero looked up at him like a kid on Santa's knee who was hoping for the right answer. "All we gotta do is hold them off from the villages long enough for the battle in space to be won, right, sir?"

Kirk placated him with a nod. "And Starfleet to send reinforcements."

He didn't estimate how much time that might take.

"What if they get past the ship?" the third ensign asked. "They could lay waste to half the planet from up there."

Kirk landed a fierce glance on him. "They won't."

Fulciero blinked into the sun. "Why not?"

"Because they won't. We don't have time for lessons, gentlemen. You have your orders. Disperse."

Being on the move with a message to deliver would be good for them. Better than sitting here, anticipating disaster and asking questions that would take time to answer.

Tense, he and Spock and McCoy watched the ensigns fan out, trying to reach companies of Starfleet forces before anybody else used a phaser. His skin crawled in expectation of the thready whine that could come any second, from any quarter. Twice he thought he heard it, and glanced at the sky, waiting for the bright pounding response, but he was wrong both times. His unit commanders were better than he remembered. He had become too custodial. Forgotten that they could see the sky too, knew a plasma burst when they saw it, and were good at their jobs. They weren't using phasers. In several places he saw his crew holstering their hand weapons and taking up the crude weapons of the planet—rocks, sticks, Capellan swords and klegats.

For a moment he wanted to tell his men not to try using the klegats. The bladed disks were used efficiently by the strong Capellans, but they took training. They were deliberately not very sharp. Injury came from raw force and bone breakage. It was a crushing weapon as much as a slicing one.

"Captain," Spock snapped, "here they come."

He pointed to the upper ground, now swelling with living enemy soldiers who were met by advanced Starfleet guards, swinging and hacking.

"Typical," McCoy threw in. "They know they've knocked out our phasers, so they're advancing." Frustration showed in his eyes as the doctor gripped the ledge and watched their own men fall wounded, and clearly he wished he could sneak out and begin treating them. "Why aren't they using their disruptors?"

"Terrain," Kirk said. "Too many obstructions."

"I believe there is more." Spock pressed a hand to the rock and straightened to look over. "Klingons prefer hand-to-hand fighting. They consider it more honorable to kill at close quarters than with a long-range weapon. If they can arrange for that, they will do so."

"So we'll give it to them," Kirk said. "We can—"

At his hip, his communicator suddenly whistled.

He snatched at it, missed, and had to grab again. "Kirk to *Enterprise*—status report!"

"Scott here, sir. We punched through the communications blanket."

"What's going on up there?"

"Battle, sir. Three cruisers. We're holding our own now. But we've got a new development. More Klingons coming in, and I don't know what to make of it."

Kirk glanced at Spock. "More Klingons. Lovely. Why don't you know what to make of it, Scotty? What're they doing?"

"Unidentified bird coming in at warp six, with wings up, weapons systems off, broadcasting interstellar distress call."

"A distress call while at warp six?" Kirk let the communicator drop a little and looked at Spock again. "Not ship distress, then."

"Unless they are under hot pursuit," Spock suggested.

"Not likely." Kirk brought the communicator up

again. "Let the situation play out, Scotty. Don't fire on them until you figure out their intent. If you don't like it when you find it out, blow them out of the sky."

"Aye, sir."

"And there's a satellite or some kind of hovering mechanism over our locality that's keyed to our hand phasers. Can you knock it out?"

"We've picked up on it and we're targeting it. If we overshoot, we could hit you there on the surface."

"Understood. Hurry up."

"Aye, sir. Scotty out."

"It's good to hear his voice." Kirk pressed the back of his hand to his bleeding mouth. "Gentlemen, I think I've finally reached my limit."

They both looked at him, and Spock asked, "Sir?"

"I'm sick of Klingons."

He pushed away from the rocks.

"On your toes. This is it." He stood up and started out into the open.

"Jim!" McCoy snatched him by the arm. "They'll see you!"

"I want them to see me. Come on, Spock."

Enemy forces were plowing over the ridge, nearly two hundred of them at a quick sweeping estimate. Their silver tunics and black sleeves were crisp in the unforgiving sunlight, their howl of charge more chilling than the whine of their disruptors. Screams of injured and dying men looped up like sirens. The survivors on both sides scrambled for new cover.

But none for retreat. It was good to see.

He knew better than to micromanage. His men knew he was here. They'd fight in pairs or triplets or any kind of unit they could form. Enthusiasm carried them up the incline to meet the enemy, and it dimmed their sight of the Klingons' fury until they could match it with their own.

He plunged out into the open and scooped up a raw wooden club and a stumpy sword from the body of a fallen Capellan.

"Spock!" When his first officer turned, Kirk tossed him the sword.

"The doctor is right," Spock said by way of warning. "They will target a commanding officer if they can pick you out."

He was plumbing for Kirk's plans.

All right.

"If I don't give them a target," Kirk told him, "they'll lay scattering fire and wound as many as they can hit. If I let them spot me, they'll concentrate on trying to knock me out, preferably hand-to-hand, for the glory of it. I can make them fixate on me. Goad them into letting me manipulate their battle plan."

With a nod of understanding, Spock let disapproval creep into his expression, but he couldn't fight the sense of it.

"Problem is," Kirk added, "they might target you too."

Spock passed the sword from his left hand to his right. "Acceptable, sir."

"I thought you'd say that. Let's go."

Chapter Four

As THE KLINGONS came roaring down the incline, disruptors holstered and daggers gleaming, Kirk and Spock charged out to meet them, pushing as close to the center as possible when they finally met the enemies head-on.

Kirk had to work to draw attention to himself, convince the swarming enemy that he was the leader. Ordinary in all ways but the fire in his mind, Kirk knew he cut no particular swash among the combatants, especially the seven-foot Capellans. But if he wanted his enemies to identify him, and today he did, he'd have to be conspicuous.

As he clubbed away the first Klingon who charged him, he loudly gave orders to his men and waved his arms with the captain's slashes on the wrists. He stayed as close as he could to the center of the action, and in moments the Klingons were looking up from their own fights, spotting him and Spock.

Around him, his own men met the howling Klingons with clench-jawed purposefulness. The Starfleet team weren't spoiled brats who couldn't fight with anything but phasers. They held clubs across their bodies like battle staffs, one hand on each end, effective for blocking or ramming, and the humans were lighter and faster than either the Klingons or Capellans. His men weren't being bogged down by their own weight, as some of the others were.

He was charged by the gleam in his men's eyes. They were enjoying this, in a twisted, unfortunate way. They had to enjoy it a little in order to survive it—stretching their intelligence, daring themselves to live up to the worst, the ugliest. . . . There was something electric in forcing an enemy back. This land fighting was refreshing in the shock of reality it gave a ship's crew, so long sequestered in the isolet of their vessel, who so rarely got the chance to fight their enemy eye to eye. Driven to impose their will on their enemies, here they were unharnessed.

They knew their duty, and Kirk knew his. It was the captain's bravery that made men face the enemy again after fighting all morning, the message in his manner that he would not only fight with them, but for them, that made them rather die fighting than scrambling. Safety no longer had flavor. None asked himself anymore the lurid question, *What am I dying for?* The question had an answer—not for this distant herd of unfriendly people nor for this speck of land on a speck in the sky. *What am I dying for?*

For the captain.

Why?

Because he would die for me.

Jim Kirk knew how they felt. He set himself constantly to live up to their devotion. He remembered his captains and what he expected of them. Determined to be worthy of what his men were doing out here, answering that ringing question in their minds over and over until they could summon their own inner fortifications, he willed himself visible among them.

Fighting twenty yards apart, he and Spock were an attractive target. Klingon soldiers were veering toward them, each hungering for the glory of killing the leaders.

A Klingon soldier charged down on him fast, not checking his speed at all as he flew down the incline. He struck Kirk with a full-body blow that sent them both bruising to the ground, then tumbling.

Kirk waited until they stopped rolling, then raised his free arm and drove the elbow into the Klingon's throat. The soldier gagged, rolled off, and crawled away on his hands and knees.

Lashing out with his right leg, the captain caught the crawling soldier's knees and knocked them out from under him. The Klingon sprawled, still choking, and Kirk snatched for the disruptor—this Klingon didn't have one. So Kirk went for the dagger at the soldier's belt. He looked up to see two more plunging down on him, and he'd better be upright to meet them.

Dust puffed up all around him from the scrape of hard soles and the impact of thunderbolt disruptor shots. So much for honor.

Some of the Klingons on the high ground were trying to aim between the fighters, but were mostly hitting the dirt as they tried to avoid killing their own crewmates. The sizzle of energy bolts raised the hairs on Kirk's arms as the shots whistled past him.

Where was Spock? He couldn't see his first officer anymore. Concentration was stolen by the two Klingons bulldozing at him through the combatants, with two more right behind them, all with their eyes on him. There were negatives to this manipulate-the-enemy theory.

They could charge him together, but unless they cooperated they couldn't hit him at the same time, and they wouldn't cooperate. He hoped.

Hoped hard as he made his bet and raised his right arm to take on the Klingon who was a millimeter closer.

Slashing outward with his dagger, the Klingon danced out of the way—Kirk had bet wrong—and faked to one side, leaving Kirk's unprotected midsection for the second soldier.

Kirk couldn't bring his dagger down in time. The second Klingon caught him in a brutal embrace and with sheer strength began squeezing the life from him, keeping him from breathing.

Adrenaline surged as Kirk felt the queasiness of death close at his throat. Over the shoulder of the Klingon attacking him he saw the other two roaring in, eyes blazing and teeth bared. He struggled to raise his knee—at least he could get one of them—

A shadow crossed his face. A bulky ensign—looked like Wilson—who had hands like bear paws and no neck at all, plunged in and took on the other two, knocking one flat with the sheer force of his charge.

A growl of anger boiled up beside Kirk. Now those two Klingons were furious at Wilson for having blocked their way, and the one on the ground slashed out at Wilson's legs with his dagger while the ensign was throwing punches at the other one. The ensign tried to dance away, but the Klingons used their combined power to drive him into the blade.

"Break!" Kirk shouted. "Ensign, break off!"

Wilson flashed a glance at him and tried to obey the order, but couldn't do it. His mouth burst open with shock as the blade chewed into his spine.

Whipped up by what he saw, Kirk found his hands between his own body and the chest of the Klingon grappling him, forced his elbows upward.

As the Klingon's body went stiff with pain and the grip on Kirk fell away, Kirk shoved the soldier over and yanked the disruptor from the belt. Now he had one, but it was warm in his hands, nearly drained.

The trick was not to waste it.

He swung around, jockeying for aim; he found Wilson still fighting, and blocking a clear shot.

"Down, Ensign!"

Wilson couldn't drop back, but managed to tilt to one side, and Kirk aimed, took a breath, let out half of it, and fired.

The disruptor buzzed in his hand and spat a clean string of energy into the chest of one of the Klingons. The soldier buckled and fell backward.

The other Klingon ignored the fate of his partner, but knew the disruptor was coming around to him and tried to shove the wounded ensign down in order to lash out at Kirk with a hard metal wristband. He would've made it, too, except that Wilson leaned back in and took the blow meant for his captain, a savage crash to the top of his head.

The Klingon's thumbnail caught Kirk's uniform and ripped into his shoulder. He felt fabric give way, then flesh, as if he'd been caught in a briar bush.

He raised a knee, kicked the Klingon backward into his disruptor sights, and fired.

The Klingon shouted an unintelligible word as the beam blasted him into the rocks and he fell hard.

In Kirk's hand the disruptor started beeping—drained. After a morning of firefights, he had gotten its last two shots. Furiously he pitched it at the skull of one of the downed Klingons and was gratified by the *crack*.

As Ensign Wilson staggered, Kirk snatched the unfortunate crewman from behind, desperate that the boy's last seconds not be his loneliest. Blood from his wounds drained across Kirk's uniform and trousers. He felt the thick body shudder in his arms, wobble, and go limp. Suddenly he slipped out of Kirk's hands. Dead or alive, there was no way to tell.

Rage boiled up behind Kirk's eyes. His disruptor was junk, he'd lost his knife, so he grabbed Wilson's club, tucked it at his side in both hands like a lance. Lips drawn back, face chalky with sweat-plastered dust, uniform torn at the shoulder, he charged into the tangle of fighting men.

He plowed through the formless battle, assisting his men and allies with his club, landing almost every blow to good effect, each time freeing another of his men to move forward. Only when he tripped and went down on a knee was his momentum interrupted—and that was when he twisted around to get back on his feet and ended up looking back the way he had come.

Against the rattan landscape a blue dot caught his eye. At first he thought he'd found Spock, but he was wrong.

"McCoy!"

The doctor had been rooted out of his hiding place somehow and was up against the rocks, defending himself against, luckily, only one Klingon. In hand-to-hand fighting, McCoy could hold his own for a minute or two, but soon he would falter. Surprise him and he would fight, but after a few moments he'd catch the eyes of someone fighting him, notice a muscle in a taut neck, and the living condition of his opponents would get to him. His inner compass would steer him away from self-preservation, and the doctor would pause.

One of these days the pause would get him killed. Kirk had learned to watch for it.

McCoy was waving a sword he'd found, but he was doing it only in defense. So he'd already crossed that line. He was backing up, tighter and tighter against the unforgiving rocks.

Any second he'll hesitate. Kirk looked around frantically, snatched the arm of a crewman rushing past him and shouted at another one. "Brown, Mellendez! About face! Help McCoy!"

"Yes, sir!"

"Aye, sir!"

They took off at barreling run.

He swung back to the shouts and clacks of men and blades and throttled his way into the fray with the club. Then he threw the club down and scooped up one of the short Capellan swords and hacked his way through to the higher ground. Disruptor fire crackled past him—a jolt of hope hit as he realized some of those shots were coming from his own men, those who had managed to lay their hands upon Klingon disruptors and were turning them on their owners. Still, the high-powered weapons could only be of so much use in tight quarters, no more use to the Starfleeters than to the Klingons themselves.

Still, the odds were beginning to balance.

Hot shale sprayed up and stung his cheeks, then went on to rattle across the rocks. As he scrambled upward, a half-dozen Klingons broke from their struggles and followed. Their ambition was getting the better of them.

It's working. They're disorganized.

Taunting them with a few swipes of the sword, he got several to follow as he climbed the rocks, then kicked two of them off balance. They tumbled and crashed to the jagged talus below, and when he saw what happened to them, he realized how high he'd climbed and that he'd better not slip.

When he glanced up to make sure he wasn't boxing himself into a trap, he caught a blue flash in his periphery. McCoy? Up there?

He looked down, across the battle area, and saw the doctor standing good ground with Brown, Mellendez, and two other *Enterprise* crewmen.

He swung around to the other swatch of blue. Spock.

The Vulcan was trapped on high ground, being funneled to the point of a slanted arm of rock by at least eight Klingons. Kirk's plan had worked to the worst—they'd targeted his first officer.

Holding his own against the Klingons but not against the shrinking footing, Spock was markedly stronger, but not faster or meaner than an angry human crew up against a Klingon force. He would try to fight logically, and that might not work against Klingons.

As Kirk frantically searched for a way to get over there, fly maybe, Spock fought with grim deliberation using the sword Kirk had given him, but he was losing. He was just plain outnumbered.

Kicking at the Klingons trying to reach him, Kirk divided his attention and picked out one of his most experienced field officers.

"Giotto!"

The lieutenant commander of Security didn't hear him, so he shouted again, and again until Giotto's squared face and silver hair turned up to him. Giotto assessed his captain's situation and shouted, "Coming, sir!"

"Belay that!" Kirk shouted. "Assist Mr. Spock!"

Giotto swung his wide shoulders, scanned the rocks, then yelled, "Security detail!"

Seven men around him, three short of a full detail, broke from what they were doing and managed to follow as Giotto charged toward Spock's outcropping.

Kirk's heart pounded. They weren't going to make it. Pebbles chipped from the ledge under Spock's feet and rained onto the unforgiving talus below. One of the Klingons had made it all the way up and was sparring with Spock, enjoying the Vulcan's situation, and the only thing saving Spock for the moment was the next Klingon down, who wanted the glory for himself and was holding on to the top Klingon's ankle and keeping him back.

Desperate, Kirk ignored the Klingons encroaching on him, took his sword by the blade, wheeled it back over his shoulder, and launched it like a throwing knife.

It wheeled through the air just beautifully, and struck the top Klingon, but not with the blade. The hilt came about and knocked the Klingon in the back of the neck. He stumbled, and the second Klingon pitched him off balance. The top one gasped audibly and skidded off the ledge to land on a shoulder below.

Kirk winced as he heard the Klingon's clavicle snap in two even under the protective vest.

Spock wasn't wearing anything like that.

Where were Giotto and the Security detail? There—they'd gone behind a clutch of overgrowth to find a way to climb the rocks. Too slow, too slow.

It's my fault. They've been fighting all morning. They're tired. They won't get to him in time.

He'd thrown his sword and now had nothing to fight with, so he kicked downward at the Klingons trying to get to him. They could shoot him off, but he saw in their hungry eyes the desire to defeat the enemy leader with their own hands. Only the fact that they were competing instead of helping each other was saving him for the moment. If his luck held out—

The crack of rock sounded clearly across the open terrain, and Kirk looked up at the exact horrible instant that Spock's last inch of footing gave way.

Kirk reached out. He saw his empty hand against the sky, Spock's form a hundred yards too far from his outstretched fingers, arms flung outward as the Vulcan toppled backward and disappeared.

"Damn it!" Kirk choked.

He stared at the empty air where Spock had been a moment ago, then shifted his rage downward at the Klingons trying to get to him.

They saw the change in his face. Though he was weaponless and at the disadvantage, at least three of them started to back down.

He put all his anger into a downward plunge. After all, there were nice soft Klingon noses to land on.

He felt a dozen impacts on his body—thighs, ribs, elbows, knees—as he body-slammed his way straight down through the Klingons and drove himself and all of them into a tangle, scraping and scratching down the slanted shelf. By the time he struck the bottom, he had scraped off at least two of the Klingons and landed on the rest of them.

His body screamed for attention. He ignored it and tried to get to his feet, but fell twice and shuffled outward on one foot, a knee, and the heel of a hand. His left arm was numb from the elbow down.

Slowly he made his way past the stunned Klingons. He had to get to Spock. If his first officer somehow survived the fall, the other Klingons would rush in and slaughter him where he lay. Inhaling dust, Kirk willed himself forward.

"Stop!"

He looked up. Who was that? No voice he recognized . . . one of the Capellans?

Out into the middle of the battling armies, striding as deliberately as if on parade, came a thick-bodied Klingon officer.

No, not just an officer . . . a *general!*

But there was no Klingon general in this sector. . . .

The wide newcomer strode into the middle of the action and held out both his short meaty arms, hands upright in a halting gesture.

"Stop the fighting! Stop! Stop this!"

The general now turned to the upper rocks and shouted—roared—at his own kind.

"I said *stop!*"

Chapter Five

LEFT ARM NUMB, his chest constricted from the dust, Kirk scraped between the stunned combatants as they stood heaving and staring, and managed to keep from going down on his knees again.

"Spock!" he called.

No answer. He didn't really expect one.

The Klingon general lowered his arms and watched as the captain crossed the battleground. The general seemed to understand and stood like Henry VIII on a jousting field, watching as Kirk came around the gravelly talus skirt.

Kirk first saw Spock as a swatch of blue and black quilted against the stones, surrounded by Giotto and his men, who ringed the fallen body and stood off several Klingons who wanted to deal the death blow if it hadn't been dealt already.

He thought the Vulcan moved, but there was so much dust. . . .

Everything had stopped, just stopped. Klingons, Starfleet crew, Capellans, all standing still—those who were still standing—looking at the Klingon general who waited like a lone monolith at their center, and at Kirk as he moved between the bodies of the fallen.

Maybe this was some kind of demand for surrender. A full general?

He glanced at the Klingon general in something like contempt or dare—even he wasn't sure—but kept to his purpose. One thing at a time.

Giotto's men parted for him, but kept their weapons up and didn't slack their stance against the Klingon soldiers.

It felt good to kneel finally. The ground had been pulling at him—it felt good to give in.

Spock was looking up, blinking, dazed but conscious, at least. His lips were pressed in frustration and effort, pickle-green blood showing in scratches on his forehead and the point of his right ear.

As the gravel cut into his knee, Kirk pressed his good hand to Spock's tattered sleeve.

"You all right?" he asked.

"Stunned," Spock said with effort, and with pain that he was trying to hide. His voice was as gravelly as the stuff he was lying on. Cautiously he raised his head, brows drawn, then in something like amusement added, "And, I believe, grazed here and there. . . ."

"Where?" Kirk persisted.

Suddenly aggravated at not being able to self-diagnose, Spock glanced up at him and belittled himself with a bob of his angular brows. "I am not certain."

Glancing up at the needle of rock above them, Kirk realized it was about two decks higher than he'd estimated from way over there. "How did you survive that?"

"Starfleet training," Spock said lightly. "I rolled."

Kirk pressed out a sympathetic grin. "Think you can get up? We've got a new development."

Faced with that, Spock pressed his palms to the stones and tried to lift his shoulders. His voice cracked as he grunted, "Shall certainly attempt it."

"Mr. Giotto, give us a hand."

In the back of his mind he could hear the protests of

common sense as he and Giotto pulled the injured first officer to his feet, but it was important to Kirk that the enemies see the Starfleet officers upright and thinking. Once they got him up it became clear that Spock couldn't stand on his own and Kirk accepted that he might be making a mistake.

He waved in a yeoman to help Giotto, then said, "Bring him over here. I want him to hear whatever goes on."

At the center of what was quickly becoming a scraggly ring of mixed combatants, the Klingon general turned in place. "Who is in command here?" he bellowed, but he was looking from Klingon to Klingon, not at the Starfleet team.

Behind the Security detail, Kirk straightened and watched. Was this some kind of crank?

"I am!" A Klingon commander came up over the incline and hurried down, clearly infuriated. "Why have you stopped our victory?"

The general's big body turned and he raised his arms in contempt. "I see no victory here. What's the matter with you? Why are you squabbling over this bit of dirt? Wasting men and munitions, and for what? A few shipments of toparine? You're a fool."

The commander waved his hand at Kirk. "They killed my representative!"

One of the big Capellans stepped forward and contradicted, "*I* killed your representative. After he betrayed us."

The blunt honesty silenced the Klingon commander, and Kirk took that as a cue to move in. He didn't care about their inner quarrels. He forced himself not to limp as he put his back to the commander as a kind of insult and raised his chin to the general.

"Who the hell are you?" he asked.

The high-ranker squared off before him. "I am General Kellen."

Behind Kirk, the other Klingons collectively gasped and relaxed their postures in respect.

"Kellen?" Kirk repeated. "Of the Muscari Incident?"

"Yes."

The general waited until his identity sank in all around. Even if they didn't know what he had done in the past, they had heard his name and they knew his reputation. So did Kirk. General Kellen . . . the only calm Klingon Kirk knew of.

That kind of thing gets around.

The general didn't seem particularly impressed with himself, but he was clearly counting on Kirk's being impressed with him.

And it was close.

They stood together on the printless stone flat, face-to-face, sizing each other up.

After he'd ticked off a measured pause, the general asked, "Your ship is the *Enterprise?*"

Narrowing his eyes in the bright sunlight, Kirk felt his brow tighten. "Yes . . ."

"Then you are Captain James B. Kirk?"

"James T. So what?"

"Then I am here to ask for your help on behalf of the Klingon Empire and your own Federation."

"Help about what?"

"We need your help, Captain. The demons have returned. The Havoc has come."

"Does this mean you're declaring a cease-fire?"

The question had already gotten its answer, but Kirk wanted his men and the Klingon men to hear it from the local top, which at the moment was General Kellen. He didn't want anyone ending up with a dagger in the back from the overzealous among them.

Peering over those funny glasses, Kellen nodded hurriedly. "Yes. And I should mention that your starship is about to punch holes in my cruiser. Instruct them not to."

Perhaps the general was fishing for an act of trust, or at least balance, or maybe he just wanted what he said he wanted. A chance to talk.

Either way, there would be a chance to pause and regroup. Never taking his eyes off Kellen, Kirk snapped up his communicator and flipped open the antenna grid.

"Kirk to *Enterprise*. Go to defensive posture . . . cease fire and stand by. If you don't hear from me in ten minutes, open fire." Without waiting for acknowledgment from Scott, he lowered the communicator sharply enough to make a point. "I appreciate who you are, General, but you can't have this planet."

Kellen held out both hands in acquiescence. "I do not want this planet. I don't know why some elements do. It has always been my standing to let the Federation tend these backward herds. Then we'll take the planets when they're worth something."

Kirk snorted. "Wanna bet?"

"It has always been a mystery to me when the Federation will fight and why," Kellen said. "That you will fight to the last man to defend something you do not care to possess. A planet like this is not worth the loss of a ship of the line. I give you this planet without contention. Congratulations. I have already spoken to your Starfleet Command. They have agreed to let me approach you if I agreed to stop this battle. It is stopped. Now I *must* speak with you, Captain Kirk."

His voice, though he was a large man, was high-pitched, Kirk noticed now, not low as one might expect a large man's to be, yet it had a certain ring of authority—probably out of sheer practice.

"You'll have to wait your turn," Kirk said. "I'll be back in when I've taken care of my men."

Kellen said nothing, but clasped his hands behind his wide back and struck a stance of impatience.

With a measured glance at Spock, Kirk swung around and scanned his surprised crewmen and the disgruntled Klingons, all standing among each other, eyeing each other's weapons, none of them sure what to do.

He turned another quarter turn and spotted McCoy, kneeling at the body of Ensign Wilson.

Good a place as any to start.

With a purposeful stride he hurried—but not too fast—to the doctor and kept his back to Kellen.

"Well," he muttered, "how do you like that?"

"Not much," the doctor muttered back, gazing at poor Wilson as he rose to his feet.

Kirk surveying quickly the surgeon's bruised face. "Are you hurt?"

McCoy blinked, frowned, rubbed his hands together, and said, "No, Captain, I'm not hurt."

"Then get started with your triage."

"Yes, sir."

As the party broke up and others gathered around for instructions, Kirk dashed off orders to others standing around.

"Log that I gave a field commission to Zdunic. He's now a lieutenant."

"Acknowledged," Spock said from behind him.

Weakness in the baritone voice registered suddenly. Kirk turned to his first officer and realized Spock had been answering him as if nothing was wrong, but the first officer was still leaning heavily on the yeoman, picking at his tricorder, valiantly trying to record the details of the aftermath and his captain's orders.

"Mr. Spock. . . . McCoy! Over here first. Yeoman, set him down." Kirk moved in as Spock was gingerly lowered to sit on a handy boulder, and carefully pulled the tricorder strap up over Spock's head to hand it to the yeoman. "Spock . . . sorry."

There was more pain in the Vulcan's face now. He was having trouble masking it. His lean frame was clenched, stomach muscles tight, shoulders and arms stiff as he pressed down on the boulder, though he didn't take his eyes from the Klingon general. Distrust pulled at him through his pain.

"Curious, Captain," he said, watching the Klingon general, "that he would concern himself with a skirmish."

"He's got me curious," Kirk acknowledged.

"What happened?" McCoy asked as he hurried to

them. If he had seen Spock a moment ago in the background, he hadn't noticed that the Vulcan was being held up by the yeoman beside him.

"He fell," Kirk said. "From up there. I can't believe you didn't see it happen."

"I was busy." McCoy ran his medical tricorder from Spock's shoulder to his pelvis. "Jim, my God—you shouldn't have moved him! He's got spinal injuries."

Priorities screwed on backward. Kirk knew he'd made a mistake. Always thinking of Spock as not just half-human, but superhuman.

Spock was pale as sea wake. Deep-rooted pain etched his face. He still watched Kellen.

"Take him back to the ship, emergency priority," Kirk said, letting himself feel guilty.

Spock looked up. "Captain, I would like to stay."

There was something behind his eyes. Havoc . . . whatever that was. Spock knew something and he wanted to hear what Kellen had to say.

And I need him here, if he knows something.

Under his swatch of dusty brown hair, McCoy was glaring at Kirk. Pretty clear message there, too.

"A few minutes," Kirk decided. "McCoy, you take care of him here for now. Contact your staff and beam down a full medical team to take over triage."

"Captain," the doctor began, protesting with his tone.

"I said a few minutes. Until we find out what's going on."

Fuming, his blue eyes boiling on Kirk, the doctor cracked open his communicator. "McCoy to *Enterprise.* Patch me through to sickbay."

Plagued not by the glare but by the reason for it, Kirk was suddenly motivated to pierce the mystery fast and get Spock to the ship.

He swung around and stepped back to Kellen. "All right, General, I've taken care of my men. Now let's talk about you."

Kellen nodded. "The Havoc has come and we have to deal with it."

Kirk eyed him. "I don't like the sound of that 'we.' What's 'havoc'?"

Spock tipped his head to one side. "In Klingon lore, 'Havoc' is essentially an apocalypse. The releasing of all captive souls to wreak revenge on those who imprisoned them."

"Yes," Kellen confirmed, wagging a finger at the Vulcan. "Yes, yes."

"How do you know it's coming?" Kirk asked.

"My squadron encountered the beginning of it. The coming of the Havoc ship."

"The apocalypse comes in a ship?" Cynicism blistered the air between them. "General, I'm not in a good mood."

"And I am not here to put you in one." Kellen's weathered face didn't change. He utterly believed that he was here for the right reasons. He looked like a latter-day Ben Franklin waiting to see whether he'd be the father of a nation or on the business end of a noose.

Kirk drilled him with a meaningful glare. "What happened to you? Start from the beginning."

"There was a mass falloff," the general began. "At first we thought our instruments were failing, but then the sun of a nearby solar system began to expand and the planets to disintegrated. This continued until all things went to zero—"

"Nothing could exist in a zero-mass environment," Spock countered, as McCoy worked on him. "Everything that moved would accelerate to the speed of light."

"We came within seconds of that," the Klingon confirmed, nodding at Spock as if anxious to be understood. "We watched as the nearest solar system broke to hyperlight and was vaporized. We managed to hold our ships to positive mass by diverting all our power to the shields. We were down to one one-hundredth percent of our mass when the effect stopped. We . . ." He paused, measured the impact of what he was saying, then decided to admit, "We did lose one ship."

Everyone everywhere was utterly still. Even McCoy

stopped in the middle of applying a field splint to Spock's back.

As they all stared at Kellen, the whine of transporters cut into the tension.

To Kirk's right, six pillars of garbled energy buzzed into place, then quickly and noisily materialized into the forms of McCoy's emergency medical staff of interns and nurses.

McCoy waved at them without saying a word, and they dispersed to triage the wounded.

"I have recordings of this," Kellen offered, pulling Kirk's attention back. He spoke with control, as if completely convinced they would want these. He raised his arm, and pulled from his belt a Klingon tricorder. "The device has a translator."

He held it before Kirk, and did not lower it.

Kirk tilted his head to his left, toward Spock. "Over there."

Without pause Kellen took the one step necessary to hand the tricorder to the yeoman with Spock, but he never took his eyes off Kirk.

The yeoman blinked as if he didn't know what to do, but a wag of Kirk's finger at the tricorder snapped him out of it. He keyed up the instrument, working as well as he could with a Klingon mechanism, then faced Spock and ran the recordings on the small screen for him.

"I was transporting back to my flagship," Kellen went on while Spock watched the tricorder, "when my beam was diverted to another place. At first I believed I was on some distant planet, for there were caves and growing moss and a source of light and heat. I explored this place and discovered solid metal walls and electrical lighting with signal panels. But also there was a corridor of skulls."

"I'm sorry?" Kirk interrupted. "Did you say 'skulls'?"

"Skulls. Bare, boiled skulls. Of inconceivable shapes and kinds—creatures scarcely imaginable, Captain Kirk. Each was set in a niche of its own from which moss bled and lichen grew. Then, it . . . came out of the wall."

"What came? A skull?"

"No. No skull . . . the Iraga itself."

The Klingon general nearly whispered the word, as if speaking the profane, yet he was trying to be clinical and scientific.

Iraga. Didn't sound familiar.

Kirk canted forward slightly enough to get across his do-I-have-to-keep-asking expression.

"A . . . vision from our past," Kellen said, sifting for words. "A gathering of evils in one body, with snakes living out of its head and flame in its eyes. It means nothing to you, but to Klingons . . . it is our past coming back."

"We have legends of snake-headed beings," Kirk mentioned, "but I don't recall anything with fire for eyes. Mr. Spock?"

"I am unfamiliar with any such legend, Captain," the science officer said. "Research may prove of service."

"Captain, please," McCoy wedged in.

Kirk gave him a shut-up nod, then looked at Kellen. "Let's deal with facts right now. You say there was a power source? Readout panels? And you could breathe?"

"Yes. I felt the engines of the ship."

"Demons don't need atmosphere or conventional power. And they certainly don't need engines."

Kellen acknowledged that with what might have been a shrug. "Whatever is going on, legends and reality have come together and this might be the end of things for us all. Whatever has been our collective nightmare for eons has now come to ruin us again. We must work together now. Compared to those, we are so much alike that I would rather be your slave than live on the same planet with them. Now that the invaders are here, there is no difference between you and me anymore."

A hot breeze coughed down the incline between the two breasts of rock and across the warm belly of the shale flats. Kirk found himself suddenly sweating under his shirt. He didn't like the feeling. He wanted to scratch his chest as perspiration trickled down his ribs.

He glared at Kellen. The sun enhanced his frown. His eyes were hurting.

"Captain," Spock called.

Kirk pursed his lips and crossed the ten steps or so to where Spock was sitting on the boulder.

Grimly Spock said, "He is telling the truth. At least, he is truthfully relating what he saw. And according to vessel-stress readings and analyses of the computer registry, there did seem to be a mass falloff. Their records also have a visual log of a solar system's burst to warp speed."

"Could his records be falsified?"

"Of course."

"But you don't think they are?"

Spock sat as stiff as an Oriental statue. "No, sir."

"What could cause a mass falloff?"

"A weapon." Kellen surged, plunging two steps closer before a handful of Security men stepped between him and Kirk and Spock. "A shot fired across our civilization's bows, Kirk. For after it, there came the vessel of demons. We have to put aside hating each other for now."

"Put aside decades of trouble just like that?"

"What do you want?" Kellen asked, becoming much more agitated than anyone would expect from the calmest Klingon in the Empire. "You want me to imprison my grandson? You want me to find a husband for your ugliest sister? Tell me! This is important, Kirk! If you could have one thing from the Klingon Empire, what would you want?"

Irritated by the pettiness Kellen seemed to take for granted, Kirk bristled. "You know what I want. The same thing the whole Federation wants. Freedom and peace for all our peoples."

"You want us to leave you alone."

"Not enough. You have to leave your own people alone too."

The whole idea crossed the general's face as utterly foreign, but he didn't laugh or show any sign that Kirk had asked for something he wouldn't consider today. Kellen seemed willing to hand over the galaxy if he could get the help he wanted.

"Just a minute," Kirk stalled. He turned his back on the general and lowered his voice to Spock and McCoy. "Opinions?"

"Obviously profound," Spock murmured, "if the effect on him is so profound that the tension between Klingons and the Federation seems childish to him now."

"Whatever's going on," McCoy nearly whispered, "it's got Kellen spooked. And from what I've heard about this particular Klingon, he doesn't spook lightly."

Kirk looked at him. "Are you saying we should go?"

"Captain, I'll say anything you want if you'll let me take Spock to sickbay."

"Captain," Kellen interrupted, and waited until Kirk turned back to him. "I do not know if I can give you the things you ask," he said, "but I give my word as a warrior—I will do everything I can for the rest of my life to work toward a treaty. You help us survive today . . . and I will dedicate my life to your wish."

What?

The Klingons around the battleground stirred and audibly choked at what they had just heard. Kirk's men held very still, cocooned in disbelief.

"You can take me aboard as hostage if you like," Kellen added, "but help us against them!"

Was this Klingon bravado? A bet Kellen was making with himself? An experienced general knew the Federation would never take hostages.

So I will.

"Fine. You'll stay with us." Through Kellen's surprise, Kirk finished, "We'll go out there, and we'll see what this is."

ing asked for something he would [illegible] for [illegible] [illegible] to introduce the girls? He could get the [illegible] started.

[illegible]

[illegible]

[illegible]

[illegible]

[illegible]

[illegible]

[illegible]

[illegible]

[illegible]

WE ARE THE IMPENDING

Chapter Six

"BONES, HOW IS HE?"

"Not good."

"Tell me."

"Vulcans have thirty-six pairs of nerves attached to the spinal cord, serving the autonomic and voluntary nervous systems. Spock has some level of damage to thirty percent of those, mostly in his lower thoracic area and lumbar plexus. No major fractures, probably because of the angle of the stuff he fell on, but there are a series of hairline fractures to the white matter of the spinal column. Add that to the impact to his muscles and tendons, a dislocated shoulder, and a fractured wrist."

"He broke his wrist?"

"The left one."

"I . . . didn't notice."

His own left arm throbbed now, reminding him of his own hurts and the hits he'd taken, and magnifying what Spock must be going through. Without thinking, he rubbed the sore elbow.

McCoy noticed. "Spock's shoulder is back in place

and the wrist bones are fused, but he'll be sore for a while."

"Can his spinal injury be fixed with surgery?"

Folding his arms, the ship's cranky chief surgeon pursed his lips and shook his head, almost as if still deciding.

But right now he was just plain galled.

"I'm not going to operate unless I have to. I'm not a neurological specialist, Captain, and we're damned far from anybody who is, let alone a specialist on Vulcan neurophysiology. The irony is that he's lucky he hit that skirt of gravel on his spine instead of his skull, or right now we'd be wrapping him up for a real quiet voyage back to Vulcan and you'd be writing a note to his parents."

A chill shimmied down Jim Kirk's aching arms. Those awful notes—he'd spend his whole night writing them, one by one, with hands scratched and sore from today's battle. He had to do them before he slept, or he'd never sleep. He would describe the situation on Capella IV and explain its importance to the Federation so families would know their young men died for something important. He would log one posthumous commendation after another, feeding them through to Lieutenant Uhura, who would launch the sad package through subspace to the parents, wives, children of those who'd given their lives today in the line of duty.

He was glad he wouldn't have to write a note like that to Ambassador Sarek and his wife.

"We're lucky," Kirk murmured. *"I'm* lucky."

"Will he recover?" he asked.

Silence told him that McCoy wanted to make the prognosis sound upbeat, but the captain was the only person on board the starship who had to be deprived of bedside manner. The captain always had to be given the cold raw truth.

"I can't tell you that conclusively," McCoy said. "We'll just have to wait and see. I've got him mounted on a null-grav pad, to keep pressure off the spinal column. He *can* walk, but I'm not going to let him yet."

"Is there anything else you can do?"

McCoy responded with a bristle of insult. "Even with advanced medicine, there are some things the body has to do for itself. His metabolism is higher than ours and his recuperative powers are different. I'm not going to tamper unless there's an emergency. Don't second guess my judgment, Captain, and I won't second guess yours."

Kirk turned to him. "If you've got something to say, McCoy, say it."

The doctor stiffened. His eyes flared and he went off like a bow and arrow ready to spring. "Fine. I processed nineteen bodies this morning and fifty-two injuries, twelve of those serious, and two men are still listed as missing in action. That's seventy-three casualties logged up to a petty skirmish of questionable strategic value."

"It's my job to defend those settlements. Would you prefer processing the corpses of innocent families or official personnel sworn to protect them? You're the one who was stationed on that planet, you're the one who knew these people personally. Would you advocate abandonment?"

"There had to be some better way, is all I'm saying, something less savage than a ground defense."

"That's not for you to judge."

"Maybe not, but my patients are filling up four wards—"

"They're not *your* patients, Doctor, they're *my* crew. And they're Starfleet officers and they know what that means. The Klingons might have slaughtered those people. That's where we come in; we were there to stop it."

McCoy's blue eyes were bitter cold by now. "Maybe there was and you chose to ignore it, just as you chose to ignore common sense when you moved a trauma victim simply because you needed another opinion. The fact is, you're likely to get to an injured crewmen long before I am, and as such it befalls you to know what to do and what *not* to do, which means holstering that dash and moxie of yours long enough to give the correct first aid!"

If the doctor hadn't been trying to whisper, he'd have been shouting.

Kirk heard it as a shout. His throat knotted and he felt his jaw go stiff, his lips tighten, the skin around his eyes crimp. He stared in challenge at McCoy, reflexes telling him to demand his rank rights to civil treatment.

But then he looked through the door toward Spock's bed.

He raised one hand and pressed his palm to the door frame.

"It was unpardonable," he said.

He felt McCoy's glare, maybe one of surprise, maybe sympathy, burrowing through the back of his head.

Evidently the doctor had gotten what he'd wanted, or perhaps he'd decided the captain was tortured enough, because he sighed, then came up beside Kirk and spoke more evenly.

"I'm controlling his pain, Jim."

"Understood," Kirk uttered, as if he did. With his tone he asked McCoy to stay behind, let him deal with this himself.

He walked into the ward.

Spock lay on what seemed to be an ordinary diagnostic bed, with all the lights and blips and graphs silently moving on the panel above, monitoring his vitals.

As he moved closer to the bed, he noted the four antigrav units locked two-each to the sides of the bed, whirring softly, keeping Spock's body hovering a millimeter off the mattress, making his organs and bones float as if he were hovering out in space. Only the pillow made any contact, and that just barely, probably because it bothered McCoy to see his patients without a pillow. A patient in antigravs didn't really need one.

Spock's graphite eyes were glazed and pinched, his face and hands still lime-pale. Sickbay's washed-out patient's tunic didn't help much, seeming to suck color out of anybody's complexion. With his sharp hearing, he'd probably heard the two of them talking out there.

"Captain," he greeted, sparing them both the awkward moment.

"Spock . . . I'm sorry to disturb you."

"Not at all, sir. Are you all right?"

Kirk shrugged self-consciously. "A few cuts and scratches. My uniform had to be buried at sea, though."

"Beside mine, most likely. Is General Kellen on board?"

"Yes, and without an escort, too. His flagship did a little posturing, but he backed them down. You should've seen it. Whatever this thing is that he experienced, it scared him enough that he's pocketing his dignity. Certainly got me curious."

"And the Capellan situation?"

"Capellan space is cleared. He sent the other ships home. That Klingon commander wasn't too happy. His career is pretty much wrecked."

"Yes," Spock rasped. "He is not allowed to start a war, but neither is he allowed to lose a skirmish. How long will we have to wait?"

"We didn't wait. We're at warp five. Starfleet's sending the Frigate *Great Lakes* and two patrol sweepers to hold ground until the treaty takes a set. I've already signed off the situation."

"And the Klingon vessels?"

"Kellen's flagship is out in front, leading the way, and the other four are tailing us. So far, so good."

He waited for a response, but there was none.

Spock's lips compressed. The pain indicator bounced at the top of the screen.

Kirk put his hand on the blanket and pressed it, as if that would help.

Second by second, the wave of pain subsided and the indicator drifted down a few degrees. Not enough, though, to make either of them feel much better.

"This is my fault," he forced out. "I wasn't thinking

clearly. I should've had you beamed directly here without moving you."

Spock blinked his eyes in a motion that otherwise would've been a nod. "Being distracted by complex circumstances and failing to think clearly are not the same, Captain."

Poof. You're forgiven. Forget it.

"We'll be approaching the location of the incident Kellen described within twelve hours. I need someone at the science station. Do you have a recommendation?"

Offering an uncomplaining gaze, Spock pressed down the undertones of common sense. "I would prefer to be there myself, sir."

A half-smile bent Kirk's cheek. "And I'd like you there. But part and parcel of dangerous duty is recuperation. McCoy deserves to have his satisfactions too, once in a while, and we've given him a hell of a day. Least we can do is let him hover over you for a watch or two. Besides, all this is going to turn out to be nothing. Something spooked a combustible Klingon and now he wants attention. That's all it is."

"General Kellen is hardly a man given to idle combustion. And a systemwide mass falloff could be considered grounds for becoming 'spooked.' I am quite eager to examine the circumstances myself."

"Don't worry, you'll get your chance. For now, stay put. Me, well . . . I've got a few things to keep me busy."

He took a step back.

"Rest," the captain said. He touched the blanket again. "Get better. I'll keep you posted."

"There it is, sir. Just popped onto our long-range."

"Visual, Mr. Chekov?"

"In a few more seconds, sir. Sensors are assessing the vessel's configuration now."

"Clear for action. Go to yellow alert. Sound general quarters. Magnification one point seven-five as soon as you can. Mr. Sulu, reduce speed to warp one."

"Yellow alert, aye."

"Magnification one point seven-five, sir."

"Warp one, aye, sir."

With amber slashes of alert panels blinking on and off in his periphery, Jim Kirk paused as his orders were echoed back to him from various positions on the bridge, a long-held naval tradition borne of common sense, to make sure orders were heard and understood over the howl of wind. Protocol was a good, stout handle to grip.

Here there was no wind, but there was the constant whine and bleep of systems working, the almost physical thrum of engines deep below, and there was the undeniable tension of the bridge. Imagined in the minds of all here with a capital T, this tension existed in some form even in the most mundane of days, for this was the brain of the starship, and the starship was the security of the sector. Down not very deep, all hands here knew that.

And the tension was different, tighter, when the captain was on the bridge, even though all orders might remain the same, course unchanged, situation stable, status unremarkable, for days on end. It was different if he stood here too.

Always had been. Centuries.

Normally he was the most comfortable here, on the bridge, but today there was the added presence of General Kellen, standing on the lower deck beside the command chair as if he deserved to be here. He was obviously used to such a position and was unimpressed by his rank privilege to stand here, even on a ship full of those he considered enemies. He said nothing, and had said very little. He watched the main screen obsessively, but with the keen eyes of a soldier seeking weakness.

"Position of the other vessel?" Kirk requested.

"Two points forward of the port beam, sir," Chekov reported. "Distance, two standard astronomical units . . . roughly eighteen light-minutes."

"Reduce to sublight."

Sulu touched his controls. "Sublight, aye, sir."

Kirk flexed his sore hands. "Mr. Chekov, where's that visual?"

"Here now, sir." The young navigator picked at his controls, tied in to the science station—not the best, but workable for now—then looked up at the screen.

There it was.

Big. Well, they could see it, but that wasn't much help. It looked like—

"Looks like a big . . . pasta noodle," Chekov said. "A little overboiled, maybe . . ."

"It's a hunting horn, sir," Sulu offered.

Uhura swiveled to look over the heads of Sulu and Chekov. "Looks like a cornucopia to me."

Engineer Scott canted his head to one side. "I think it's a giant purple foxglove kicked on its side. Y'know, the flower part."

"Enough," Kirk droned. "You're at alert."

"Aye, sir," Uhura, Chekov, and Sulu uttered, each suddenly attentive of stations.

Satisfied, Kirk rubbed his elbow again and eyed the new ship. It *did* look like all those things. Like a porridge of those things. Huge collars of hull material set in a pattern, purple plates fanned out like playing cards. Maybe Scott was the most right. The structures were like flower petals, winding down to a point. Yet there was a decidedly nonfloral ferocity about it.

He could see why Kellen would be shaken. The ship was the color of Klingon blood—plum fans shimmering in the light of the nearest sun, twisting down, around and around, into shades of night orchid, etched in sharp black.

"All stop. Hold position relative to the other vessel. Communicate orders to the Klingon ships."

"All stop," Sulu said as his hands played the helm. "Compensating for drift, sir."

"Fire!"

General Kellen's big voice became a thunderbolt under the low ceiling.

Kirk spun and belted, "Security!"

Kellen plunged for the helm console, his wide hand aimed specifically at the phaser controls. Another inch—

Sulu pressed upward out of his helm chair, driving his knobby shoulder into Kellen's chest and almost disappearing under the bulk. Ensign Chekov lunged sideways from the navigator's position and pushed his own skinny shoulders over Sulu's head and under Kellen's chin, while Kirk himself made a grab and caught a handful of hair and silver tunic with his weakened left hand. With the other hand he clutched the arm of his command chair and hauled away.

The chair swiveled, then caught and gave him purchase. He drew back hard. It took all three of them to hold Kellen away from that critical inch.

An instant later the two Security guards made it down from the turbolift vestibule and grappled Kellen by his arms, muscling him back from the helm and plunging him against the bright red rail until his great bulk arched and his face screwed up in anger. Not too soon, though, for Kirk's mind flashed over and over that Kellen's hand had been halted directly over the phaser control. No guesses. Kellen knew exactly where those firing controls were, though there were no markings.

Once the Security men hit the lower deck, the crisis ended, but Kellen strained against them and bellowed, "Shoot while you have the chance!" He pivoted toward Kirk. "Fire on them!"

"I don't *know* them!" Kirk pelted back, squaring off before him.

The big Klingon's face bronzed with excitement. "But I have seen what they are!"

Angry now and reminded of it by the screaming muscles and throbbing bones in his left arm and both knees, Kirk said sharply, "You've described a Klingon legend. I told you before, legends don't use conventional power ratios. Barbarians don't drive around in ships like that."

The general stopped hauling against the red-faced guards. He seemed to accept Kirk's charge of the moment, and fell again into that disarming, nearly bovine self-control which had garnered him a reputation even in Starfleet circles.

"What are your intents?" he asked.

As the passive bright lights flickered in Kellen's spectacles, Kirk said, "I intend to hail them."

"You will give us away."

"I've already done that by entering the sector, General. We neither explore nor protect by stealth. Will I have to call more guards?"

The general squinted at him as if in challenge, but let his arms go slack in the guards' grips and acknowledged with his posture that this was not his bridge. The power of such a concept rang and rang. Command. One per ship, one only.

"Bring us into short-range communications distance," Kirk said, without taking his eyes from the general's.

"Aye, sir," Sulu responded, and beneath them the ship hummed its own answer.

"Shields up, Mr. Chekov. Keep weapons on-line."

"Phaser battery on standby, sir. Shields up."

"Captain," Communications Officer Uhura spoke in that crystal-clear teacher's English, "Mr. Spock is calling from sickbay. He requests to speak to you."

Kirk allowed himself a smile, but didn't allow Kellen to see it. "Somehow I'm not surprised. On visual."

Spock's angular face appeared on the darkened monitor on the upper bridge, just above the library computer access panel. Kirk stepped up to meet it as if his first officer were there, at his post, as usual.

"Captain," Spock greeted. "Permission to monitor the encounter with the unidentified vessel."

Kirk eyed the face on the screen. "And just how did you know we were approaching the unidentified ship at all, if I may ask?"

But he already knew, and glanced at Chekov, hunkering down there at his navigation console and scouting Kirk in his periphery.

"Collusion, sir," Spock admitted.

"I see. And once you've monitored?"

"I shall analyze the information and make recommendations."

"As usual. I see again. You intend to do all this from sickbay?"

"As necessary."

"How?"

"If Lieutenant Uhura will give you a wide view . . ."

Without waiting, Uhura skimmed one hand over her board, and Spock's monitor clicked to a wide side view of the Vulcan laid out on his diagnostic couch, with the antigravs working silently at his sides, but with a new development. Above him was mounted a small monitor.

"And who did that?" Kirk asked, as if asking which of the kids put the soccer ball through the bedroom window. "Scotty."

Burying a wince, he turned and glanced up at the port aft station, main engineering, where Chief Engineer Scott tucked his chin guiltily and peered out from under the squabble of black hair.

"Wouldn't want him to get bored, sir," the stocky engineer excused, letting his Aberdeen accent make him sound quaint, "lyin' there, an' all."

"And which of the ship's heads did you lock McCoy into while you were doing this?"

Scott held his breath. "Don't recall mentioning it to him, sir."

"Nor do I," Spock confirmed.

"They both forgot to mention it to me."

McCoy sauntered out of the turbolift when Kirk looked toward the voice, and came to join the captain on the starboard deck.

"Flummoxed," the doctor said. "Right in my own sickbay. That's what you get when you try to hold down a pointed-eared bunco artist." He cast a glower at Scott. "Or his sidekick, Jock the Jolly Tinker."

Scott actually blushed, and Kirk crushed back a grin.

"I should be able to assist effectively," Spock said, and there was unmistakable hope behind his reserve. He managed not to frame a question with anything but his eyes, gazing across the silent circuits at his captain.

McCoy didn't approve, according to his expression,

but he said nothing, and Kirk felt the decision go *thunk* into his hands from the chief surgeon's.

"I'd go stir-crazy myself," he allowed. "Glad to have you on duty, Mr. Spock. I'll leave it to your better judgment not to overburden yourself."

"Oh, he won't be overburdening himself," McCoy said. "He's scheduled for a sedative."

"When?"

"The minute I decide he's overburdening himself."

"Oh, of course. You heard it, Mr. Spock. You're on duty, but you're also on medical probation."

"Thank you, sir."

Kirk nodded to Uhura. "Keep Mr. Spock's channel open, Lieutenant." While cannily watching Kellen press his hair back into place, Kirk left McCoy's side, swiveled toward Uhura's communications station, and spoke very quietly to her exotic, expectant face. "Note to Starfleet Command, scramble. Klingons have intimate knowledge of our bridge control configuration. Suggest necessary changes in color code and location with next design upgrades. Kirk, commanding, *Enterprise,* stardate . . . so on. And while you're at it, give them our location."

She turned her eyes up to him. "Right away, sir."

"Captain," Sulu interrupted, "coming into short-range comm, sir. Thirty seconds."

"Open channels. Let's see if they'll talk."

"Talk," Kellen snapped. Cranking his thick arm around his own body, he dug between the silver tunic and the protective molded vest that Klingons had started using only lately and only in battle, and yanked out his personal communicator.

"Stop him!" Kirk shouted, but the Security men weren't fast enough in snatching the communicator from the big fist.

Snapping it to his lips Kellen spat, "Aragor! *HIgh! Tugh!*"

The guard grabbed the communicator and Kellen's hand and cranked hard. Kellen's face twisted into a grimace, but he knew he'd gotten his message through and gave up the communicator before arms were broken—a toss-up just whose arms.

"Captain, the Klingon ships are moving around us!" Chekov gulped. "Attack formation!"

"On screens!"

The main screen and four subsystems monitors changed to show the five Klingon ships swinging freely around the *Enterprise* as if swung on strings. In open space, the starship could easily have outmaneuvered them, but in these tight circumstances the lighter-weight Klingon ships were like hornets buzzing around a swan, racing away toward the unidentified vessel at full impulse, and they got the best of the bigger ship on short notice.

"General, order them back!" Kirk demanded.

"They have their orders," Kellen answered, strangely calm now. He watched the screen as a man watches a house burning down.

Kirk grabbed for his command chair's shipwide announcement control. "Red alert!"

Bright poppy-red slashes lit the bulkheads in place of the amber ones as the alert klaxons rang through the lower decks, announcing to the crew that the ship was coming into action. On the main screen, the Klingon ships shot into the distance and closed on the unidentified ship and opened fire the second they were within range, pelting heedless and relentless lancets of phaser energy onto the wide purple fans of hull material.

Sparks flew and bright energy wash pumped down the fans, but was quickly drained away. There might've been some spray of debris, but it was difficult to see from this distance, moving at this speed.

Spinning full-front to the main screen, Kirk cast his order back to Uhura.

"Warn those ships off!"

Chapter Seven

"THEY WILL NOT go off, Captain," Kellen said. "You have no choice now. You will have to fight with them."

"We'll see about that. Mr. Sulu, ahead one-half impulse. Mr. Chekov, take the science station. Ensign Donnier, take navigations."

The assistant engineer blinked in surprise and dropped to the command deck. Chekov jumped up to Spock's library computer and science station. Donnier slipped into Chekov's vacant seat and barely settled all the way down. He was a competent assistant for Scott, but he'd never been on the bridge before. He was young and particularly good-looking, which got him in many doors, only there to stumble over his personal insecurity because of a stuttering problem that he let slow him down. He'd requested duty only in engineering. That was why Kirk had ordered him to put in time on the bridge.

The unidentified ship began to return fire—one, two, three globular bulbs of energy that looked more than anything like big blue water balloons wobbling through space toward the Klingon cruiser. Two missed, but one hit and drenched the cruiser in crackling blue, green, and white destructive power. The cruiser wasn't blown up, but fell off and spun out of control.

"Heavy damage to the cruiser, sir," Chekov reported. "Main engines are seizing."

"Analyze those bolts."

"Analyzing," Spock's baritone voice answered from up on that monitor.

Kirk glanced up there. He'd been talking to Chekov.

He stared at the main screen, where the remaining four Klingon ships were dodging those heavy blue globes and pummeling the unidentified ship so unbrokenly that Kirk winced in empathy. "Stand by photon torpedoes."

"Photon t-torpedoes r-ready," Donnier struggled, barely audible.

As if he were standing at Kirk's side, Spock read off his analysis. "The unidentified ship's salvos are composed of quadra-cobalt intrivium . . . phased incendiary corosite plasma . . . and, I believe, plutonium. They also seem to have some wrecking qualities based on sonics."

"Everything's in there," Kirk muttered. "Fusion, phasers, fire, sound . . . effective, but not supernatural. Double shields shipwide."

"Double shields, sir."

"They will use their mass-dropping weapon if you give them the chance, Kirk," Kellen rumbled. "They can negate the gravity in the whole sector. You must attack them before they use it."

"If they have that kind of technology, General, then we're already sunk," Kirk responded, watching the action. "And they don't seem to have it."

"How can you know?"

"Because your ships are getting in some good punches and the visitors haven't used that 'weapon' again. They're using conventional defenses. If they have hand grenades, why are they shooting with bows and arrows? Helm, full impulse."

"Full impulse, sir."

"Good," Kellen whispered, then aloud said again,

"Good. Fight them with this monster of yours, while we have the advantage."

"Just keep back," Kirk warned. "Helm, come to three-four-nine. Get between those Klingon ships. Force them to break formation."

"Kirk!" Kellen pressed forward and the guards had to grab him again.

Around them the giant Artemis hummed as she powered up to her full potential and all her systems came online. A choral song of heat and imagination, she took a deep bite on space and moved in on the clutch of other ships, cleaving them away from each other with the sheer force of her presence and her sprawling shields.

Two of the Klingon ships were pressured to part formation, while one other was forced off course and had to vector around again, which took time.

In his mind Kirk saw his starship plunge into the battle. He'd put her through hell in their time together and she'd always come out with her spine uncracked. She'd picked herself up, given a good shake, and brought him and his crew back in under her own power every time. This was one of those moments when he felt that esprit with sailors from centuries past, who understood what a ship really was, how a bolted pile of wood, metal, and motive power could somehow be alive and command devotion as if the heart of oak actually pumped blood. How fast? How strong? How much could she take? How tightly could she twist against the pressure of forces from outside and inside? How far could they push her before she started to buckle? How much of herself would she give up before she let her crew be taken? How *tough* was she?

Those were the real questions, because the ship was their life. If she died, they died. When a ship is life, it becomes alive.

"Port your helm, Mr. Sulu, wear ship," he said. "Mr. Donnier, phasers one-half power and open fire."

"Wear the ship, aye," Sulu said, at the same time as Donnier responded, "One half ph-phasers, s-sir."

Firing bright blue streamers, the starship came about, her stern section and main hull pivoting as if the engineering hull were held on a string high above.

Kirk gripped his own chair with one hand and Donnier's chair back with the other. "Ten points more to port."

"Ten points, sir."

"Good . . . twenty points more . . . keep firing, Mr. Donnier."

The ship swung about, showing them a moving panorama of stars and ships on the main screen, swinging almost lazily from right to left.

When he couldn't see the unidentified ship on the main screen anymore, he said, "Midships."

"Midships," Sulu said, and tilted his shoulders as he fought to equalize the helm.

Donnier glanced at Kirk, plainly confused by the term "midships" on something other than a docking maneuver. Good thing Sulu was at the helm instead of someone with less experience. Maneuvering a ship at sublight speeds, in tight quarters, had entirely different characteristics from maneuvers, even battles, at warp.

At warp speed, the helm maneuvers were very slight and specific, designated by numbers of mark and course, and even moving the "wheel" a pin or two had sweeping results of millions of light-years.

But at impulse speed, things changed. And changed even more in tight-maneuvering conditions. Helm adjustments became more sweeping, bigger, sometimes a full 180 degrees, or any cut of the pie. "Midships" meant "find the navigational center of this series of movements and equalize the helm."

Forcing her crew to lean, the starship dipped briefly to port, then surged and came about to her own gravitational center and ran her phasers across the hulls of the *Qul* and the *MatHa'*, knocking them out of their attack formation. The point of Donnier's tongue was sticking out the corner of his mouth and his backside was hitched to the edge of his seat as he concentrated on his phasers, following not the angle of his phaser bolts but the position of the moving Klingon ships out there—it was exactly the right thing to do. Like pointing a finger.

The two Klingon ships wobbled, shivered, nearly collided, and bore off, one of them forced astern and down. Kirk hoped Kellen took note that the starship's punches were being pulled.

"Good shooting, Mr. Donnier," he offered. "Maintain."

Sweating, Donnier mouthed an aye-aye, but there was no sound to it.

The other two cruisers—he forgot their names—kept wits and plowed in again, opening fire now on the *Enterprise.* The ship rocked and Kirk had to grab his command chair to keep from slamming sideways into the rail. His scratched fingers burned with the effort.

Full phasers.

He didn't want to respond in kind. He wanted to make a point, not chop four other ships to bits.

Well, not yet.

Problem was that their commanding general was here, out of communication. They might take that as final orders and fight to the death.

Qul was back in the fight now, firing on the unidentified ship, and Donnier was doing an amiable job of detonating the Klingon phaser bolts before they struck the giant fan blades. He managed to catch three out of four bolts. Not bad.

Kirk pulled himself around the helm against the heel of the starship. "Keep it up, Mr. Donnier. Photon torpedoes on the Klingon vessels, Mr. Sulu. Fire across their bows and detonate at proximity."

"Aye, sir."

New salvos spewed from the *Enterprise,* making a spitting sound here within the bridge, much different from the screaming streamers of phaser fire, much more concentrated and heavy-punching, exploding right in front of the *Qul.* The *Qul* flinched, probably blinded by the nearby explosions, and bore off on a wingtip, forced to cease fire and try to come about again.

"Call them off, Kellen," Kirk said. "I'll open up on them if I have to."

"What right have you to do that?" Kellen bellowed. "I brought you here to be my ally!"

"But I'm not going to be your mercenary. Call them off."

But Kellen only glared at the screen and clamped his mouth shut.

"Fine," Kirk grumbled.

As the firing intensified, the fans on the unidentified ship's long twisted hull began to close inward, lying tightly and protectively upon each other and creating a shell instead of a flower. The curve of the hull itself began to straighten out, like a snake uncoiling its body, thinning the field of target and making it harder to hit. Talk about looking like a living thing . . .

The strange ship continued to fire those sickly-blue globes on the Klingon vessels that strafed it.

"All right, General, have it your way," Kirk ground out. "Mr. Donnier, phasers on full power. Mr. Sulu, photon torpedoes full intensity, point-blank range. Fire as your weapons bear on any Klingon vessel."

Kellen cranked around against the guard's hold on him and glared at Kirk. "No!"

"It's your decision." Kirk met the glare with his burning eyes. "Call them off!"

The Klingon's lips parted, peeled back, then came together again in a gust of frustration. He all but stomped his foot. Yanking one arm away from the guard on his left, he reached for his communicator, still being held by the other guard. As if it were all part of the same order, the guard let him have it.

Kellen snapped the communicator open and barked, *"Qul! Mev! YIchu'Ha."*

Short and sweet.

Worked, though.

The Klingon vessels swung about, joined each other at a notable distance, then dropped speed and came to a stop in some kind of formation Kirk hadn't seen before. Good enough.

"You seem to have the ear of your squadron, General," Kirk said. "Mr. Donnier, cease fire. Helm, minimum safe distance, then come about and all stop."

"Aye, sir," Sulu said tightly.

"Safe distance," Kellen protested, shaking his big head. "Warriors coming home shredded and shamed, spewing tales of a Federation devil with hands of fire and steel in his eyes. 'I fought Kirk! My honor is not so damaged as if I fought a lesser enemy!' It's become an acceptable excuse to lose to Kirk. Some want to avoid you, some want to challenge you because it would be a better victory. I expected you to come in and shake planets. And *this* is you? Talk? I wanted a warrior. All I find is this—you—who will not act. I will go home and slap my commanders who spoke of you."

"Your choice," Kirk said, ruffled less than he would've anticipated at the Klingon's lopsided insults that actually were kind of complimentary. Matching the general's anger with his own control, he countered, "When you met them before, did you try to talk to them at all?"

"No!"

"So you opened fire without announcement."

"They kidnapped me. My fleet came in and took me back. Of course we fired. I brought you to fight them, not to defend them."

"You brought me here to handle the situation. So let me handle it."

"I am disappointed in you, Kirk," the general said. "You do not deserve to be Kirk!"

"That's your problem." With a bob of his brows, Kirk raised his voice just enough. For a moment he gazed at the alien ship, then cast Kellen a generous glance. "Be patient. Mr. Sulu, move us in again. Let's see if they'll talk to us."

* * *

"How many ships?"

"We count six ships, Vergozen."

"Count again, Morien. Sweep the area. Be sure. They have stopped firing?"

"Yes, Vergozen."

"Farne, hold position. Make no movements."

"Yes, Vergozen."

"Morien, speak to the engineer. Have him take some time repairing the damage done to the ship as we came through the fissure."

"Time?"

"Have him go slowly. Keep the power down. Otherwise Garamanus will expect me to destroy those vessels instead of simply closing the cocoon and firing a few light shots at them. I do not want the repairs complete until I am ready for them to be complete."

"I understand, Vergozen."

"Speak to him personally, Morien, not on the communications line."

"I will."

The doors of the bridge were low and wide, and took several seconds to open, then to gush closed again, and this time they seemed to take longer. When they closed, Morien was gone, yes, but something else had changed too.

"Zennor . . . so you have found them."

"Garamanus—I did not expect you to come to the bridge yet."

The mission commander turned to meet his vessel's Dana and resisted any movement of his facial features. Briefly he thought the Dana had heard his instructions to Morien, but as he forced himself to be calm he realized that Garamanus had just come in as Morien was leaving.

Garamanus was watching him too carefully.

That was the Dana's purpose. Not the ship or the danger, but the commander and the mission. To make sure the latter two meshed as the chieftains instructed. And the chieftains did as the Danai told them, for the Danai had special gifts.

Holding his long hands before him in a relaxed position, with the traditional white streamers falling softly from his wrists, Garamanus bowed his heavy head. Over many years his horns had grown thick and bent his shoulders noticeably, but even so he was taller than Vergo Zennor by a hand's breadth. His presence chilled Zennor, and chilled the bridge.

"You have made contact with the conquerors," the Dana said. "Play the tape."

"They have not yet identified themselves," Zennor countered, speaking with cautious measurement. "I prefer to make personal contact first. Otherwise we will be assuming we are in the right place and that these are the people who deserve our coming. After so many centuries, after the millennia indeed, we should be prudent. Look—those ships are not familiar in any way. Some fired on us, but the large one stood them off. I would like to comprehend their conflict. We will give them a chance to speak to us before we give ourselves away. I appreciate your flexibility in my decision at this very special and important moment, Garamanus. Thank you."

The vapor-pale face and heavy horns dipped slightly under their own weight as Garamanus turned to look from the screen at Zennor, and Zennor knew he had lost.

Garamanus nodded as if in polite response, but his manner became a subtle threat.

"Play the tape," he said.

"Witness you conquerors . . . we the grand unclean, languishers in eternal transience, come now from the depths of evermore. Persistent . . . we have kept supple, fluid and . . . changeable . . . because we were destined to return. You have . . . cowered through the eons, knowing this day would come. . . . It has come. Because we are forgiving, we shall give you the opportunity to leave this . . . sector . . . or you will be cast away as we were cast away . . . or you will be destroyed as you have done to us. With your last moments you will know justice. We are . . .

the impending. Now gather all you own, gather your kin . . . and stand aside."

The message thrummed and boomed through the low rafters of the bridge, then echoed into silence. Not ending, just silence. Waiting.

Everyone held still, and watched the captain.

The sound of the heavy, eerie, haunted-house voice remained in every mind, and spoke over and over. *Stand aside . . .*

Tightening and untightening his aching arm, aware of McCoy watching him because he'd never reported to sickbay for his own treatment, Kirk indulged in a scowl and tipped his head to Uhura. "Lieutenant, what's the problem with that translator?"

"I don't know, sir," she said, playing her board. "Having some trouble distilling the accurate meaning of some of their words and phrases."

"Fix it. I don't want to have to guess."

"Trying, sir. I don't understand why—"

"Was it a living voice, far as you could tell?"

"Given the inflections and order of sentiments, I believe it was a recorded message, sir. Or it's being read to us."

"I thought so too."

He moved away from her, back to where McCoy was staring at the screen, eyes wide.

"That's a mighty poetic mouthful," the doctor uttered. "Any idea what it meant?"

"I'd say they're inviting us to get out of their way."

"I told you." Kellen stepped forward, but made no advances toward the helm this time, especially since the guards flanked him snugly now. "Attack them, Kirk. Your chance will slide away under you. Do you see it sliding? I see it."

"Something tells me I'll get another chance, General. Mr. Spock, are you reading any shielding on that ship?"

"No, sir," the upper monitor said. "No energy shields at all, except for the way clover-leaved hull plates fold down."

"Not battle attitude, then," Sulu offered.

"Not ours," Kirk said, stepping down to his command center and slid into his chair. "But we don't know theirs yet, other than the defensive posture we've just seen. Maintain status."

"Aye, sir," Sulu and Donnier at the same time, and tensed as if they'd realized they were relaxing too much.

Kirk moved back to the rail, where McCoy stood over him. "Opinion?"

"Pretty lofty talk," the doctor said. "But there's a ring to it. I can't put my finger on it."

"Mr. Spock?"

By not looking at the monitor, he could imagine that Spock stood up there, next to McCoy, bent over his sensors, adding his deductions to the information being drawn in by the ship's eyes and ears. Spock wouldn't have admitted it, or wanted it said aloud, but there was a lot of intuition in that man.

"There is a common tone in the phrases," Spock said, his voice rough, underscored with physical effort. " 'Witness you conquerors,' for instance. 'Eternal transience,' 'destined,' and the suggestion that we have been expecting them, that they have been wronged, and that they believe they are returning from somewhere."

"Conclusion?"

"We may have a case of mistaken identity."

"That may not make a difference," McCoy warned. "They're inviting us to leave, remember? They might not take our word for our intentions."

"They can't take anything for anything until we've identified ourselves."

"Captain," Spock's rough voice said from the monitor, "I suggest you answer their immediate request first."

"Set the parameters? Yes . . . I agree."

There it was. The reason he needed Spock here. He hadn't thought of that. Just answer them. The simplest answer had almost slipped by. Set the line of scrimmage before he offered anything else.

"Challenge them!" Kellen insisted. "Demand they

stand down and allow us to board and inspect! Then we'll be inside!"

Kirk rubbed his hands and, gazing at the screen, shook his head.

"I think Mr. Spock and I have something else in mind. Lieutenant Uhura," he said slowly, "tell them . . . 'No.' "

Chapter Eight

" 'NO'? THAT IS all they say?"

"Nothing else. The translation has no error, Vergozen. They say only 'No.' "

Vergo Zennor gazed through the smoldering constant vapor at the wide band of screen curving halfway around his bridge on either side of where he stood. He thought he had gotten used to the moisture necessary for some members of his crew, but today, for the first time since years past, his skin began to itch.

This was a beautiful portion of space. Or perhaps he only wanted it to be beautiful. Ordinarily he would sit, but with Garamanus on the bridge, he felt compelled to stand.

Shrouded in the mystique of his order, the echo of subtle power held dear by all Dana, Garamanus made no comment as the answer came in from the conqueror ships.

No?

Zennor bowed his own heavy head. His horns tingled. So he was more tense than he let on, even to himself.

His own feelings were lost to him. Simple desires of a

straightforward mission had become suddenly and almost instantly entangled in the mechanisms of those ships out there. He had hoped to explore awhile before facing those who lived here. He wanted to search around.

No longer possible. Now there were beings to be confronted, the tape had been played, and the answer had come back. No.

How strange. How simple. He had trouble with simple things.

The ship at the front was a sizable arrangement of white primary shapes—a circle, an oblong, two cylinders, joined to each other by graceful necks of white pylons. Behind it were ships more familiar to him in raw form, more like the green dawn silhouettes of creatures in hunting flight, heads down, wings arched, muscles tight and tucked.

None was moving forward now. *No,* they had said.

No.

Zennor forced himself to turn away from the Dana and shiver down the waning-moon eyes that followed him. Unlike Morien and the helmsman Farne, Garamanus was of Zennor's own race, the horned ones among the many, yet Zennor felt nothing like him and when Garamanus was on the bridge the place became as foreign as this space.

"They want us to speak to them," he said quietly.

"You have had more communication than this with them?" Garamanus rumbled.

"I sense they want to speak. When they contact us again, I will answer them myself."

"That is not the procedure." The Dana's voice was like wind. Low wind.

Zennor tightened his thick neck muscles and tensed his shoulders, which raised his head and the curved horns upon it. He saw his own shadow move like a wraith against the oblong helm as he turned to face the Dana.

"This is not your forest grove or sacred Nemeton," he said. "This is my ship and my mission. We can never go back, and now the situation complicates. I have done your bidding and played your sanctimonious tape. Nothing else is required of me yet. The next decision is mine. And I want to speak to them. When the time comes to destroy them, that will be my decision too."

General Kellen fumed with disappointment, but he was standing on the port side of the command chair, flanked by the Security team, saying nothing. He cast the guards no attention and as such seemed to understand why they were here.

At least he wasn't insulted by the fact that he was being treated like a delinquent.

Kirk offered him a glance, as if to communicate that he understood what the general was feeling, whether or not he intended to act upon it.

"Two minutes, sir," Sulu reported. "No action out there."

"Nothing on the open frequencies, sir," Uhura confirmed.

Kirk nodded, sighed. "All right. We'll do it by the book. Uhura, ship to ship. Universal Translator on."

"Tied in, sir. Go ahead."

He moved to his command chair, but despite his raging muscles did not sit down. Not with another fleet's general on his bridge.

Clearing his throat, he parted his lips to say the words that were so practiced, yet so different every time he said them, because they were said hundreds of light-years away from the last time, and each utterance was something completely new and critical.

"This is Captain James T. Kirk, commanding the *U.S.S. Enterprise.* We represent the United Federation of Planets and request you communicate with us on peaceful terms. We await your reply."

Channels remained open as he paused. There was a different sound about it, an openness, like a cave without an echo, a tunnel waiting for someone to shout through it.

They waited. All the others took their cue from him, and he didn't move or make any sounds. Let the greeting distill, see what would happen. Let the listeners hear the ring of his voice and decide on its honesty, let them decide what to believe.

A full minute. Nothing came over the waves.

Ten more seconds. Sweat tickled his spine.

Finally he asked, "Recommendations, Mr. Spock?"

Gravelly and contemptuous, Kellen spoke before Spock had a chance. "Recommendations," he intoned. "Recommendations. The great shipmaster asks for recommendations. The cavalier of Starfleet asks of his subordinates what to do. The Federation's headmost uphelmer parries to his rear and mocks the rash faith given to him by those he flies before. Recommendations. Certainly the stories that come back to my people of Starfleet's Argonaut will be different after today." He gestured to the deck at his feet and added, "The arrogant falls before me."

Kirk glared at him without really turning his head, but with only his eyes shifted to the side.

Kellen was sizing him up and was no longer impressed. That bothered him.

It shouldn't, but it did.

"I am . . ."

The bridge changed suddenly. All eyes turned to the screen, to the alien ship holding position out there.

The two words were long, sonorous, even distorted, like distant foghorns sounding over a cold ocean. Then the voice paused as if listening to itself, testing the open frequencies.

Or maybe they were just changing their minds.

Kirk felt the eyes of his crew. He kept his on the screen.

"I . . . am . . . Zennor . . . Vergo of the Wrath."

There was a sense of echo. Something about the tenor of that voice. Like the last upbow on a cello's low note.

He glanced up at McCoy and mouthed, *Vergo of the Wrath?*

The doctor shook his head and turned one palm up. No idea. Uhura the same.

On the science station monitor, Spock's brow furrowed, but he said nothing yet.

Kirk shifted his feet to take some of the ache out of his back. Maybe it was empathy. What a morning.

Square one.

"Thank you for answering," he said, though it sounded clumsy. "Where are you from?"

"Here."

Kellen bristled, but didn't interfere, though he stared a burning hole into Kirk's head.

"According to our history, our laws and treaties," Kirk attempted, "this area is claimed by the Klingon Empire. Nearby is a neutral area of space, beyond which is space charted and occupied by the United Federation of Planets. We have no records of the configuration of your ship, or any planets in this vicinity which could support advanced life. Can you give us the location of your home planet?"

"We do not . . . know it."

Putting one foot on the platform that held his command chair, Kirk cranked around to Uhura. "Can't you fix that translator? We're not making sense here."

She shook her head in frustration and touched her earpiece. "I don't think it's in the system, sir. I think it's endemic to their language or their brain-wave patterns."

"Scotty, take a look."

"Aye, sir."

As the engineer crossed the deck behind him, Kirk pressed an elbow to his chair's arm and grimaced. What would help?

"Our communications equipment has visual capabilities," he said, speaking a little slower and more clearly. "Will you allow us to open our screens so we can look at each other?"

Another pause.

Kellen looked at him. Kirk ignored him.

"It is against our custom," the booming voice came finally, *"to display living faces on screens. . . ."*

The voice drifted off as the translator struggled along after it.

All right, next step.

"Very well," Kirk responded, measuring his tone. "Perhaps we can meet face-to-face. Will you come to this ship as our guests?"

"No—" Kellen choked, balling his fists.

Waving him silent, Kirk went on, "We have the ability to transport you here in minutes."

He stopped and waited. Over the years he'd learned that extra talking didn't usually serve. Make the statement, and wait.

Hell of a long pause.

Were they making this up as they went along?

Why not? I am.

The alien ship turned passively on the screen, drifting not from power but on a breath of solar wind from the distant red giant sun that drenched its purple fans in bloody glow, and the leftover momentum from the battle so shortly arrested.

"You may . . ."

The voice paused, as if listening. Kirk held his breath. His crew did the same.

". . . come here."

"One moment please."

A gesture from him caused a click on Uhura's control board that cut off the frequency.

"What's the atmosphere like over there?" he asked.

Chekov started looking for that, but from the subsystems screen, Spock already had the answer. "Scanning . . . reading oxygen, nitrogen, argon, with faint traces of methane and other gases . . . rather thin and quite warm. Breathable for controlled periods of time."

"How controlled? Bones?"

The doctor flinched as if coming out of a trance. "I'd recommend an hour at a time, Captain."

"Noted. Lieutenant Uhura, inform the transporter room that we'll be visiting that vessel out there. I want the coordinates kept updated at all times, in case we have to come back in a hurry. The transporter officer'll have to stay on his toes."

"Yes, sir."

"'Vergo of the Wrath,'" he muttered, narrowing his eyes at the big quartz ship on the screen. "Could that mean 'captain' of the *Wrath?* Could *'Wrath'* be the name of the ship?"

"Possibly," Spock answered from the monitor. "However, I caution against applying our own use of words and concepts based on something that sounds familiar, sir."

Kirk sighed. "Never mind how complicated it might end up being to deal with people who name their ship *'Wrath.'"*

He avoided looking at Kellen. The Klingons named their own ships with words like that.

"Dr. McCoy, you come with me, and I want a Security detail with us also. Palm phasers only. I don't want to appear too threatening."

Placing a hand on the rail, he climbed the three steps to the quarterdeck and stood over Uhura's station. She continued to look at her board and tap at her fingerpads, and that bothered him.

"Ship to ship," he said, and waited for the click from Uhura's board before he spoke again to the unknowns. "This is Captain Kirk. I will come to your ship with a greeting party. We will come directly to your bridge, unless you have other instructions."

Silence fell in. He got the feeling things were being discussed over there and anticipated their changing their minds, but—

"Come."

"Thank you. We'll be there in a few minutes. Kirk out. Mr. Sulu, drop the hook. We'll be staying awhile."

"All systems stabilized, sir. Holding position."

"Secure from red alert. Stand by at yellow alert. Damage-control teams get to work. General Kellen, you may communicate with your ships and assess their damage. If they need any lifesaving assistance, we'll provide it."

Kellen raised his neatly bearded chin. "Imagine my gratitude."

"Inform them we're going aboard the unidentified ship. If they make any aggressive movements, Mr. Scott will drive them back again. Is that clear, Mr. Scott?"

"Crystal clear, Captain."

"General, do you want to join the boarding party?"

"I?" Kellen's face turned horrible. "I will never go there again."

"Fine." Kirk turned away and looked at Uhura again. "I need a linguist. Do we have one on board?"

"Yes, sir. Me."

"You?"

Her almond cheeks rounded in a smile. "What do you think 'communications' means? 'Small talk'?"

"Sorry," he said. Then he hesitated. Take her along?

He paused for a moment and pressed down the twinge in his stomach. "Lieutenant, I'd like you to join the landing party."

Uhura's face lit up. She didn't get asked very often, and the couple of times before had turned out to be near-disasters. Still, she seemed excited.

"Aye, sir," she said, for the same reason Scott had said it, and in almost the same tone.

"Very good," he offered, and moved around her. "Mr. Spock, you have the conn."

The crew's eyes came up to him in a nearly audible snap. Silence from the monitor up starboard. Uneased, nobody spoke. How inappropriate it would have been for anyone, however well intended, to point out the captain's colossal error.

Kirk scowled at himself. "Mr. Scott," he corrected, "you have the conn."

Scott nodded with more sympathy than was comfortable for either of them. "Aye aye, sir."

It was the eternal ideal response to a commanding

officer, the one that saved any situation and would get anybody off the hook. Didn't work quite so well at the moment. It got Scott and Spock off the hook and relieved the bridge crew of their tension, but did nothing for the captain who had made the blunder.

He charged over it. "Uhura, bring along a tricorder tied directly in to Mr. Spock's computer access channel, so he can see what's going on. Let's go."

"Captain," Kellen broke in, coming to the rail below the bright red turbolift doors, "you are out of order here. I organized this mission. I am its commander."

"You're a guest on my ship," Kirk corrected. "You can act that way, or you can go back to your own fleet and all bets are off."

"This transport is folly," the general insisted. "No one with any sense goes over to an enemy ship in the middle of a battle!"

"It was your battle, not theirs. They didn't fire on us until you opened fire. And part of the mission of this vessel is to contact new life forms on an amicable basis if at all possible."

"It is *im*possible. This is the Havoc. There is no amicable basis."

"We'll see. I'll be back in an hour. Gentlemen, let's take a look at who these people are."

What's the mission of this vessel? To seek out and contact alien life . . . and an opportunity to demonstrate what our high-sounding words mean.

—James Kirk

Chapter Nine

SOMETIMES THE STUNNING ART of transporting seemed to move beyond physical science and into magic. And sometimes it seemed to take days instead of seconds.

This was one of those times.

Jim Kirk tapped a mental foot during those seconds. It was always like this when a new form of life lay in wait for discovery on the other side of immaterial state.

As his mind gathered itself and the transporter room of the *Enterprise* dissolved into fog, he realized he couldn't see and wondered for a heart-snapping moment if something had gone wrong. When he felt his feet beneath him again and his arms at his sides, the fog was still there. Had the transport been completed?

There was moisture here. He felt hot. At least all his nerve endings were still with him.

Starting to think like McCoy. Scientist though he was, McCoy was a medical biologist and physics often intimidated him, especially when physics separated biology into a billion bits of molecular energy and claimed to reassemble it in perfect order. Some people still didn't believe that planes could fly.

Kirk blinked the anxiety away and waved his hand at the fog in front of him, not so much to clear it but to sense its texture. The tendrils of cloud moved like smoke rather than moisture, but felt like moisture. What did that mean?

Smelled like a pond in here. The deck under his feet felt pulpy, but it was definitely flat as a floor and hard underneath. There was a source of low light, but he couldn't pin down the location. Immediately before him were two more sources of light, one cranberry red, the other a bleeding purple. He glanced to his left, at McCoy.

Washed in the blended light, the doctor stood staring and disconcerted by the strange surroundings. The back of his head and shoulders were bathed in soft pearly light—another light source, this one behind them. Kirk didn't look around. That would be the job of the Security team.

For a moment he held still, with his hand up in the middle of a wave, and listened.

A faint vibration came up through the soles of his feet, a throbbing of mechanical regularity. Engines. Kellen had been right. Motive power and tangible hardware. Obvious now that the ship had been seen, but the sensations here were familiar enough that Kirk guessed the power sources might be similar to those of conventional ships. At least they weren't dealing with a race so different from their own as to make the contest one-sided.

Nearby was the murmur of other mechanical systems, though much more subtle than any on the *Enterprise*. He saw no ceiling, and though he felt the deck he couldn't see it. The fog was thick up to his knees, then became a lazy haze.

There was a smell too, but not like a ship smell. Fungus? Weeds, mosses, moisture. Algae. Spock probably could've told him what species. Yet the foresty smell was overlaid with a chemical presence too, almost industrial, like glue or cleanser, and it insisted there was a technical presence here.

His gut began to shrink, giving off warnings.

I've seen aliens before, plenty of them. Some unthinkably strange, defiant of any known evolutionary pattern. I haven't even seen these people yet. Why am I already flinching?

He knew the answer. Kellen. What could shake an experienced spacefaring Klingon general with a long record of bravery and a reputation for disarming composure?

Had Kellen set him up? The thought flashed, unwelcome and distasteful, that he was falling into a trap. Was he so distracted that he hadn't thought of that dimension? Exhausted, losing so many crewmen, worried about Spock—

Not good enough. There wasn't anything that would take him off the hook for the entirety of his job, and here he was, beamed in with a team, and only now thinking of a seriously viable possibility.

On the other hand, this ship *was* here. Might as well throttle up. If he had to strangle Kellen later, well, an option was an option.

"Is this their bridge, sir?" Uhura asked just behind his right elbow, speaking low, as if walking through a graveyard and worried about waking someone.

"That was the plan," Kirk answered. "We homed in on their communications signal. Tricorder."

She raised the powerful little unit hanging from the strap over her shoulder and clicked it on. "Reading lifeforms, sir, lots of them."

"Proximity?"

"Nearby . . . the readings are . . ." She paused, frowned, tampered with the instrument. "I can't get a fix."

"Jim," McCoy murmured at Kirk's side, scarcely above a whisper. His blue eyes were wide, unblinking, bizarre in the glowing fog.

Kirk looked at him.

"They're here," McCoy said, his throat tight. "They're in here now."

Put on edge by the doctor's intuition, Kirk lowered his

right hand until it hovered near the small phaser hidden on his belt. He didn't touch the weapon, but he kept his hand there.

He took one step out from his boarding party and raised his voice.

"I'm Captain Kirk," he said through the choking humidity. "Is there anyone here?"

For several moments, possibly a minute, there was no change at all, as if he had spoken firmly but pointlessly into an empty cave.

The fog began to shift. For an absurd instant he entertained the idea that the fog itself might be the life-form they were seeking. A fog with a voice, though? McCoy would have something to say about the vocal chords of a fog.

No, not the fog. There was physical movement beyond it. Shapes of upright beings began to form, broad shoulders, high heads, like gray chalk etchings on concrete.

About our size, he noted instinctively. *Six feet . . . seven . . . not out of line for humanoids.*

The huge numbers of humanoids discovered by the Federation in its outward expansion had upheld theories of scientists who believed that intelligent industrial life had to be of a certain size, not too big, but also not too small, in order to develop industry and eventually space-flight. There would have to be some form of propulsion with which to go against the stream—legs—and some form of sensors at the other end with which to avoid running into walls—hands and eyes and sometimes a nose. There would have to be at least two hands with which to alter their environment, and at least two eyes for depth perception.

So despite the thousands of planets out there, it hadn't turned out so unusual that there were Klingons, Romulans, Terrans, Orions, and others, each with roughly the same appendages and a head each. Also not so strange that the horta, a creature based on silicon, with no arms, legs, head, or eye, though intelligent, had no industry. Like Earth's cetaceans or Alpha Centauri's big mammaloids. Didn't matter how smart they were if they had hooves or fins instead of hands and couldn't manipulate their environment.

All this flashed through Kirk's mind as he waited for the beings to show themselves. He lay in the hope that he was dealing with humanoids, with whom he automatically had some common ground. For a civilization to advance, there had to be some level of cooperation, they had to take care of their offspring, and they had to have common goals. Those communal elements were his anchors in exploration. He could make himself understood to beings who understood those.

He motioned to his boarding party to stand very still and let the next movement be those of this ship's crew. That was how he would want it on the . . .

Eyes. Yes—there they were.

Like a cat's stare catching candlelight, a dozen sets of eyes came toward them. A cold stake of shock bolted from Kirk's stomach to his feet. His innards shriveled at the forms moving from the fog toward them.

McCoy stiffened beside him. Uhura drew a sharp breath and tightened her arms to her sides, but didn't step back.

A Pandora's box of demons pushed the vapor aside. Ill-shaped and colossal, three of them were an amalgam of triangles, with long bony faces and eyes the shapes of sickles, and huge twisted ram's horns upon their heads, as elegant and horrifying as could be. Between those, other creatures appeared with dozens of serpentine white tentacles undulating from their skulls as long as a man's arm and freely moving, caressing the faces and shoulders of the beings they decorated as if searching for something.

To Kirk's left, another creature had two sets of arms and an elongated face like a jade tiki. Behind that one there were others, some skeletal, others swollen, and at least one had no face at all that Kirk could see. This was an utterly amalgamated crew.

And there were others he couldn't make out yet,

except for the distorted shapes of their heads and their masklike faces cast in shadows and highlights, caressed by fog.

Most of them wore some kind of clothing, and lots of jewelry. Recumbent half moons, demon-headed brooches like the things carved into the walls, and each one wore an engraved bronze medallion about three inches across with scrolled designs and a small handle, dangling from a long chain.

Two of the creatures moved forward of the rest. They were both of the same species, each head heavy with arching horns, but one was a watercolor ghost of the other. Totally different colors. One had eyes of rum yellow and a complexion of bronze and rattan. The other was paler, with face of bony moon-gray and ivory slashes for eyes.

Kirk cleared his throat, but paused. Did they want to make the first gesture or not?

Stiff as a statue, McCoy managed to lean toward him. "Come on, we got used to Spock, after all. . . ."

At the doctor's mumble, the splendid golden demon moved one of his elongated hands. At least he only had two of those. So far so good.

The heavy voice thrummed, the same voice they had heard on the message over the *Enterprise*'s comm system.

"Are you having trouble . . . seeing?"

What a voice. Translators were working all right at the moment. Any little reassurance in a storm.

Kirk found his own voice. "Yes. A little."

The creature turned his disturbing head. Fog rolled around his horns. "Light."

A mechanical sound, not a beep but more of a twinkle, chittered in the background, though they saw none of these creatures move. There must be others here too.

Almost imperceptibly at first, the haze began to change. Slow as dawn, the area around them became easier to see. The sources of colored light intensified gradually until distinction came to the place where they stood and the creatures before them gained dimension.

Like the *Enterprise*'s bridge, this bridge was a circle and possessed two command chairs and a coffin-shaped helm console, but there the resemblance ended. This place was more like a voodoo temple than a mechanized vehicle's brain trust. Forms were carved into the bulkheads of animal-headed trumpet—might've been the alarm system or just decoration. Shields and wheels and double-headed metal masks, mostly of animal types separated by scrolls, banded the ceiling all the way around. Other facelike stone carvings stood in punch-outs in the bulkheads themselves, empty eye sockets staring, with grotesque head shapes and orifices barely notable as mouths or noses.

"Skulls, Captain," McCoy murmured without moving his lips more than he could get away with. "Real."

Kirk glanced at him. How McCoy knew those things were real and not just carvings, he had no idea. Maybe he saw tracks of veins or something other bio-clue. That was the doctor's job and Kirk didn't question the call.

The skulls of enemies, possibly? Not the best doorbell.

The golden creature took another step toward them.

"I am Zennor," it said. "Vergo of the *Wrath.*"

Kirk matched the step forward, in case such a motion turned out to be a custom of some kind.

"I am Kirk," he responded evenly. "Captain of the *Enterprise.*" When the aliens didn't say anything, he added, "We appreciate your welcome."

The huge horns bowed. "I cannot offer you welcome, until I know you are not the conquerors."

Could be the translator. Or use of the word. Zennor hadn't said "conquerors," but "*the* conquerors."

Kirk let that one go. No sense claiming not to be the conquerors until he had some idea who these people thought were the conquerors.

"Then we offer our to welcome you," he said instead. "You're new to this space."

The creature like Zennor, with shell gray horns and a banshee face, parted his lips and asked, "This is your space?"

"This space is claimed by the Klingon Empire," Kirk said, trying not to sound as if ownership would move the moment. "My ship and I represent the United Federation of Planets. Our space is not far from here."

He moved forward now, and squared off with the white creature, then paused and with his posture asked the unasked question.

Zennor angled to face them both. "This is Garamanus Drovid, Dana of the *Wrath.*"

Kirk started to respond, but only nodded, because he now noticed something very quizzical as his eyes adjusted to the eerie light. Each of these beings wore a stuffed doll on a belt, each doll about eight or ten inches long. Zennor's doll had little twisted horns and a bony face with glossy snakish eyes, as did the dolls of each of the beings who looked like him. Garamanus's doll was the same height as Zennor's, but about twice as stuffed.

A horned wraith with a fat doll? What kind of day was this turning out to be?

On the beings with the tentacles moving in their heads were dolls bearing long wiry strings on their stuffed heads. The creature with the rocky jade face had a doll with a green face and the same kind of clothing. The dolls had the same kinds of clothing the aliens wore, right down to tiny crescent necklaces and animal-head brooches. The only trapping missing from the dolls seemed to be the circular medallion on the long chain.

Kirk felt completely baffled. Here he stood, among horrific beings with a strong ship and heavy weapons who wore soft little toys on their belts. And why was Zennor's doll skinny? Was Garamanus's fat doll a rank thing? Social order?

Suddenly he started paying more attention to who said what, and why Zennor had included Garamanus in a conversation barely begun. What was "Dana" of the *Wrath,* and in what designation compared to "Vergo"?

Made a difference.

As the questions flashed through his mind, he decided to lay some questions at the aliens' feet too.

"This is Leonard McCoy, Chief Surgeon of the *Enterprise,* and Lieutenant Uhura, of Communications. When you appeared in this space," he began, "there was a drop in mass to zero. A solar system was completely disrupted. The Klingons assume this is a weapon."

"We have no such weapon," Garamanus rumbled.

"Then can you explain what happened?"

"To your solar system?" Zennor spoke. "No. We have nothing to change mass."

Kirk paused. One plus one usually equaled two, but when things came down to push or shove, was there any way to prove correlation between the mass falloff and the appearance of this ship?

They said they couldn't do such a thing. There would be no point in insisting they had.

"Then," he began carefully, "perhaps you should tell us why you're here. Tell us what you want. We may be able to help you find it."

Zennor and Garamanus stared at him like wall paintings for a moment; then Zennor simply said, "We have come from a great distant place to this place to see if it is ours."

His deep voice took on an abrupt tenor of threat.

It could have been his imagination, just those shining marbled eyes, or the firedog horns scuffing the ceiling.

"If it's *yours?"* Kirk echoed, then realized he had spoken too sharply. Instinct had made him match that sense of threat. At once he was glad Kellen hadn't come here, or there'd be another incident. "We have a history of more than two centuries in these areas of space."

Garamanus dipped his rack once, slowly. "Our history is more than five thousand years."

Kirk felt his eyes widen. The translator got that one all right.

Five *thousand* years. That was a lot of years.

If that's what impressed them, he had a few extra centuries to pull out of his back pocket.

"We do have a history of over a hundred thousand years on our various home planets, proven by detailed archeological and cultural evidence. Perhaps we're better served by your telling us where your home planet is?"

"We do not know it," Zennor said again. "We know only where we have been for five thousand years."

"Jim . . ." McCoy murmured, but when Kirk looked at him he said nothing more. His face suggested a troublesome suspicion, though he seemed not to be able to back it up now, and remained silent.

Making bets with currency he didn't have yet, Kirk turned to Zennor, taking "Vergo" for what he guessed it was. Command couldn't be done by committee, so he addressed the one he thought was the captain, and would let Zennor handle the affront.

"Why don't you tell me your story?" he asked, and held out a beckoning hand.

Perhaps it was the hand, perhaps his tone of voice. Zennor's strange eyes moved this time as he pondered what he heard, then blinked slowly, and Kirk suddenly realized he hadn't seen Zennor or Garamanus or the other one with the horns blink at all until now. That, possibly, was why they appeared more like engravings than living creatures.

Zennor looked at Garamanus and for a brief time the two seemed alone here, though they said nothing to each other.

Then Zennor turned a shoulder to the being he called his ship's Dana and faced Jim Kirk instead.

"Five thousand years ago," he began, "there was a war between two developed interstellar civilizations. When the war ended, one civilization lay in defeat. The survivors of the vanquished, many races from many planets, were banished to a far distant place in the galaxy, 'relocated' well away from the victors, dropped in the barren middle of nothing, with nothing. No technology, no science, no supplies.

"Many millions perished in the first few decades. The civilization fell apart, fell back to barbarism, splintered, regressed to the primal. There were plagues, wars, and ultimately a massive, extended period of dim, raw survival.

"As they began to crawl out of this thousand-year dimness and to populate three of the planets to which they were banished, a belief emerged about another place, the home space, where they were meant to be. As society and science clawed upward again, the splintered spurned began to draw together under one common belief.

"This belief has become the driving force of our culture as we evolved once again to high technology. Because of the thousand-year dimness there are no records with facts of locations, but only words passed from descendant to descendant. On the parent's knee every offspring learns of the fury to regain our place. It is our unifying purpose—to reach out and repossess the section of space from which we were evicted.

"We are the unclean, the out of grace, ill-bidden castaways with the fury in our minds, disowned and cast down, thrown together by our collective loss of war, with only one thing in common—our singular commitment to find the way back. It is a culture-wide investment . . . and we are here to spend it."

Jim Kirk had stared at a lot of inhuman creatures in his life, but somehow none of those moments ever exactly repeated itself. This one was completely new. Evidently there was an invasion of sorts going on, but it was the most polite invasion he'd ever witnessed.

He shifted his feet, stalling for a moment to think, to bottle and distill all he had just heard and decide what to say back. "So you aren't sure you're in the correct . . . area?"

"We are sure," Garamanus spoke up. "Our Bardoi and the Danai have studied for centuries."

"Studied what?"

"Legends, history, biology, customs, and the designs we saw in the skies. The positions of stars in the galaxy as they have moved over the centuries."

"Of course, stars lying on the fabric of space," Zennor said, "may appear side by side while being lifetimes apart. *I* would like hard proof."

Garamanus glared fiercely and the others in the alien crew stared at their captain.

Kirk looked from one to the other and sensed Zennor was taking a mighty risk. But Zennor hadn't said anything any sensible spacefarer wouldn't know. Why were they staring at him that way?

To keep distraction on his side, he elected to take the wildest, least predicted step available to him—the one McCoy would really hate.

"Let me invite you to our ship," he suggested, "where there are extensive historical and scientific records more easily at hand."

Ignoring Garamanus's silent assault, Zennor gazed at Kirk for a moment, during which the sulfurous eyes seemed not to see. The Vergo and his Dana could easily have been etchings on these bulkheads. But for the undulation of the tentacles on the heads of those other creatures, the whole gathering might have been merely fresco.

"You may find our ship too cool. We'll go ahead of you and prepare the atmosphere so you'll be more comfortable. I'll inform our various divisions and labs. Join us on board and we'll . . . look."

"Morien, when they take us to their ship, I want you to analyze this beam of theirs. Find out how it is done, to adjust the body and make it travel through open space. Then make sure our adjustments to the ship's surface cannot be brought down unless we bring them down. One mistake, and we could be destroyed from within.

Centuries of scientists designed this ship to be invulnerable, and within minutes of arrival we found ourselves vulnerable. What other surprises await us? We must anticipate everything."

Morien gazed at him in rapt appreciation, then uttered, "I will check it all, Vergozen!"

With his tentacles twisting excitedly, he rushed away into a clutch of other technicians, who also gazed at their leader with disclosed awe at his suspicions.

Zennor nodded to them modestly, then freed himself by turning away, and found he had made the mistake of turning toward Garamanus. "And we should send the analysis back through the wrinkle, so it can be studied and copied. Then our people will also have the ability to go through open space without a vessel."

"You are intelligent to think of that," the Dana said.

"It is my role to think of it," Zennor responded, looking at the ships on the curved screen before them. "I must imagine ways for the enemy to use his own talents, or he will think of it first."

"Are they our enemies, then? These people with whom you speak so freely?"

Zennor looked at him without turning his head, sliding his eyes to the side as far as they would go. "Until it becomes proven that they are not."

His judicious answer apparently satisfied the Dana, or at least even Garamanus was inclined to wait for a different moment before designating enemy status. Now began a struggle for the hearts of the crew, Zennor knew, between the day-to-day leader and the leader of eons, between the Vergo who made the mission real and the Dana whose spiritual strings had kept the people unified and motivated. The crew would be devoted to Zennor for the crude purposes of the mission, but these were the most fervent of the fervent and would follow Garamanus too, should Zennor falter.

In his knowledge of this, Zennor carefully said nothing else.

The Dana moved slightly forward, so Zennor had no

choice but to look at him. "You told Vergokirk too much."

Evidently he was not so satisfied after all.

"That is my option as Vergobretos of the mission," Zennor said. "We have no reason to hide our past."

"You implied this may not be the right place." Garamanus lowered his voice. "The Danai have studied for generations. You have been a mechanic in comparison. It is not in your realm to decide what to do, but only when to do it."

"I may not be Danai," Zennor said, "but I know the sacrifice of our people. I will not have it wasted."

Garamanus hovered in place. "The crew is not sure why you hesitate. These are the conquerors. Conquer them."

"The crew will not agree to aggress against the innocent. We have waited a hundred generations. We can wait a day longer."

"You gave up advantage when you told him who we are."

"Others will not tell us who they are if we do not tell them who we are. And Vergokirk took the first risk. Now we will take one. Aralu, Farne, Rhod, Manann, you will go with the Dana and me. Make the formation here around me which they explained to us. Rhod, this way another step. We must be correct. Very good. Aesh, maintain defender status until we contact you. Farne, signal to them that we are ready."

The transporter room seemed unaccountably bright after the auramine bridge of the other ship. Fresh air flooded into their lungs in place of the pungent, moldy stuff they'd been breathing for the past few minutes.

Leonard McCoy plunged off the platform and let out a huffing breath and brushed at his sleeves as if to cast away hidden weevils. "I felt like all my granddad's stories came to life before my very eyes! That bridge was like a cross between a temple and its catacombs. And

I've never seen a crew like those people before. Did all that make you as nervous as it made me?"

"Not once they spoke up." Jim Kirk followed his chief surgeon off the platform and reached over the transporter console to the comm. "It's when they *won't* speak that I get nervous. Kirk to environmental sciences."

"Environmental. Ensign Urback speaking, sir."

"Adjust the ship's temperature up by eight degrees and increase humidity to ninety-five percent relative."

"Are you cold on the bridge, sir?"

"Visitors coming aboard, Ensign."

"Oh—right, sir, sorry, sir."

"And inform the crew so nobody tries to repair it."

"Right away, sir."

"Carry on. Kirk out. Lieutenant, did you get anything out of that?"

Uhura blinked her dark eyes. "Only that I don't believe 'Wrath' is what we think it is. I do think it's their ship, but I'd like to zero in on the translation. And I'd like to work on the terminology 'Vergo' and 'Dana.' I could also run the visuals of those carvings and their clothing and jewelry through the library computer. I may be able to have something for them when they get here. Assuming, sir, you want me to help them."

"Until we have a reason to oppose them, we should help them. Do it from sickbay. Give your tricorder to Spock and let him get what he can out of it."

"Aye, sir."

"And dismiss the watch. Send them to breakfast. I want a fresh team on duty while these people are visiting."

"Aye, sir," she said, and stepped between the two guards without a glance at either of them.

Kirk waved to the guards. "Security, stand by in the corridor."

"Aye, sir."

"Aye aye, sir."

He swung to the transporter officer. "Mr. Kyle, prepare the transporter to bring aboard six visitors from the bridge of the other vessel. I told them what to do and they should be in position in another minute."

"Aye, sir," the lanky blond lieutenant said, then politely attended to his console and didn't look up again. That was one of the things Kirk liked about Kyle—his "ignore" mode. Sometimes a transporter room needed to be as intimate as the captain's office, and a transporter officer with discretion was worth his weight in precious metals.

Kirk stepped around the console to the auxiliary screen, where one tap pulled up an unassuring view of Zennor's massive ship and two of the Klingon vessels.

"Captain," McCoy began, "I know you like to bring 'visitors' aboard because there's less chance of their taking potshots at the ship with their own people aboard, but, if you don't mind my asking, are you out of your mind?"

"Probably." Kirk gazed at the ships. "But I know how I'd like to be treated and they reminded me of us."

"Only if 'us' are looking in a fun-house mirror."

"It's their similarities to us you're reacting to."

The doctor scowled. "Pardon me?"

"The scariest aliens are the ones who are distortions of ourselves. We look at them and see something vaguely familiar. An upright silhouette, the same kind of movements . . . arms and legs, mouths, an eye or two . . . a verbal language. Aliens like the horta or the Melkots aren't as frightening because they're so completely unlike us. It's those like Zennor and his crew that shake us up, and all because we see a glaze of something we recognize that's been stretched out of shape. Once we get over that, we can look at the similarities for what they are."

McCoy folded his arms and canted his head. "That's what's different about you, Captain."

Kirk looked at him. "About me? I don't follow."

"Yes," the doctor sighed. "No matter how far out we go, or how much space separates us from somebody else, you always see how we're all alike instead of how we're all different. And you talk to strangers as if you've known them a year. That's what sets you apart from me and Spock and all the rest of us. Even from the other starship captains. Everybody else goes out into space expecting to see things that are alien and weird. You look at the alien and weird, and you see a piece of us."

Basking in the compliment, somewhat embarrassed that there wasn't a veiled insult in there somewhere, Kirk leered at him. "You're a frustrated psychoanalyst, McCoy."

The doctor tightened his arms and bounced on his toes. "I'm not frustrated at all."

"Those skulls over there . . . you're still sure they were real? Not just decor?"

"Dead sure. Ah—bad choice of words."

"Noted. I want you to check on Spock now, while we have the chance."

"Yes, I intended to do that."

"Do it right away. Mr. Kyle, hail the bridge and inform General Kellen that we're having visitors from the other vessel. Have Security escort him down here if he feels like facing his fears."

"Yes, sir."

"Then clear the board and energize. Let's take the bull by the—uh—"

"Sir?"

"Just bring them over."

Chapter Ten

"AH, GENERAL."

The corridor suddenly turned burlesque with possibilities as Jim Kirk led the vagabond demons out of the transporter room.

Kellen said absolutely nothing. Behind him, two Security guards stood at attention, but they couldn't keep the shock out of their faces at the diabolical creatures following their captain.

Impressive in his tense stillness, Kellen stood with his thick arms tight to his barrel-like body, the wide silver tunic shimmering under the corridor's soft lighting. Only now did Kirk notice that the general had left his body armor behind when he'd beamed aboard. A convenience? Or a gesture of some kind that Kirk had failed to read? Too late now, if so.

The big Klingon didn't move a muscle, but there was abject horror plastered on his face as he stared at the gaggle of visitors, his eyes growing large. He stood dead still, his lips pressed into a line, and glared with all the appeal of a broadax.

Kirk slowly—perhaps too slowly—led the way toward

the general, hoping the extra seconds would give them time to get used to each other, and was gratified when Zennor, Garamanus, and their crew followed him like a clutter of travel-stained gypsies.

He stood to the side and gestured between the general and the aliens, and hoped for the best.

"General, this is Zennor, Vergo of the *Wrath,*" he said, careful of pronunciation. "Vergo Zennor, may I introduce General Kellen of the Klingon Imperial High Command."

Sometimes it could be that simple. Just introduce them. Push them past that bump, and maybe there'd be communication.

"You are allies?" the ghostly Dana asked, his voice a growling sound that engulfed the corridor and startled the Security team.

"We are not allies," Kellen quickly said. He seemed to be making good on his promise to be ashamed of having asked for Kirk's help in the first place and having it all come to this, a pointless parlay in a ship's corridor. "You must turn around and return to the depths from which you emerged. We will fight you if you do not."

"General," Kirk interrupted sharply, "they're my guests at the moment. I brought them here so you could see firsthand what you were attacking, in hopes that an understanding might come about."

"I already understand them," Kellen snapped back. "They are the Havoc. The tainted souls released from imprisonment, returned to torture us with their poisons. *Look* at them!"

Furiously he pointed at the being with the white tendrils on its head, then at the tall thin one behind Zennor with expanding skin flaps that moved in and out with the appearance of wings.

"Iraga!" he belted. "Shushara!"

"Yes, I see them," Kirk said, and stepped between Kellen and the visitors. "Are you prepared to strike up a dialogue?"

"There is no dialogue, Captain," Kellen ground out.

"I came here to destroy them before they destroy all of us. If you will be this foolish, then I will take my leave of you and return to my flagship."

Kirk squared off before the general's wide form. "You'll stay here until the sector is secured."

"Are you holding me hostage?"

"I'm holding you to your agreement to stay here until I decide the situation is no longer volatile. Ensign Brown, escort the general back to the VIP quarters and maintain watch there."

It was a polite way of telling the ensign to stand guard and keep the Klingon under house arrest. Brown glanced at him, then snapped to attention.

"Aye, sir!" the guard's deep voice boomed. "This way, General." A meaty six-footer, Brown stepped aside to let Kellen pass by, and it seemed for a moment that the corridor was filled from wall to wall with just Kellen and the guard.

Kirk hoped it wasn't too obvious that he had picked the bigger of the two ensigns to stand guard over Kellen. He wanted to make a point, but not to be rude. Not yet, anyway.

"Ensign Fulciero, please conduct our visitors on a general tour of the primary section and labs. Inform Mr. Scott and request he show them around main engineering."

The other ensign nodded, still wide-eyed. He held out a hand, gesturing down the corridor. "This way . . . please . . ."

Turning to Zennor, Kirk held out his own hand, in the opposite direction.

"My quarters, Captain," he invited. "We'll have a chance to talk privately."

Without the gawkings of my crew or the hauntings of your Dana.

He was glad there were relatively few crewpeople striding the corridors. The few they did pass managed to choke back their shock at Zennor's size and volcanic appearance, but Kirk was relieved to finally usher the alien commander into his quarters and have the door whisper shut behind them. He hoped Scott would warn his engineers that there were visitors coming and prepare them for just what that could mean in deep space.

Then again, the chief engineer would probably do his share of gawking. Scott didn't trade much in discretion.

"Excuse me one moment," he said, and tapped the desk comm. "Kirk to sickbay."

"Sickbay, Nurse Chapel."

"Nurse, is Dr. McCoy still down there?"

"Yes, sir. He's with Mr. Spock. I'll get him. One moment, please."

"Standing by."

He let quiet settle as he waited and as Zennor moved away from him and looked around the quarters. There was a constant aura about Zennor, a sense of omen, perhaps, and a sound in the back of Kirk's head like a tuning of cellos before a performance of *Faust.* He had no idea what he was sensing, but in this creature and those others, there was a sorcerous spirit of the familiar.

"Captain," Kirk began, "if you'll look at the computer screen on the desk, I'll call up a visual tour of the starship and other Starfleet vessels. You can adjust the speed with that dial on the side of the monitor."

Zennor turned to the desk, and Kirk keyed up the program, careful to call up the nonsensitive data tour, the one reserved for dignitaries without telling too much. Then he edged away to let the ship show itself off.

"McCoy here."

He blinked and shook his attention back to the comm. "Bones, how's Spock? Any better?"

"He's no less stubborn. I was hoping to have that organ removed, but I don't have a long enough drill."

"Give me a report, please."

"I've reduced the level of antigrav and begun to put weight on his spine again. If there's any more swelling around the disks, I'll have to increase it again."

Kirk let his chin drop a little as his gut twisted. Like the first gnawings of space sickness in his teenage years, the feeling of being without anchorage rushed in. "Has he had a chance to review the information Lieutenant Uhura brought back?"

"Yes," McCoy said, *"and he wants to go over it with you at your earliest convenience."*

"Understood. Tell him I'll be there soon."

"Yes, Captain. Lieutenant Uhura says she has a few things for you also."

"Very well. Kirk out."

He cut off the comm before McCoy had a chance to give any details. The doctor didn't know Zennor was here, and Kirk wasn't ready to tip any of his hand.

Zennor continued to gaze at the computer screen as it scrolled—damned fast—before him. He had it on full speed and was apparently soaking up all it could give in spite of the fact that Kirk could barely make out the photos at that speed. "Your ship is clever. Many technologies we have not thought of. You and this Klingon . . . you are enemies?"

"Yes, traditionally we're enemies. Occasionally we have an uneasy truce, as we do today."

"Strange that you would be enemies. You are so much the same."

"You see no difference between Kellen and me?"

"No difference between any of you. You, your crewmen, your Klingon . . ."

"There's a big difference between us and the Klingons," Kirk said, letting flare a touch of defense. "For instance, just today we were engaged in a land skirmish between an aggressive Klingon commander and my crew. We had to hold them back from innocent people they would've annihilated, all because those people refused to do business with them."

"You were on a planet?"

"Yes."

"Could the Klingon not simply lay waste to the planet with those long-necked vessels?"

"Yes, but they wouldn't. That would be an act of war.

In a skirmish, they can always claim they were ambushed."

"I do not understand this." Zennor's voice was heavy, deep, as if speaking through a long tube.

Kirk couldn't quite read the ferocious bony mask of the other captain's face, or the smoky reddish orbs of his eyes. "Klingon command is set up in cells," he explained. "The area commanders have a great deal of autonomy in their areas, but aren't allowed to commit the Empire to interstellar war. Each is responsible for a specific area, and can conquer it if it's within his skills to do so, but if he fails in his aspiration, then all the Empire doesn't suffer for it. The commanders aren't allowed to drag the Empire into a war. That's for the High Council to decide. If the local commander oversteps his authority in the course of his ambitions, he can be demoted rather than promoted. They could have reduced the planet to a blackened char, but they know the Federation would never put up with that. As it turned out, General Kellen overruled the local commander because he was more worried about you."

"About us . . ."

"You saw how emotionally you affect him. And he is a particularly cool customer among his kind. His restraint is famous."

"He claims we are . . . trouble?"

"Havoc. It's a Klingon myth about an apocalypse. A final reckoning."

"Myths can be powerful. Given enough time, myth becomes religion. Mysterious legend becomes immutable fact. My culture moves on this kind of sea also. That is why he hates us so."

"He fears you." Kirk offered a cushioning grin. "He doesn't know you well enough to hate you."

"If it comes to be proven that we are not in our space, we will destroy the Klingons for you."

The grin fell off Kirk's face and he almost heard the crunch. "I can't sanction that."

"But if they are conquering, they must be stopped. Why would you allow them to continue?"

Oh, tempting, tempting . . .

"We prefer other pressures. A war brings a high death toll. People can and do change, given time. We're working on them in other ways."

"I do not understand that," Zennor admitted. "Perhaps I will eradicate them anyway."

Despite the words, there was something sincerely well-meaning in the way the alien leader said what he said.

Enjoying the whole idea for a raucous instant in the privacy of his own heart, Kirk nodded in some kind of arm's-length comprehension, then got control of himself and calmly pointed out, "We protected you from the Klingons. We'll protect them from you for the same reasons, if you force us to."

Zennor's heavy head lay slightly to one side. "You are . . . spirited," he said admiringly. His almond-shaped eyes flickered and actually changed color, like camp matches flaring briefly in the woods. "When my ship's power is fully restored, you will not be able to stop me."

That grin came sneaking back to Kirk's lips, and he felt his own eyes flare a little. Undercurrents of mutuality ran between them. Dare though this might be, still there was something about Zennor's convictions that ran close to Kirk's heart, and he understood what Zennor meant and wanted, the intense sense of right and wrong that might have been a bit skewed but still smacked of strong decency.

And underlying all this, a spicy challenge, as when Spock asked him to play chess.

"Let's hope we don't have to find out," he deferred gently. "Vergo, I'm curious about where you came from. You say it's a great distance. Can you tell me the area?"

The twisted horns tipped forward and cast a shadow as Zennor's triangular face pivoted downward. "On the opposite side of the mean center of the galaxy from this place."

"And yet you said it wasn't a transporter that brought

you here. Not a mechanism of the sort that we use to move from ship to ship."

"We have no such instrument. We came here from the far distant side of the galaxy, using a device that causes space to wrinkle, thus offering passage of large distance in a short time."

Kirk waved his hands in casual beckoning. "Explain the technology."

"We do not understand the technology. We only know that it works."

Kirk felt his brow pucker. He had always assumed that people using a science at least understood the science.

When he didn't offer much sympathy for that, Zennor picked up on it and evidently decided he wanted to say more.

"For many centuries this thing hovered in space above my people's central planet. It passed between us and our sun, regularly throwing its elongated black shadow upon our planet. Because it was known to be the machine that delivered us to our banishment, it became a symbol of evil and doom, a god that glowered upon us and kept us in misery. Anything bad was credited to it, this great black shape dooming our sky to ugliness. Our women conjured spells against it. Young men dreamed of flying up to destroy it. We said it was of the conquerors."

"The conquerors—you said that before. Who do you think the conquerors were?"

"Those who cast us out. To my people they are the highest evil. My people are from many tribes and groups and clans—"

"I noticed that."

"We warred for eons with each other, blaming each other for our conditions, claiming collusion with the conquerors, until finally we realized we were all cast out together and it was no one's fault but those who exiled us. Worse than killing us, they took the place where we were born. *Took* it. If we fail to take it back, then justice has not been served. Gradually this became the driving force of our unity. Century upon untold century, the shadow of the conquerors' machine passed over us, forging our unity stronger and stronger with every pass. Ultimately our scientists figured out what it was. Only a ball of mechanics. What for eons we had dreamed of destroying turned out to be the tool of our future. Fortunately we came to our senses before we could react emotionally and destroy this valuable piece of lost technology. We found out it uses time as a dimension, and thus allows interdimensional travel. And we figured out how to activate it."

"Your entire culture turns on this one cog? Don't you find that a little . . . obsessive?"

"Yes, I do. But a culture must have a common purpose. We spend generations storing enough energy to push this ship through, packed with sensory equipment. We have no idea what powered the machine originally, and have been centuries developing enough power to pass through to where we believe we came from. We do not know why it goes, but we know how to make it go."

"That much energy must be a powerful space distorter," Kirk said. "It explains the mass-drop effect."

"Which was not our intention."

"That doesn't repeal your responsibility for it. Every ship's master is responsible for his own wake."

"I do not understand that reference."

"According to our laws of space travel, it befalls you to anticipate the effects of your ship's passage."

"These are insignificant things you speak of. We have spent a hundred generations preparing for this. The Danai and the Bardoi of our cultures have spent uncounted years, centuries, on the direction and purpose of my mission. I must keep perspective."

"What if they're wrong?"

"Then I will go against them myself. I am willing to cast away the work of a hundred generations if we are wrong."

"You must suspect they could be," Kirk said, "or you wouldn't be here, talking to me." He paused, using his senses to decide how hard he could push. "Am I right? Do you have doubts?"

Turning away from him, Zennor's long hands coiled the chain of his medallion as he scanned the simple decor, the military trim of the bunk and desk, the lack of carvings or haze, and his strange orange eyes narrowed.

"If the belief in the giant shadow god was silly," he said, "what about the rest of our legends? If that was wrong, what else is wrong? Shall I kill everyone on this side of the galaxy based on myth? Was that the only part of our mythology that we misinterpreted?"

Probing like a sea lawyer, Kirk asked, "Is there something specific you're suspicious about, Vergo?"

As he swung around, Zennor's dangerous eyes scoped him and for a moment Kirk thought the amicability might be over. Then Zennor admitted, "I am not entirely sure we were thrown across the galaxy. It *appears* we did not evolve together, but who knows? We could have been moved to save our lives and grew the opposite belief out of fear and superstition. The Danai seem to me to have made many leaps. I would not wish to see my civilization expending all its wealth and energy to make war on strangers based on legends."

"But you do believe your civilization was wronged and unnecessarily banished?"

"We certainly were banished, most coldly and without resource. Many millions died, including some whole races, because they could not survive the changeover."

"What must be proven to you?" Kirk asked carefully.

"That we were cast out . . . that this is the space we were cast out from . . . that these are the descendants of those who cast us out. Unlike Garamanus, I am unwilling to assume. I think we are in the wrong place. I hope to prove that. Then my people can begin to live a future, rather than endlessly hunt for the past."

Seizing his chance, Kirk offered, "You can do that now. Give up the idea of conquering the conquerors and embrace the idea of cooperation. You can settle here, start a whole new civilization. There are many planets crying for colonization and development. We'll help you."

Zennor's great horns scuffed the ceiling as he nodded slowly. "For myself, that would serve. For my people, certain steps must be taken first. If I can prove the Danai wrong, the crew will not attack anyone who is not the conqueror. They will not become what they hate. Then the Danai will be obsolete."

"How do you know your people won't just try again?"

"The Danai insist this is the right place. How can they insist again about somewhere else?"

"It's that simple?"

"Yes. But how do I disprove a thing? The Danai say this is the place. How can I say it is not?"

"One step at a time." Kirk watched Zennor for a moment, then asked, "What's the first step?"

Zennor kept to the shadows of the captain's quarters, perhaps seeking instinctively the shrouding veil that twisted in his own ship, but moved toward Kirk and deposited on the desk his crescent brooch. When he had taken it off Kirk had no idea, but now it was in his long-boned hand, and now it was on the desk.

With one pale fingernail, Zennor flipped the crescent over. Etched on the inside of the curve were dots and a series of curved lines. Kirk recognized it instantly.

"Star chart?"

Zennor nodded once. "We can tell from a few preserved etchings how the stars looked at differing periods five thousand of your years ago. The Danai have based their decision on these pieces. The surviving originals are very old, but there is a definite arrangement of stars. What you see here is an extrapolation of stellar motion over the generations, and how those stars should be arranged now. These are regarded as absolute. This one is the most certain, and it shows what the Danai believe is the home system of the creatures like Manann."

"Manann . . . the ones with the wings?"

"Wings? Those membranes are for temperature adjustment."

"Yes, of course. . . . General Kellen told me those creatures are called 'Shushara' in the Klingon legend of Havoc. Does that word sound familiar to you?"

"No."

"Perhaps that's good."

"Perhaps it is. This is the strongest piece of solid evidence we possess. If this is disproven, then the Danai's theory will collapse. If there is no planet there which has had life in the past five thousand years, Garamanus will have to back down."

"If those creatures lived on that planet only five thousand years ago," Kirk said, "there's got to be evidence of it. Let's overlay this and see if there's a correlation."

Without waiting for Zennor to comment, Kirk scanned the piece of jewelry into the computer access, then said, "Computer."

"Working," the flat female voice replied back.

"Identify this star system."

The machine paused as if shut down, but he knew it was searching, and in moments a star system appeared on the desk access screen. The arrangement of stars wasn't exact, but this was evidently the closest the computer could find. Abruptly the odds struck him—anything could look like anything, given enough monkeys and enough years.

"We must go there," Zennor said. His maize eyes remained unchanged, unimpressed.

"Computer," Kirk continued, "specify location of this star system."

"It is the Kgha'lugh star system, located in sector nine-three-seven, Province Ruchma, Klingon Star Empire."

A low protest rose in Kirk's throat.

Deep into Klingon space. Deep, deep.

Zennor read his expression and evidently understood. "For me to balk would be suicidal. It is not what we spent so many generations to do. If I do not go there, Garamanus will take over, and our people will go there."

"You're talking about violating entrenched Klingon space, Captain," Kirk told him. "You'll be beaten back before you make it halfway there."

"We will get there. My *Wrath* can broach any challenge."

"You're underestimating. All you've seen is a few midweight border cruisers. You don't realize what a fleet of heavy cruisers can do to your ship."

"I can destroy their fleet," Zennor assured, not seeming to intend the bravado with which Kirk read the claim. "When we came through the wrinkle, our power slackened somewhat and the Klingons inflicted some minor damage, but that is no longer a problem. My ship is no longer in any peril from you, but you, Vergokirk, are in grave peril from us, and that is my concern. If I fail to do this, or if the Klingons push an attack too much on me, I will have to destroy them. If I do not destroy them, Garamanus will take over and destroy all of you. And that is my concern."

Kirk shoved off the desk and stood straight. "Vergo Zennor, you're either a very skilled liar or you're putting a great deal of trust in me."

The fiery eyes looked down at him. "I have made a decision to trust you. And you must honor that trust, Vergokirk, and help me keep control," Zennor finished with slow impact, "or you will be dealing directly with Garamanus."

"Yes, well," Kirk said with a guttural response to what he read as a dare. "You have Garamanus and I have Kellen. For the moment, they're both quiet. While they are, my officers are putting the ship's considerable resources to work on information you've given them. Your party will tour the ship and with luck gain some understanding of us and see that we're not these 'conquerors' you speak of. Meanwhile, I think you and I should attempt to iron out this problem between your people and the Klingons."

"General, these are your quarters. I'll be right outside if you need anything."

"Thank you, but I need only this."

With his back to the husky young Starfleet guard, and without even bothering to turn, Kellen used a new dagger and an old trick. He raised his chin and braced his feet for balance, locked his elbow, and thrust his arm straight backward. In his fist was the warm hilt, behind it the blade.

Without even witnessing his own act, he felt the blade pop the skin of the guard's body and grate against a rib. The guard's breath gushed out against the back of Kellen's head and the boy fell forward against Kellen's shoulder.

Only then did he turn to see the boy, to turn him over quickly so there would be no telltale blood upon the deck, and finally to drag the body into the quarters where Kellen was supposed to wait in complacence, which was as much his enemy as Starfleet itself and almost as alien to him.

So much more alien than he expected—this complicatory inaction was unexpected and he cursed it. Kirk was a thorough disappointment. As the door of the VIP quarters hissed closed behind him and hid his kill for the moment, he thought about how far he could push the Federation. It had always been in his mind, through all his years in the Imperial fleet. Klingons had not survived so long by being stupid. He knew the Federation tolerated much more than any Klingon would, but when they did turn and fight they were not a pleasant enemy. They would fight ruthlessly and methodically. There were other Kirks out there who deserved to be Kirk, and one disappointment would not fool Kellen. Unlike Klingon honor, the Federation had a sharp sense of right and wrong as their barometer. When they believed they were right, they fought with unmatched ferocity.

This had always been a mystery to Kellen—when the Federation would fight and why. Always a minefield to walk. He could spit in a human's face—something a whole Klingon family would go to war over—and the human might shrug and walk away. Yet step on the toe of something they had no interest in and the Federation would marshal all its forces to defend a thing it did not care to possess.

Like this Kirk. Why had he refused to fight so obvious a threat? Certainly there were primogenial memories in the Federation of those demons, just as there were for the Klingons. Even time beyond recall could be recalled when the common danger was disclosed.

Some predictions could work, though. He had gambled and won that these people were too polite to make a body search of a visiting dignitary, even a Klingon dignitary. They hadn't. He had kept his dagger hidden, and beside it a shielded communicator which he now withdrew and powered up.

"Qul . . . Aragor, do you read me? Come in, *Qul."*

Communicator shields often worked in both directions and impaired broadcast. He kept the signal weak, not sure how much of a signal would trigger this ship's security systems and notify them that he was attempting to reach out from here to his own ship.

He started walking. No turbolifts. Too entrapping. There would be ladders, tubes, other ways to go down.

"Qul . . . Qul . . ." Over and over he murmured the name of his ship, slowly adjusting the gain on the communicator until they would hear him calling.

And here was a tube—with a ladder. He asked and was answered.

He peered down the tube to be sure there was no technician coming up whose head he would have to crush, and swung his thick leg around the ladder.

"General . . . this is Aragor. Where are you?"

Clinging to the rungs and wedging his way into the tube, which barely accommodated his girth, Kellen paused. "I am in the starship. I believe Kirk is about to betray us. Call for reinforcements, as many as you can find. Make no obvious movements, but be ready to attack. Contact the *Jada* and tell that idiot Ruhl to prepare the squadron's defenses, but quietly."

"Sir . . . the commanders will not be allowed to attack a Starfleet ship under a flag of truce without provocation or gain. How will we make them believe you saw?"

"I must be believed! Or it is disaster."

"I believe you, General, but the commanders will demand proof."

Anger welled and he wanted to shout at Aragor, yet he knew this was not Aragor's doing. His science officer was neither fool nor petty stooge. A truth was a truth.

"There will be proof. I will find it somehow. You call them. Give them the facts as we know them. Show them the tapes. I am going to main engineering to disable this vessel. Make preparations to beam me back when I make signal. No more communication."

"Understood. Out."

The tube was narrow but bright, and he felt closed in, trapped, even as he moved freely downward through the veins of the starship. The voices of the crew from deck to deck were his only contact with the Starfleeters, giving him reason to pause now and then to be sure no one saw him pass through the open hatchways and companionways. He could be easily cornered here, but his size forced him to move slowly, with cautious deliberation. To slip and tumble because of nervousness would be shameful.

Tours. Guests. Open arms to demons and friends. Havoc embraced. A Kirk who was no Kirk. Seek out the unshatterable and discover only crumbs.

The rungs were cool against his palms. Rung after rung, the ship peeled away beneath his hands and boots. Nearer and nearer he climbed down toward the pulse and thrum of the warp core. He felt it vibrate through the ladder and heard it hum in his ears. That was the power source he must cripple, or the starship would once again stand in his way.

When the thrum was strongest, he went one deck more to make sure he had indeed zeroed in on the main engineering deck, then climbed back up and cautiously extracted his bulk from the tube. This was a wide-halled ship, with room to stretch his arms from bulkhead to bulkhead even in the passages. They wasted space, these people, attempting to create an environment too much like planetary architecture. They came into the depths of space, then tried to pretend they were otherwhere. They coddled their comforts too much in sacrifice to efficiency and quickness. No one needed this much room. And with every extra bit of indulgence, there had to be that much more thrust, so they wasted energy to accommodate their waste of space.

That could mean they had power to spare. He would have to consider that in his sabotage.

He moved slowly through the offices to the functioning engineering deck, keeping himself hidden from humans in red shirts who moved from panel to panel, reading and measuring what they saw, and crossed walkways overhead. At the far end of the deck he saw the cathedral-tall red glow of the warp core throbbing placidly, off-line as the ship lay at all-stop.

Finding an angular elbow between three tall storage canisters, Kellen paused to assess what he saw and decide how best to inflict injury that would be hard to find and take time to fix.

As he studied the movements of the engineers and listened to their faint conversations, wicking general information about these panels, he almost failed to notice the most important change when it came—the demons were here.

There . . . nearly obscured by the thing he was hiding behind, but they were here! On their *tour* . . . doing just as he was doing, seeking information and scanning the uncovered consoles and all this technology these idiots kept out in the open and freely showed to any and all who came. Even demons could see.

That other ensign now tagged behind. The gaggle of

evil was led instead by a senior engineer, who seemed uneasy at the creatures following him. He spoke little, but gestured for the creatures to disperse about the deck and gaze about.

The other engineers paused in their work and stared at the ghastly amalgam who came here now, the long-faced horned beasts, the winged Shushara, the hideous Iraga with those white snakes in its head. Even the vaulting humans who spoke so large and pretended nothing bothered them today could not hide their disgust. They acted as if they did not remember these ill-biddens, did not recognize what they saw, but it was in their eyes and the tightening of their shoulders as they looked upon the evictees who now returned unasked.

No matter how they lied to themselves, they did remember. It was their Havoc too.

Kellen held his breath as the Iraga crossed the deck, shuffling upon its ugly limbs toward him, coming to look at something on this side of the high-ceilinged chamber. Its leprous face was more terrible than any mask, crowned with those arm-long snakes that moved independently, reaching and retracting, as if tasting the air.

He backed into his nook and held very still. There was a cool and convenient shadow here, not quite big enough to engulf his entire body, but dark enough to obscure him.

The profane thing passed by him and moved into a secondary chamber, passing within inches. He smelled its licheny body and drew his chin downward in disgust, wincing as the tentacles whipped toward his face and licked at the canister's edge. If they had eyes, the Iraga would know he hid here.

What would the horror be, to be overrun by these, the condemned, even to survive and be forced to do their filthy bidding? The thought shuddered through him. He held his breath.

But his shadow served him. The beast moved past.

Kellen raised his right hand and sifted through his outer robe for the familiar palm-filling shape of his dagger's hilt. It was a good dagger, not his family dagger, which he had already given to his son, but a good weapon that had known too little use. Now it would have its moment.

The general rolled out from between the canisters, walking casually across the open archway because that would gain less attention than if he attempted to sneak across.

Without changing his stride he walked up behind the Iraga, reached as high as he could, snatched a handful of the gory tentacles moving in the creature's skull, and drove his blade into the haze of white gauzy cloth covering the creature's body.

Chapter Eleven

UNLIKE THE BODY of the ensign whom Kellen had just killed, the Iraga's wound gushed no liquid onto his fist, but instead puckered around it. He felt no spine, but assumed there was one in there somewhere, and aggravated the blade across the body from side to side.

The Iraga gasped and arched backward against him. Its mouth stretched open and its limbs thrust outward. Kellen pulled it down until he could twist the tentacles around the creature's face and stuff them into its mouth and down its throat, guttering any cry it tried to make.

He waited for it to die, but it would not die. It cranked to this side, then that side, trying to pull itself free of his grip and the blade digging into its back. Soon it began to go pliant in his arms and he let it drop.

It slid down his legs and rolled to the deck at his feet, staring up at him with bitter green eyes that had no pupils.

"Security to Mr. Scott. Emergency."

Kellen looked up, and stepped to the archway. The senior engineer was reaching for the nearest panel.

"Scott here."

"Sir, Mr. Giotto here. Captain says to notify you of intruder-alert status. We've had a call from deck four. Yeoman Tamura went to ask the Klingon general if she could bring him dinner and she found Ensign Brown on the floor of the VIP quarters. He's been killed, sir, and there's no sign of the general. We're attempting a bio-sweep for Klingon physiology, but we haven't pinpointed anything yet."

The engineer's face turned stony, and for a moment he glared at the comm as if it had done the killing. When he spoke his voice was like metal grating on metal. "Acknowledged. Scott out." He looked up and snapped his fingers. "Mr. Hadley! Go to Security alert status two in the lower section. Double guards at every entrance. Let's clear this deck of all but assigned personnel. Arm the lot and set up in teams."

"Yes, sir, Mr. Scott. Johnson, come with me! Elliott, come down here!"

Suddenly there was confusion all over. The demons were rounded up and shuffled out of Kellen's sight. Guards with phasers jogged through, and his plans for sabotage were snuffed before his eyes.

So the plans must be altered.

He stepped back to the poisonous body, yanked his dagger clear of the Iraga's back, and quickly retracted the two claw extensions. Taking the hilt in both hands, he braced his legs wide, raised the heavy center blade as the creature looked up beseechingly at him, and brought it down with all the power in his thick upper body. The blade crunched through the Iraga's throbbing neck and went a finger's length into the deck.

Sawing deliberately, he ignored the free flood of white fluid and gray organs. Finally he twisted his left hand into the frantically jerking tentacles and pulled as he cut. The eyes flared as if the demon knew what was happening to it. The lips moved open, closed, open, closed, as if trying to speak to him, and there was sound from the ravaged throat that soon dissolved into a froth.

He sawed relentlessly. In moments the beast's eyes began to roll and the tentacles began to coil around and around Kellen's hand and wrist, growing thinner as they tightened. He was disgusted at the greasy sensation, but forced himself to maintain his grip and continue to pull and cut.

The neck muscles were twisted like cord and resisted even the razor-sharpness of his dagger blade. The bones of this demon's throat grated fiercely, but he gritted his teeth and applied his strength, and soon the Iraga's lips peeled back to reveal its pointed teeth, and its head flinched off into his hand.

Kellen stumbled back with the force of his own pulling as the last of the ligaments snapped. Before him the Iraga's body winced and jolted, its long fingers scratching at the deck, air sucking with futile desperation into the exposed tube endings through which it had been breathing only moments ago. It was trying to live.

He had no idea whether it would succeed, but he had its head and that was what he needed. Now there would be movement, action against the Havoc, which he had let slip through his grip by failing to destroy the Havoc ship from within when he had the chance. Since then, everything that had happened had done so because of the price of his own life.

He would not make so great an error again. The Klingon who stopped the Havoc would be the icon of the next age.

And more, far more, the disaster to his people and all people would be shoved back into the maw of legend.

With his gut-stained hand he shoved his blade into his belt and clawed for the communicator. The instrument nearly slipped between his wet fingers. If it fell, it would ring the deck as loudly as a klaxon and they would come and find him.

He brought the instrument to his lips. "*Qul. Qul.* Activate transporter. I have the proof!"

* * *

"This is a mighty odd invasion, as invasions go."

McCoy adjusted the antigrav on Spock's diagnostic bed down another few degrees, then tilted the upper-body section of the bed so Spock could at least feel as if he were sitting up some.

The science officer's computer accesses were still at fingertip convenience and Spock wasn't moving much, but his face had lost its sea-foam pallor. The therapy of work had done him good.

McCoy wished there were something that could do some good for a furious captain whose arms were knotted at his sides and who couldn't seem to stop pacing in bitter rage.

"I've got a crewman murdered by a dignitary with whom I made a treaty, and a potential flashpoint on my hands," he snarled as he swung around and started back toward Spock after coming nose-up to a shelf full of vials. Every time he paced over there he caught a sour vision of himself in a mirror behind the shelves.

It made him madder.

He struck the nearest comm unit and for the fourth time clipped, "Kirk to Security. Progress report."

There was a pause, though he could tell through raw experience that the line was open.

"Captain, Giotto here. We've completed our bio-sweep. There's no Klingon on board anymore. The general must've gotten off the ship somehow."

Big surprise.

"Understood. Shields up. No more beaming unless I authorize it personally."

"Aye-aye, sir."

He snapped the comm off without acknowledging and twisted back to Spock. "Have you got anything? Anything at all?"

Spock's straight brows furrowed some as the responsibility hit him squarely between them, but he tapped on his keyboards and brought up on the screen a stylized watercolor painting of a creature disturbingly like one of Zennor's party.

"In Klingon legend, the Shushara was a winged demon, or group of demons, given to consuming unsuccessful warriors, beginning with their feet and eating its way up the body while the victim witnessed this and contemplated his failures. Like many other demons, they were ultimately banished, but promised to return with the Havoc to consume the weak. Kellen may see Zennor's crew as a manifestation of the Empire's failure to expand since the establishment of the Neutral Zone by the Federation."

"Havoc is their punishment for having let themselves be contained?"

"Yes," Spock said. He moved his hand to his lap, rather gingerly, slowly, and scooped up the crescent brooch, looking at the scratch of stars and comets upon which Zennor's civilization set its hopes. "Regarding this etching, taking into account the ten differing periods of their standard year and the speed and movement of stars, there is a legitimate corollary in the Danai research. They seem ready to jump to a conclusion, but nothing is disprovable yet. Any arrangement of stars may look like something else five thousand years later from any angle of your own choosing. I must admit, though, this is an excellent correlation to this particular stellar group, given the millennia and the constant movement of celestial bodies. I find myself deeply impressed that they managed to do this, especially from across the galaxy, Captain. The technology—"

"Not the technology now, Spock. How likely is it that this is the actual place?"

Spock let the brooch slip back onto his thigh and moved his eyes to Kirk. "Not very likely."

Kirk flattened his lips. "As I understand it, Zennor and Garamanus are competing for the loyalty of their crew. Garamanus is, more or less, the spiritual force aboard, like the priests who went on board the ships of the Spanish Armada and were the political force that the captain had to deal with. When Zennor didn't move to destroy us and the Klingons, Garamanus had a reason not to trust him. Zennor's required to take certain steps. If he doesn't take them, Garamanus can have him removed."

"And one of those steps," McCoy prodded, "is to prove that we're the conquerors, whoever they were?"

"Or that we're not. 'Conqueror' to them is like saying Kodos the Executioner to us. We have to establish that we weren't involved in the conquest that banished their civilization and that they have come to the wrong place to look for their home."

"They have ferocious religious beliefs, evidently," Spock said, "and these have taken care of them over the generations."

"But Zennor seems to be some kind of agnostic," Kirk added. "He wants our help to disprove that we're the conquerors. Their priests have settled on this area for their own reasons, and the scientists have been afraid to challenge. They put all their cultural energy into coming here, but Zennor doesn't want to come here and become just another conqueror. He has a mission inside his mission—to disprove the mission."

"Interesting," Spock murmured. "The galaxy is prohibitively huge, Captain, and they have risked everything to come to this one area. Either way, the trip is one-way for Zennor and his crew. No matter what happens, they cannot go back. They are here now. Such commitment takes great fortitude. I am impressed with Vergo Zennor for taking on convictions above and beyond belief in his assignment."

"So am I," Kirk said with a reckless sigh.

"The priests of their culture are taking this as hard fact," McCoy said, holding out a hand to Spock. Then he looked at Kirk. "They'll only take hard fact to knock it down. What're we going to do?"

Kirk glowered at the edge of the bed, not really seeing it. "If we go there and there's no such planet around the star they've targeted, or there is a planet but there's never been life on it, then their plan falls apart. Zennor wants it to fall apart, but we have to go there to pull it down."

"Vergo Zennor believes his ship can stand up to a Klingon fleet attack," Spock said. "I have checked and double-checked their vessel, and yes, it is powerful and may be able to stand down a squadron of patrollers. But a fleet of heavy cruisers—I tend to doubt."

"I don't want to find out," Kirk said. "If it comes to that, I'll have to side with Zennor. The Klingons are being completely irrational about this. They're acting on an instinctive level."

"I can understand it," McCoy offered. "Our crew's having the same reaction. And so am I. These people look . . . I don't know, familiar somehow. Even though I've never seen anything that looks like any of them before."

"Regardless, I've got a decision to make. Do I violate Klingon deep space now that I've put my foot in this? Or do I abandon Zennor at the Neutral Zone and see to myself? No, scratch that. I've made a commitment to the situation."

The doctor frowned. "Jim, shouldn't you ask permission from Starfleet Command before you make any tactical movements farther into Klingon space?"

"I've already been given permission once. Why ask again and give them a chance to say no? Those orders aren't withdrawn. The mission isn't over. It's still my option. I won't hand that option away to a bureaucrat. All right, Spock, you've found a thread—follow it. In the meantime, I'm going to let Zennor set the pace. He knows the pressures he's dealing with and I believe him when he says he wants to knock the knees out from under the driving forces. There's a short road to defusing this situation and unfortunately it leads directly into Klingon territory."

Scooping up the crescent brooch, Kirk rubbed his thumb across the etching on the inner curve, then held it out before them.

"This is it, gentlemen," he said. "If we can disprove this, the invasion falls apart."

The crew of the Imperial patrol cruiser *Qul* shrank back like beaten children, huddled into the recesses of the bridge, and covered their faces with shuddering hands. Before them writhed the unthinkable, the incarnate, twisting between the fingers of General Kellen as he held high the proof of Havoc.

Kellen felt like a living beacon as he held the straining tentacles of the Iraga before his witnesses.

"All screens on! Broadcast this on all frequencies to the squadron and on long-range to the fleet and all Imperial receivers, wide dispersal! There will be no more doubt!"

No one moved. Aragor, Mursha, Karg, Rek, Horg—they all stared with eyes like eggs at the thing in his hands, which stared back with its slowly blinking green eyes and moved its lips in ghastly beckoning at them.

"Quickly!" Kellen roared. "Before it dies!"

There sat auld Nick, in shape o' beast;
A tousie tyke, black, grim, and large,
To gie them music was his charge:
He screw'd the pipes and gart them skirl,
Till roof and rafter a' did dirl.
Coffins stood round, like open presses,
That shaw'd the Dead in their last dresses . . .

—Robert Burns
"Tam O'Shanter"

Chapter Twelve

"THE SHIP IS RUN at sublight speed by an internally metered pulse drive. We call it impulse."

"We have something similar."

"I know you do. There's quite a bit that's similar about your civilization and ours. If we can reach an understanding, perhaps your people will be satisfied to settle here and exchange knowledge, share a few things."

"Vergokirk . . . you underestimate the passion of my civilization. You are too comfortable in your identity. You and your friends, and the Klingons and others here, all have a sense of home. You all know where you came from. You have no doubt in your souls about defending it. When we find our space, we will defend it."

Each corner of the captain's cabin and office had been thoroughly roamed, and now Zennor had found himself the most amenable corner from which to contemplate the place and people among whom he now found himself. He hovered behind the perforated privacy partition, which cast a gridlike pattern of shapes and shadows upon his face and form. Standing there in the dimness, he was as bizarre a visage as Jim Kirk had ever seen.

"You say that with great conviction, but I'm not sure I accept what you say," Kirk told him. "You've admitted you think the evidence is too scant."

"Scant or not, it is taken as religion now." Zennor turned to Kirk, and his bony face was terrible as it caught the brittle shadows. "I do not believe you are the conquerors."

Strange how his words were so antithetical to the appearance of this enigmatic alien. He was indeed a ghastly visage hovering there in the shadows, the light designed mostly for humans stamping in confusion across the angles and twists of his skull and horns. And it had no idea what to do with those eyes.

"If we find this is the wrong space, we can live among your Federation. There is something here upon which to build, and my people are builders."

"And we'll welcome you," Kirk said. "We'll welcome you right now, if you'll let us."

Before Zennor could answer, the comm unit behind Kirk twittered and he turned to it. "Kirk here."

"McCoy, Captain. As soon as you can, would you please come down to sickbay? I've got an emergency and I believe you should know about it."

Abruptly interested, Kirk pressed his elbow to the comm and leaned closer. "Is Spock all right?"

There was a pause. *"It's something else, Captain. Please come alone."*

Come alone? What was that supposed to mean?

Instantly he knew what it meant. Leave Zennor up here, something's been found out.

"If you'll excuse me," he said quickly, "my first officer was severely injured this morning and I think my ship's surgeon is trying to cloak any weaknesses in my staff. If you wish to leave here, push this button and Security will answer. They'll escort you back to the bridge or to the others in your party. As I understand it, they're enjoying their tour of the ship."

* * *

"Bones? What's going on?"

Sickbay's main door panel to the corridor closed behind Kirk.

"I'm in here, Captain," McCoy called, and appeared in the doorway of an auxiliary examining room.

Kirk glanced into the main ward, where Spock was confined, but didn't go in there. "All right, what's your crisis?"

"Captain," the doctor said, "there's been a murder."

As he looked at McCoy's sober face and hoped for a punch line, Kirk felt his feet go cold. "You mean, other than Brown? A second one?"

"Yes. But not one of our crew. This is one of Captain Zennor's people. It was just discovered about twenty minutes ago. Security delivered the body down here and I instructed them that I would notify you."

Ramifications tumbled across Kirk's mind, piling one upon the other. A visitor from an alien vessel in a volatile situation, murdered. Here.

Horrible.

But only a little more horrible than the body McCoy led him to. This wasn't just a murder. This was a slaughter.

Kirk stood over the mutilated cadaver lying on its slab in the lonely and so rarely used morgue, unfortunately today occupied by the bodies of crewmen killed in the land battle with the Klingons. In a few days, they would be buried in space with full honors, once matters at hand were dispensed with and the crew could adjust to the loss of shipmates. It was never easy.

This, though—this thing on the slab . . .

He cleared his throat. "Where's the head?"

"I don't know," McCoy said straightaway. "We haven't been able to find it. I suspect—"

"That Kellen took it with him."

"Then you *do* think he did it?"

"We'll know in a minute." He reached for the comm on the wall, the least-used one on the ship. "Kirk to Security."

"Security, Hakker."

"Do a biosweep of the ship for Klingon biological readings. Hail sickbay with the results."

"Right away, sir."

"Kirk to bridge."

"Bridge, sir."

"Bring the ship to double yellow alert. And hail the Klingon fleet."

"One moment, sir."

The moment was a long, ugly one. Kirk stared at the remains, and McCoy stared at Kirk, both supremely aware of each other.

"What're you going to do?" McCoy finally asked when the pressure got to him.

"I don't know," Kirk said. "But I have to decide the next move, or Kellen will decide it for me."

"How could he get off without tripping some alarm somewhere?"

"I'd get off."

"Captain, bridge. The Klingons refuse to answer our hail, sir."

"Any movement out there?"

"None yet, sir."

"Notify me if there's the slightest change. Kirk out."

Stiff-lipped and severe, he circled the foot end of the corpse.

Its pale hands were chalky with lack of life, long fingernails nearly blue now, and there seemed to have been very little blood, or whatever fluids this creature possessed. Its clothing was nearly pristine. There hadn't been much of a struggle, but considering Kellen's strength and experience, that was no surprise.

"You didn't do an autopsy, did you?"

"I wouldn't do that without consent," McCoy said with a touch of pique. "I sterilized the body and had the scene of the crime searched and sealed off. If they want it back, or want back any of this jewelry it's wearing, we're prepared to comply. By the way, look at this." He plucked up the round bronze piece hanging from the chain, similar to Zennor's and all the others'. "This medallion isn't a medallion. Did you notice? It's a mirror."

He turned the oblong disk over to the undecorated side, and sure enough there was a crudely polished surface there that could be used as a mirror when held up by what now looked like a small handle.

"They each carry a little mirror?" Kirk looked, but didn't touch. "Why would they do that?"

"I certainly don't know. Would you carry a mirror if you looked like that? But, Jim, there's something else. If you'll come with me . . ."

He led the way into a smaller examining room, where a normally clean metal experimentation table was cluttered with a matte of shredded cloth and separated piles of what appeared to be dried leaves, nuts, hair, and some kind of chips.

"What's all this?"

"I found it on the body. Take a look."

At closer examination Kirk realized what he was looking at. "It's the doll. Each of them carries one. You dissected a doll? This is a new low for you, isn't it?"

"It's more efficient than reading the handwriting on a wall. Besides, it smelled funny and I wanted to see why. Now, take a closer look."

"Yes, I see it. It's got strings in its head and clothes like that. The doll looks like them."

"No, no. It looks like *him.*" McCoy pointed at the headless corpse. "With the head on, I mean. Look at it."

Irritated and impatient, Kirk pointed at the doll, whose guts lay spread all over the table, but whose little wormy head was still mostly intact. "I don't get your meaning."

"That corpse is of that species and the doll is also, but look closer. It's got the same features, the same coloring, the same hair—well, yarn—and it's missing the same finger that the corpse has been missing for most of his life."

"You mean, if one of them loses a finger he cuts it off his doll?"

"A finger, or whatever they've got. And one leg is a little shorter than the other, just like the corpse, and it's got the same scars marked on it as the real body has. And it's wearing tiny versions of the same jewelry that's on the body. Jim, this doll isn't just any doll. It's a poppet."

Kirk looked up and let silence ask his question before he barked it out.

Getting the message, McCoy held one hand over the piles of hair and leaves and bits. "All these things filled the doll. It's not just stuffing. You could throw this in a pot and make soup. Here you've got bits of hair, fingernails—not from the same person—buttons, something that might be a kind of bullet, pulverized nutshells, candle wax, caraway seeds, dried rosebuds, berry leaves, various worts, cloves, spider's web, and over here is the dried heart of some kind of small animal. And these things didn't all come from the same planet." The doctor looked up at him and meaningfully said, "I think this is a chronologue of this creature's life. They're relics of his experiences. If I didn't have the body, I could even roughly guess his age from just this mannequin. It's a facsimile of that very person over there."

"Yes," Kirk murmured, glancing back. "Zennor's has little antlers, a crescent brooch, bands on its wrists, and it wears his clothing. If it gets filled gradually, over a lifetime, older beings would have more items inside their doll than younger beings." He paced around the table again, thinking. "So Garamanus is older than Zennor."

Seeming satisfied that he was getting his analysis across, McCoy sighed and nodded. "Very likely so."

"What was that other word you used?"

"Poppet. I was getting to that. It's a medieval practice that came out of witchcraft and sorcery, which basically was the first practice of medicine. Poppets were one method of mixing mysticism with herbal medicine, invoking sympathetic magic."

"But that's Earth. It's trillions of miles away from where these people come from. What're you getting at?"

"That's what I'm getting at." McCoy leaned over the table. "I'm talking about Earth. That other one—they introduced him as Garamanus Drovid, right?"

"Yes. So?"

"I did a little skipping around in my medical-history files and there's a match. The word 'drovid' has roots in Old English, and that was where I found the references to poppets and midwives and sympathetic medicine."

"Bones, make your point before I stuff this mess back in the doll and stuff it down your throat."

"First ask me where the other two wise men are."

The doctor stood back a step, pointed at the piles of herbs and bits, then swept his hand toward the corpse on the table in the next chamber.

"Drovid," he said. "*The* drovids. The 'infernal of our past, the sinister, the banished'? Jim, don't you hear it? These people are druids!"

Chapter Thirteen

"THAT'S THE WILDEST leap of logic I've ever heard," Kirk accused. "As near as we can calculate, it's a leap across two galactic quadrants."

"I agree." With typical sleepless diligence, Spock scanned the information McCoy had handed over for analysis.

Druids?

Every time Kirk heard the word in his head, he squinted as if looking through a fog. How many times in his career had he been faced with the inconceivable and asked his crew to believe? Now he couldn't seem to give himself that much cooperation.

He rubbed his sweaty palms and waited for Spock to do the dirty work.

Spock's hands and eyes moved as he keyed information into the monitor mounted over his head. The screens rolled with gory pictures of ancient myths that bore startling resemblances to Zennor's crew.

"With uncharacteristic efficiency," the Vulcan barbed, "the good doctor has stumbled upon some interesting data."

"I do not 'stumble,' sir," McCoy aggrandized. "I am a superior scholar in my field. I know my poppets."

Abandoning what may have been an effort to ease pressure on the captain, Spock became suddenly clinical and looked at Kirk with disclosed sympathy. "Lieutenant Uhura is still working on some of the nomenclature and linguistics using Dr. McCoy's theory, focusing on the crossover between the old woodland religions of western Europe and the encroachment of Christianity. The simple folk of those times easily believed in both."

"Old religions die hard," Kirk said. "Zennor's people are living proof. They're hanging on to theirs and looking for scientific data to back it up."

"Real scientists do not form a theory first and look for data second, Captain," Spock said. "However, I would be deluding myself to deny the surprising similarities between Zennor's race and the pantheon of Celtic folklore."

"Specifically?"

Spock hesitated, as if walking on thin ice, but offered his typical straightforwardness. "Specifically, the Horned God, ruling deity of winter and the hunt. It was a beastly vehicle, usually portrayed in stag form, with horns."

"And Zennor . . . sure has horns," Kirk said. "But some of those beings have wings. Doesn't make them angels."

"No, of course not," the doctor agreed, "but I think this is the key to a peck of trouble. You've been going about this all wrong, Mr. Spock, looking at arrangements of stars and searching for archaeological evidence. These beings look a lot like common archetypes in humanoid culture, but not just any archetypes. Specifically archetypes of evil. Antlers, horns, snakes, skulls—they'll find so much that looks like them that they'll say, 'See? We're from here.' People who are this much into their myths will be *very* convinced by ours. Jim, you'd better disprove this, because if I were them, all this Celtic stuff would bother me."

"Celtic," Spock said unsparingly.

McCoy looked at him. "Pardon me?"

"You said 'Seltic,' Doctor. The work is 'Keltic.' The 'C' had a hard sound in the ancient Gaelic language. It is often mispronounced by the ignorant."

"Now wait a minute, Mahatma. Didn't there used to be a baseball team called the Boston 'Seltics'?"

"Basketball," Kirk corrected, and was instantly mad at himself for bothering.

Keenly Spock raised one punctuating brow. "An ideal case in point."

McCoy's squarish features deployed a barrage, but he didn't say anything.

Tilting a scowl at an innocent wall, Kirk squeezed back a headache and reached for the nearest comm. "Kirk to engineering."

"Engineering, Hadley, sir."

"Request Mr. Scott join me in the sickbay right away."

"Yes, sir, I'll find him."

Impatient, Kirk paced a few steps away, as if to distance his officers from the stain of his responsibility and the tilt of this conversation. Myths . . . gods of this and that . . . poppets and witchcraft . . . he didn't like any of it as a basis for any decision.

"Zennor's people seem very fierce, but tolerant of each other, as races go. They've had to live together and work toward this common cause, and as such they've had to believe in it, proven or not. It forced them to respect each other's various cultural habits. They're actually better at tolerance than the Federation, except for this one clubfoot. This group-space idea. Zennor is smart enough to realize the holes in all that."

"Who did they have this war with?" McCoy asked. "Do we have the foggiest idea?"

"It was five thousand years ago," Kirk mourned. "Maybe more than that."

"Could it have been one of the early Klingon cultures, and maybe that's why it seems to fulfill a legend of Chaos?"

"Havoc," Spock adjusted. "I doubt that. The Klingons had no spacefaring capabilities in their sectors that long ago. I suspect it was some advanced race, now long gone."

"Or still there, in some other part of the galaxy," Kirk pointed out. "Don't make their mistake and assume this is the right place. Zennor said their archeologists pretty much proved they didn't evolve on their planets. They were all transplants. After all this time, there's no way even to know whether they were persecuted, or if they lost a legitimate war."

"Legends become distorted over five thousand years," Spock said. "The people writing them tend to skew them in their favor. Havoc, heresy . . . all these are inventions of those who wish to maintain control through threat of supernatural punishment. In fact, the word 'heresy' is from the Greek. It means 'free choice.'"

"Well, they're exercising free choice right now, that's for sure."

Kirk scuffed his boot heel on the deck and anchored himself to the sound, the hard sensation of his ship around him. The hollow ache of having lost crewmen, especially young Brown, ate at him. And what was he going to do with that headless body in there?

"Spock, what about their ship? What exactly are we up against?"

"I have done extensive sweeps, but there is much sensor masking. The ship remains essentially an unknown. I do believe they have the raw power to push back the *Enterprise,* but could they push back all of the Klingon squadron and us as well? I have no conclusions."

"Neither do I," Kirk told him, "and I can't put my finger on it, but there's something about his ship that Zennor's not telling."

"Intuition, Captain?"

"If necessary."

The Vulcan frowned into his monitor screens. "I am also questioning Garamanus's astronomical data regarding the Klingon solar system as seen from the other side of the galaxy, given the distortive nature of the galactic core. It can not even be seen through. To send out a probe of any effect would take hundreds of—"

He moved one arm to tap an order to his computers, and apparently moved too much. He suddenly stopped speaking, choked silent by a spasm somewhere in his injured body. Kirk covered the space to the bedside in one step, but somehow McCoy got there first and hurriedly adjusted the antigravs to take some pressure off. So much for pain being a thing of the mind.

"Are you all right?" Kirk asked.

"Well enough, Captain." The voice was a scratch now, still twisted with effort, and more seconds passed before the pinch left Spock's narrow eyes and his hands began to relax again on the fingerpads.

As they waited, the outer door parted and Chief Engineer Scott thumped in, looking untidy and frustrated with the day's tensions. His emblematic red shirt was rumpled and bore the burns of a splatter of sparks. He clearly didn't want to be here.

"You wanted me, sir?" He reached up to check the mountings on the monitor. "All right with this, Mr. Spock?"

Kirk squared off behind him. "Scotty, what do you know about Celtic mythology?"

Scott twisted around, one hand still poised overhead. "Celtic what, sir?"

"Druidic myths of supernatural beings," Spock filled in, burying his effort. "The primary deity of hunting and survival. The Horned God."

"Me?" The engineer looked from each to the other. "Not much. Where'd you ever come up with all that, sir?"

"We just wondered if all this meant anything to you," Kirk told him, keeping his tone even, not wanting to hedge his bet.

"Because I'm Scottish?"

"Any port in a storm."

"Oh . . ." Scott's expression turned pained. "Sir . . . you're barking up the wrong kilt. That Celtic druid stuff, that's a lot of hooey!"

"That hooey may be the key to our situation. You have druid ruins in Scotland, don't you?"

"Have we. We hang our laundry from 'em. That'n postcards is about all they're good for."

Kirk simmered. "You don't know anything at all about that folklore."

Glancing with a pathetic face, Scott's round eyes bobbed in a shrug and he looked like a street urchin being asked where the neighborhood hiding place was. "Well . . . give or take *Tam O'Shanter,* not a blessed thing."

"What's that?"

"Everybody's heard the story of Tam O'Shanter's ride."

"Give me the high points."

"Oh . . . well, it's a Robert Burns poem about a fellow who takes a look inside a haunted kirk—oh, sorry, sir—a haunted church." Uneasy at relating folklore instead of phase inversion ratios, Scott struggled to scrape the dust out of his memory. He made a disapproving sound in his throat and forced himself to speak. "Inside are demons and unconsecrated dead dancing about, and perched in the window is the devil, shaped like a beast, wheezing his pipes for all he's worth. I saw a reenactment of it once, right there near the actual kirk in Alloway—"

"Wait a minute!" McCoy cut in. "The devil plays bagpipes?"

The engineer screwed a glare at him. "Welcome to heaven, here's your harp, welcome to hell, here're your bagpipes."

"Oh, fine."

"Can I go now, sir?"

"No," Kirk snapped. "What other details are there?"

Scott shifted his feet. "I don't rightly recall, sir. . . . I'm sure it's in Mr. Spock's computer someplace. This Tam has to get away from the demons, and there's something about how demons can't cross running water, so he makes for the bridge."

"Logical," Spock fed in.

McCoy shook his head. "Logical!"

"Scotty," Kirk pressed, "*why* can't demons cross running water?"

"I wouldn't have a clue, sir."

"Is there a point to it happening in the ruins of a church?"

Desperate, Scott shrugged. "Why does *Hamlet* happen in a castle, sir?"

McCoy leaned forward. "Why's the devil in the shape of a beast?"

"Doctor," the engineer groaned, "you're not talking to a man who thinks there's a monster in the loch."

Unsatisfied, Kirk let his brow crimp. "Very well, Scotty, dismissed."

"Aye, sir!" Flushed with relief, Scott vectored for the door, then abruptly looked back. "It's all got to do with that lot we beamed over, doesn't it? If ever a bunch needed a ruined kirk about 'em, those are the ones."

Before anyone could stop him, he dodged for freedom and the sickbay door hissed shut on empty air.

"Well, there's one generalization gone up in smoke," McCoy commented.

Kirk paced, embarrassed. "I shouldn't have disturbed him."

"Gentlemen," Spock said with an anchoring tone, "this is interesting information, but it is entirely anecdotal. Still only folklore."

"But dangerous information, Mr. Spock," the doctor insisted. "Sometimes myth can be much more explosive than fact."

Kirk turned to Spock and waved his hand. "McCoy's right. You and I need hard evidence, but Zennor's crew may well be satisfied with anecdotal evidence. We can't take that chance. All this will become a moot point if we can get to this Klingon solar system and find no proof that it's their home system. That's my intention. We are not having a war. We're not having these people warring against the Klingons, the Klingons against them, and the Federation scrambling in the middle. I'm not having it. I want both of you to—"

"Red alert. This is the bridge. All hands, red alert."

Suddenly angry that his aggravation was being interrupted, he assaulted the comm. "Kirk here."

Sulu's voice came through, sounding tight. "The Klingon squadron, sir, they're moving into attack position and swinging under us toward the other ship."

"On my way. Contact Security and have them bring Captain Zennor to the bridge. Kirk out. McCoy, Spock, you two keep on this line of research. And hurry it up. If this is legitimate, I want to know it. If it's not, I want something concrete that I can put in front of Zennor and Garamanus to show them that it's not."

"Yes, sir."

"We'll do our best, Jim."

"Status, Mr. Sulu?"

"The Klingon squadron swung around us to attack the visitor's ship, sir. They've opened fire several times, but seem to be only making glancing blows. They may be looking for weak points. Impulse power's on-line and helm is answering."

"Mr. Donnier?"

"Phaser batteries on standby, sir. Photon torpedoes powering up."

Hardly had the tube cleared when it opened again and Zennor came out into the shadowed area beside the glossy red doors. Kirk glanced at him.

As the Klingon squadron separated into a new attack formation on the forward screen.

Kirk dropped to the recessed deck and gripped his command chair, but didn't sit. He couldn't quite make himself do that, not with Zennor haunting the upper deck's turbolift vestibule, looking quite zombieish with the soft bridge lights teasing his bony features, sulfurous eyes, and twisted horns and glinting off all that carved jewelry.

"Sensors full capacity. Come full about starboard, impulse one-quarter. Intercept course. Gentlemen, I thought I ordered change of watch. What are you all still doing here?"

Donnier swung around as if he'd committed a crime, but his mouth hung open without making a sound.

Sulu turned too, but didn't take his hands from the helm. "The order just came up, sir. We were waiting for our relief to show up. I think the lower decks have all changed over."

Kirk glanced over his shoulder. "Vergo Zennor, I assume you'll want to return to your ship to confront this action."

Zennor's horns caught the bridge lights and played with them. "My ship is strong, Vergokirk."

"As you prefer," Kirk said, a little irritated. He'd want to be here, and suddenly that seemed like a sign of weakness. He trusted his crew, but this was his responsibility, not theirs.

Strange, though, to be so completely unconcerned . . . as if a bunch of delinquent children were hitting his ship with sticks. Zennor was either very confident in his ship's technology or he was putting on a hell of a show.

Grudgingly Kirk accepted the first divisions between himself and Zennor that weren't physical.

The turbolift door gushed open and an engineer came out, but didn't go to the port side. Instead, the short and thickly built fellow stepped down to the helm and looked at Sulu, then at Kirk.

"Lieutenant Byers, sir, relieving the helm."

"Not now."

"Sir?"

"Not in the middle of action. Stand by."

"Aye, sir." Byers blinked at him self-consciously, then at the screen. He was new to the bridge and Kirk guessed that a department head somewhere below was pushing him. Happened sometimes. Sooner or later the lowliest technician got a hitch at the wheel, just to see what it felt like, not to mention in case of some catastrophe that blistered the whole crew and left one confused yeoman to steer. That happened sometimes too. Usually those were historical accounts, but one could never tell.

Byers rubbed his wide hands on his thighs and shifted from foot to foot, not knowing whether to vacate the bridge and wait to be called, or take a position on the upper deck and wait there, doing nothing.

"Up *there.*" Kirk pointed sharply to the engineering systems station. He couldn't keep the irritation out of his voice, nor did he want to take the time to explain that the lift tube should be kept as clear as possible during action, especially not to someone who should know it.

Maybe I expect too much of them, he thought vaguely as the ship swung full about and space turned on a pendulum before them. In a moment the pinecone form of Zennor's ship swung into full view, harassed by the Klingon cruisers.

In the privacy of his mind Kirk damned Zennor's calm and set himself to match it.

Too competitive?

Maybe.

Too bad.

He glared at the screen, at the Klingon ships, four of them, sweeping up and around the horn-shaped vessel. He could almost hear the *whoosh.* They laid fire down across the visitor's hull, then spun wildly toward the *Enterprise.*

"They're trying to keep us from increasing speed," Sulu muttered aloud as he countered the moves of the Klingon ships.

"Doing it, too," Chekov put out of the corner of his mouth as he looked down from Spock's station.

Kirk ignored them. There had to be weakness. There had to be one moment when those ships weren't all coordinated, when at least two of them weren't sure what the other two were doing. He was waiting for that moment. "Mr. Donnier, prepare to open fire."

"Ready, Captain."

"Captain Zennor, are you agreeable to evasive action? High speed to your target solar system?"

He turned enough to look.

In the lift vestibule, Zennor appeared as still as a gargoyle and moved not at all to answer. "Yes."

Had his mouth even moved?

Telepathy?

"Would you like to inform your crew?"

"They know it."

He didn't offer how that could be possible.

Kirk didn't ask, sensing that the answer would be vague and his crew would become uneasy.

"Mr. Donnier," he said instead, "reduce phasers to two-thirds. Mr. Sulu, one-half sublight."

Donnier looked over his shoulder. "Two-thirds, sir?"

"We'll have a reserve if we need it. And there's no point draining everything we have to destroy those ships when all we have to do is get away from them. Prepare to dump a wash of heavy radiation behind us once we get clear. While they choke their way through it, we'll make distance. All right, gentlemen, let's drive them away from the other ship and make our getaway. I've always considered ass'n elbows a perfectly legitimate battle tactic."

"Aye, sir," Sulu said, and grinned.

Donnier nodded and smiled too. "Yes, sir."

The attitude on the bridge went up two notches.

The ship groaned with the effort of snug turns, a long-legged foxhound trying to turn like a basset. She was powerful, but she was no road-hugger. The Klingon ships worked a baffling pattern that kept one always in the starship's path while the others cut across her lateral shields and fired on her. Every few seconds a hit racked across her hull and sent tremors through it. Every time he said "fire" Donnier tried to coordinate phaser controls with the flash-by of whatever ship was in range.

Engulfed in a shameless relief that the so-called truce was over, broken by the Klingons' first shot—if there were any doubts—Kirk flexed his hands as if they'd just been unmanacled. The old kids' excuse from any playground was at perfectly good work here: He started it.

Zennor's ship took relentless strafing in the most leisurely fashion Kirk had ever witnessed, and it annoyed the hell out of him. He wanted movement, panic, retaliation from the other ship. That was how Klingons needed to be treated. But Zennor's vessel did virtually nothing but turn its aft end to the incoming Klingon fire and let the destructive energy wash across its folded hull plates.

"Make tighter turns and continue evasive," he said, authorizing a risk Sulu couldn't take on his own. "Come about."

"Coming about, sir."

On the screen, the Klingon ships veered out from each other in a practiced formation, then began angling erratically, so their patterns couldn't be plotted. Then two of them broke pattern and swept toward the *Enterprise* as it came in firing and knocked the other two off course.

The two steady cruisers kept their heads, executed a perfect maneuver, and laid into the starship's upper hull, strafing the bridge.

Kellen knew what he was doing. Decades of experience could serve in a pinch.

He had drawn a breath to give a maneuvering order to Sulu when a huge wing suddenly appeared in the forward screen, blanketing their view of everything else—Kellen's flagship!

Where had he come from? Some daring twist Kirk had failed to anticipate, he realized as his gut twisted as if to show him what he'd missed. Disruptor fire danced across the starship's brow, splintering the shields and piercing the hull above the bridge before double shields could be put up there.

The forward half of the ceiling blew downward in shards and sparks, engulfing Sulu in a flush of electricity. Donnier plunged sideways and was only scorched, but Sulu was shaken hideously, then slammed to the deck and fell limp.

Kirk shielded his face. "Sickbay! Get him off the bridge!" The second order really canceled out the first, indicating that he didn't want to wait, or have an injured crewman to trip over in the middle of ship's action. The upper-deck technicians and engineers understood, and three of them shuffled Sulu toward the turbolift.

"Mr. Byers! Here's your chance. Take the helm."

Byers had almost gone into the turbolift, but now turned back to the center of the bridge and picked his way to the helm. He brushed the smoking shards off the seat and gingerly sat there on part of his backside. He stared at the helm for a moment, his hands hovering over the instrumentation without making contact.

"Put your hands on the controls, Mr. Byers," Kirk said firmly, and knew his own work was cut out for him, taking an inexperienced helmsman into battle. "Come about starboard . . . that's it. . . . Mr. Donnier, fire. Good . . . all we have to do is clear the way for Zennor's ship."

Did the other ship have warp drive? It just now occurred to him that the subject hadn't come up. Fine time to think of it, James.

They had to have warp drive, or some force of science that allowed them to go to hyperlight speeds. Examining a quadrant at sublight would take thousands of years.

They had it, they had it. Stay the course.

Enemy fire crackled like pulsebeats over the ship's deflectors, but she stood up to them. Returning fire was a different trick and took more than just a stuck-out jaw.

Byers hunched forward and concentrated on keeping hold of the bull elephant in his hands, tapping maneuvers through to her impulse engines in a manner that was making the power center heave and howl.

"Fire as your weapons bear, Mr. Donnier. Target the ship abaft starboard and fire. Mr. Byers, don't let them work our stern like that again."

Byers pressed his hands to the controls and attempted a dry swallow before speaking. "Sir . . . I . . . I can't do this very well . . . respectfully submit you call up somebody with more experience. Shouldn't Mr. Chekov—"

"Mr. Chekov's needed at the science station." Kirk stole a moment from the battle and said, "We pilot the ship by changing the field geometry of the warp-coil timing. How well each helmsman can do that is a personal thing. It's the closest thing to subjective activity on the ship. Experience is a factor, but it's not all there is. Sulu does it his way. You do it yours. We'll deal with it."

Byers stared at him a moment, then nodded and faced the helm again. Permission to screw up, if necessary.

That done, Kirk shifted his concentration to the movements of the ships outside, arranging them in 3D in his head and anticipating every movement he could see as the sensors on the upper monitors read the courses of each ship.

On the main viewer, Zennor's ship had come full about and was facing Klingon space. Just a few more seconds. Just a chance to get past Kellen—

"Down more, starboard . . . mark two . . . Don't use the sensors, Mr. Byers—follow them with your eyes and feel your way through. Three degrees port . . . present our profile to them. . . . Mr. Donnier, fire . . . good . . . Byers, if you see a window don't wait for my order. There—get through it! Quickly, angle ten degrees port. Midships . . . fire."

For an instant there was silence, and then the whine of the phaser controls cutting across the power-packed Klingon ships. Two of the ships bloomed in hot strikes. Another swung past, launched a shot, then veered off as if afraid it too would be hit at proximity.

"Two good hits, sir!" Donnier said, surprised that he'd done so well.

"Good, Mr. Donnier," Kirk awarded. "Now if we can push aside the others, we'll get past them."

"Sir," Chekov called over the pounding of unforgiving disruptors, "their upper hull plates are only double-shielded."

"Noted. Mr. Donnier, there's your target. Mr. Byers, get us in over their heads. Ten degrees port . . . good . . . midships."

"Midships," Byers murmured, his lips dry.

"Hold that . . . fire . . . five degrees starboard."

"Five starboard, aye . . ."

"A little more starboard."

"Little more, aye . . ."

"Midships."

"Midships . . ."

"Fire."

With one hand on Donnier's chair and the other on Byers', Kirk drove his ship as though rushing whitewater in his favorite canoe. He moved his shoulders with the rhythm of the ship, flexing his knees as the deck rose and dropped, tipped and rolled around them.

"Sir, they're dogfighting us," Byers choked. "I can't get past them."

"You don't have to. Just distract them until Zennor's ship gets past."

Phaser blast after phaser blast vomited from the ship's ports and crashed across space to torment the Klingons, who returned fire shot for shot without remittance.

"Static pulses, sir!" one of the engineers gasped from upper port side. "Shield power's fibrillating!"

"Ignore it. It'll hold."

As they were hit again the engineer's response was swallowed in howling alarms and a puff of chemical smoke. Metal splinters rained on them and for a few seconds all they could see of each other were hunched, headless shoulders.

On the main screen, Zennor's dark ship loomed enormous, so big that Kirk had to shudder down a desire to duck.

"Sir, I . . ." Byers stopped, unwilling to say the obvious. He couldn't get past the swarming cruisers, not and protect Zennor's ship at the same time. The starship was simply too big and too sluggish at low sublight speeds to handle a well-manipulated squadron of lighter, quicker, tight-turning buzzards.

"Stay with it, Mr. Byers."

From the upper deck, Zennor's bass voice hummed. "Vergokirk."

Kirk turned.

Zennor looked down at him, and came forward a step. "Allow me to clear the way for you."

An instant before he would've told Zennor to hold position, that the *Enterprise* could take these ships with the right maneuvers and a certain amount of sacrifice, Kirk clamped his lips. Here was a chance to see what that uninvited vessel could do, and he suddenly didn't want to give that up.

He gestured to the communications station. "Would you like to contact your ship?" he offered again.

"I have," Zennor said.

"Sir!" Chekov pointed at the forward screen.

Kirk cranked around.

The giant ship of purple shadows and tightly laid shingles was turning color—not overtly, but as if some mystical stagehand were backstage, changing the spots and footlights. The purple colors bled to hotter electric blue, then bundled together and ran down the pinecone-shaped hull to blast out the twisted point and blow into space.

Two Klingons vessels were hit directly and knocked violently off course, and the others were kicked into a spin, left struggling to regain their gravitational balance.

"Sir! We're clear!" Chekov called suddenly, and then coughed on a puff of chemical smoke. "Sir!"

"Captain Zennor, I hope your ship knows to follow us," Kirk called.

"They know."

That voice. Like cellos and concert basses moaning in another room.

Damn it, *how* could they know?

He refused to ask.

"Very well. Chekov, dump that heavy radiation."

Chekov plunged four feet down the starboard side and hammered the controls. "Dumped, sir!"

"Mr. Byers, warp factor five, right now."

Chapter Fourteen

"THE KLINGON SQUAD is falling behind, Captain," Chekov clipped, unable to keep the victory out of his voice. "The radiation is choking their thruster ports. Captain Zennor's ship is matching our speed."

"Very good. Go to warp six, Mr. Byers."

"Warp six, sir," Byers answered.

"Captain," Lieutenant Nordstrom spoke up, her hand on her earpiece receiver, "General Kellen is hailing us."

"Is he. Put him on."

"Go ahead, sir."

"General, this is Captain Kirk. You're seriously over-stepping."

"Are you out of your inadequate mind?"

"I beg your pardon?"

"You are streaking into Klingon space with those fiends. Why?"

"Because there's a chance of resolving the conflict. I request you secure clearance for us from your High Command."

"I refuse. You are giving asylum to a threatening

species. I have summoned the Assault Fleet. You turn around and leave."

"I'm here at your request," Kirk pestered steadily. "You're the one who came aboard my ship, then murdered a visiting dignitary from another government. That will not go unanswered, I guarantee. If I turn around and leave without resolution to the problem, you're going to look pretty foolish, not only in front of my government, but in front of yours. Who in the Klingon Fleet will take your word for anything anymore?"

"They have taken my word, and they are coming. I asked for help from you and this is what I've been given. We will take care of the Havoc ship ourselves. If you interfere, then there is war between us."

"I hope to have this resolved before you and your fleet can reach us. In any case, I'm lodging a formal protest with the Klingon High Command, stating that we have been invited here and attacked while authorization was never officially revoked."

"Lodge what you want. I would expect no better from such as you. I did not attain my position by waiting for my bidding to be done by others."

"Sir, he cut us off," Nordstrom said before Kirk could answer, as if he had an answer.

They had left behind the immediate problem, but not the lingering question. With a sigh, Kirk scratched the back of his head and wished he had time for a backrub. Or somebody around whom he wanted to give it.

He glanced back and caught in his periphery the sorcerous form of Zennor in the lift entrance.

No point avoiding the inevitable.

Gripping the bridge rail for sustenance, he pulled himself to the upper deck.

"Vergo," he began, "we have a situation in sickbay that demands your attention."

* * *

"Let me apologize ahead of time for what I must show you."

Jim Kirk led the way into sickbay. Zennor followed, having said very little on the way down, as if he anticipated something dire and unmendable. Kirk understood that. A captain's sixth sense. He could *feel* when something was crooked.

He avoided the area where Spock was recuperating and instead gestured in the other direction, toward the morgue.

"If you'll come with me . . ."

McCoy appeared at the door of his office, his face suddenly blanched as he saw Zennor. He didn't say anything, but stepped out as if to follow them.

Before they reached the specially sealed doorway of the morgue, the hiss of the outer door panel made them turn.

Kirk had been anticipating speaking to Zennor alone about the murder, but that wasn't going to happen now.

Garamanus's tall form filled the doorway, chalky and bloodless, his skullish face and animal eyes immediately untrusting.

How could he know?

"Gentlemen," Kirk said, and gestured again.

McCoy silently stepped forward and keyed in the security code. The morgue door slid open on a breath of suction.

Without ceremony he led them to the body of their crewmate—the headless body.

Zennor came a few steps into the room, then stopped. Garamanus never made it past the doorway.

"We believe General Kellen did this before he arranged to have himself beamed off our ship," Kirk said. "I want you to know that none of my crew would ever be involved in such an atrocity and that I stand in utter condemnation of this act. I intend to log an official request for extradition of Kellen for trial at Starfleet

Command, although . . . the Klingons don't have a stellar history of complying with Federation law."

Sounded too prepared, though he hadn't prepared it. Some things had to be said, logged for official reasons, no matter how stilted they sounded.

Neither of the horned beings said anything. No response at all. They simply stared and stared. They didn't blink.

McCoy stood aside, also not blinking, but he was staring at the two of them instead of the body.

Kirk allowed them a couple of silent minutes—long, long minutes—to absorb what they saw. He had no way to tell how they felt about the dead person, whether their astonishment was couched in loyalty of one crew member to another, or actually in the devotion of friendship. For all the clues he read in their faces, it could've been a female and married to one of them. He just couldn't tell.

Finally he stepped between them and the body. "Can I help explain this to your crew, perhaps?"

"We could never explain this," Zennor said tightly.

Slowly Garamanus shook his large horned mantle. His voice was like gravel turning in a drum. "We could never bring Manann back this way."

Zennor quickly said to Kirk, "You will have to dispose of him before any of our crew sees this."

"As you wish," Kirk assured. "We'll do everything we possibly can to ease the situation. How would you like us to dispose of the body?"

Zennor looked at Garamanus for a moment, then turned to Kirk and for the first time seemed dubious about which course of action to take. "What . . . do you do with your dead?"

In his sudden desire to offer at least one straight answer, Kirk said, "Most of our cultures bury the body. Some burn them. On the ship, if possible, we launch the remains into a sun."

"Burn . . ." Garamanus visibly shuddered.

Zennor's eyes paled from red to sulfur. "In our culture, we burn only the living."

Kirk stiffened. "The living?"

"Criminals," the Dana said. "Burning is punishment. The dead must be honored."

Zennor added, "Some of our groups require keeping the skulls of the dead with us for four generations before they can be smashed."

Kirk didn't ask. They'd probably just explain and he didn't want to hear that one.

Garamanus turned from the body and didn't look at it any more. "Where is the soul?"

Perplexed, Kirk glanced at Zennor, then back to Garamanus. "I'm sorry?"

"Manann's soul," the Dana said. "We must have it."

"I don't understand."

Suddenly McCoy's face went as white as Garamanus's robe. "I think I do . . . gentlemen . . ."

He motioned toward the experimentation room and led them to the archway.

Garamanus and Zennor had to dip their horns to go inside, and once there they stopped in their tracks and stared at the table.

Stared and stared, as if slugged. Far worse was this stare than that with which they had looked at the remains.

There on the cold table lay the piles of herbs, nuts, clippings, hair, and assorted other relics, and the cut-open remnant of the poppet itself, its limp arms and legs no longer supported by stuffing, its open chest showing loose threads, its tiny head and those yarn tentacles canted to one side.

Garamanus turned away from what he saw, and his eyes were terrible on Kirk. "What *are* you people?"

Silence fell like an ax blade.

Feeling suddenly unwashed, Kirk felt patent shame at not having trodden his course more delicately. They had transgressed more sensitive ground than mere territory, and he had let it happen.

"We meant no insult," he submitted. "We didn't

realize how important this is to you. To us, it's just a stuffed doll."

"Vergokirk," Garamanus chafed, "do you devour your young?"

Kirk weighed the question, but saw no other way to answer it. "No, of course we don't."

"Neither do we. But if we did, this is what it would be like."

"You're joking!" McCoy reacted, then suddenly realized he might be committing another error, glanced at Kirk, and clamped his mouth shut.

"The mannequins are representatives of each of us," Zennor told them slowly. "Wherever we go, they tell our life stories. When we go into battle, we leave them behind, or send them in a safe pod. It is honored as if it is the person. This . . . it is desecration."

"Oh, no," McCoy uttered, so softly that only Kirk heard. His face blanched, his eyes like a cat's in a flashlight. "I'm truly sorry," he said genuinely. "I didn't realize!"

With a crisp warning Kirk began, "Bones—"

"No, no, it was my blunder. Please don't blame Captain Kirk for this, or any of our crew. I take full responsibility. I had no idea this would be any kind of affront. Is there some way I can apologize to your crew? If there's anything I can do, I'll gladly do it."

"McCoy, stand down," Kirk snapped.

Irritated and jaundiced with deep mortal panic, McCoy started to speak again, but caught the captain's glare and managed to stop himself before the error compounded.

Kirk smoldered with the level of tension he'd been driven to, but an instant later demanded better of himself. He understood what McCoy was going through. As a starship captain, his successes had always been magnified, but so were his blunders. He'd learned the hard way that a well-maneuvered pause could ease a bad situation and ordered with his eyes and posture that

McCoy give himself that pause before anything else happened.

What else could happen? He had trouble imagining the shuddering rage in Garamanus's face compounded any more than it already was. Not only was the victim's head gone, but McCoy had cut apart the poppet.

Measuring each word with what could only be caution, Zennor looked at Garamanus and declared, "Accidents were inevitable."

Feeling his skin contract, Kirk bit back the weighty declaration that this was no accident, but damned cold-blooded murder. He knew instantly how lucky he was, and Zennor also was, that Garamanus chose not to point that out himself.

Kirk had no way to establish, even for his own comfort, how dangerous that silence was. And when he couldn't think like those around him, he had no anchorage. That bothered him. Bothered him big.

In a last bid for compassion, for both crews, for both civilizations, he turned to Zennor.

"Let me help," he pleaded.

A shadow cast itself upon him and he stepped back. Garamanus was beside him, above him.

The Dana's voice was like the slamming of a gavel. "We will wait to see what the stars say."

"Absolutely nothing? You're sure?"

"We're sure, sir."

"Give me the rundown again."

Chief Barnes, head of the astrogeology, gave him a pained look and pointed again at the row of bridge monitors on the science side. "There's not much here, sir."

Beside the chief, stellar cartographer Amanda Alto and her brother, solar chemist Josh Alto, both looked too young to be able to do the kind of jobs they were doing.

"As far as we can tell, sir," Josh said, "this sun went through its first red-giant stage three to four thousand years ago and incinerated all its inner planets, which is where life generally occurs. Actually, we don't even have any way to know if there even were inner planets—"

"Except for the number and orbits of the outer planets, which may have changed considerably during the expansion stage of the star," Amanda filled in. "There *had* to be something there."

"But there's no way to prove it," her brother added, not to be outdone.

Kirk turned. "Any of the rest of you?"

There were seventeen science specialists and staff technicians on the bridge, crowding both the upper and lower decks. As he gazed at them, all the young faces, peppered with a few older ones, all their minds crammed with numbers and probability and measurements, extrapolations of known data and theories of unknown data, the culmination of thousands of years of learning and in fact the very reason the starship could be out here doing what it did, he was struck with the sad realization that all these people were needed just to replace Mr. Spock.

And he still needed Spock anyway.

From beside the command chair, Astrobiologist Cantone broke the silence. "The remote cluster quark resonance scanners, spectrometers, and thermal imagers just aren't picking up anything that indicates there was ever life in the solar system, sir."

"That doesn't mean there wasn't," Specialist Angela Godinez from the astral life sciences department pointed out. "It only means that any evidence of life was destroyed when the sun went red giant."

"Chemical compositions of asteroids that might once have been planetary matter don't give us any clues either, sir," confirmed Astrogeologist Ross.

Others just nodded or shook their heads in canny agreement. They all knew what he needed, and none could provide it.

"If there ever was life here, sir," said Chief Barnes, "there's no possible way to know it anymore."

Destitute. Billions of miles into space, and there was

nothing to show for it. An unthinkable risk, flying haphazard into Klingon space, using the thinnest of permissions to do so, likely as not a revoked permission, and like an errant child Kirk had a chilling sensation that the worst was yet to come.

He looked at the forward screen, showing Zennor's ship cruising at warp speed two points off the port bow.

"They came to search for the past," he uttered, "and there's none to find." He parted the sea of blue tunics and pressed his thigh against the bridge rail.

"We'll keep looking, sir," Chief Barnes said with unshielded, and rather pathetic, sympathy for him. "But we won't find anything."

"I understand that," Kirk told him grittily, aggravated that a stellar incident four thousand years ago should have so biting an effect on the eighty-odd years allotted to him in which he might get something done.

He turned toward the turbolift. "Captain?"

Against the shiny red lift doors, Zennor was a living gargoyle, with one errant shadow creasing his horns. Beside him, Garamanus was like something out of a reversed negative in an old photograph, the image of Zennor, with little of the color. Pale skin, white robes, and for the first time Kirk noted that his pallor might very well be from a life indoors, poring over historical information, piecing together details, with little intimacy to the outdoors and the brightness that bestows russet cheeks. Even on the other side of the galaxy, things couldn't be all that different.

"I'm sorry," he said to them both. "You've seen the data. There's nothing left here to use as proof for any of our theories."

He watched their faces and realized he was beginning to glean expression from those bony, deerlike features and the chromatic eyes. He thought of what McCoy had said to him about seeing aliens as like himself instead of unlike, and saw it now. Just a matter of getting used to them, and then space began to grow smaller between peoples.

Was Zennor pleased? Was that the expression Kirk was reading? If so, the other captain was trying not to show it in front of Garamanus.

Made sense.

"If there is no proof," the deep voice began, "then we must change our plans."

"There is no proof against us," Garamanus spoke up, not facing him. "The Danai will not change yet."

But Zennor did turn. "This evidence is insufficient. I will not launch invasion based upon poor data. We must have absolute proof."

"No proof is nothing," the Dana said, gritting his—whatever those were. "This is our space. All things lead to this area."

Zennor seemed to grow taller. "You wanted it to."

The two massive beings squared off as the Starfleet audience watched from below, and it was as if the two were alone, as if Kirk and all the others had skidded away on the thin ice beneath them.

"I always suspected you of being an unbeliever," Garamanus charged. "Why, if you did not believe, did you sign for this mission? The most important mission of all our civilization's history?"

"Because I do believe we were cast out. But I do not want our civilization impaled upon that belief. There is no greater evil than that which was done to us. I will not have us become what we hate."

Sensing that he was losing control of the bridge, if not the situation, Kirk yanked it back by stepping toward them and saying, "No one says you can't come here. If your civilization wants to move, there are ways to do that. There are habitable planets in Federation space. You're welcome to them. We'll help you. You can live in peace, settle, raise your—"

Flocks, herds, spawn?

"Young."

They were both looking at him now, and if he could indeed read their expressions, then the expressions were very different.

"You two can debate about this later," he plowed on, "but we've got to get out of Klingon space. I know you think well of your ship, but you don't know what the Klingon fleet really is. We'll give you sanctuary, but we must leave now."

"I've seen your ships," Garamanus rumbled. "You have no idea what you stand against. You are less than an annoyance to us."

Angry, Kirk raised his voice. "I don't stand against you. Not *yet.*"

Zennor stepped between them, raised his long clawed hand to Kirk, but turned to face Garamanus again. "Are these the conquerors? The drooling, snarling visions of evil you have held up to us for generations? Every essence of meanness and torture, delighting in agony? Why do you not admit you are wrong? The stars are not here, the proof is not here . . . the crew will be against you when I show them this. We have come to find evil and found the opposite. Can we fail to grow?"

He paused, waited to see if Garamanus would speak, and when the Dana did nothing but stare, Zennor gestured again at Kirk.

"We tell the conqueror we come to drive him out. He offers us sanctuary. We are damaged. He offers repair. We are attacked. He defends us. We tell him we have no home. He offers to make room for us. Garamanus Drovid, Dana of the *Wrath,* Keeper of the Magic Eggs and the Gold Sickle, call up your wisdom and not just your research, and tell me . . . is *this* the conqueror?"

The large tawny hand clenched so tightly that the long fingernails seemed nearly to break the skin, then fanned open and made a sharp gesture at Jim Kirk's chest.

Challenge boiled between the two impressive creatures. Tension rolled heavily across the bridge, bringing an ache to every head and a clench to every throat. No one moved.

Standing on the tripwire, Kirk knew better than to move and hoped his crew would take his example.

Reaching critical mass, Garamanus glared in bald

provocation, but despite anticipation there was no spring of attack, no roar of rage. When he finally spoke, his voice was as passive as a foghorn. His decision, evidently, had been made in those tight seconds, and now he would abide.

"I wish to go back to my ship and be with my people."

Unsure to whom the sentence was directed, Kirk took it upon himself as host to respond. "Transporter room two will be standing by when you want it."

"Go back to the ship," Zennor sanctioned. "We will send a message through the wrinkle. The conquerors are not here. Our place is not here."

Without another word or look, Garamanus flowed toward the turbolift and like some piece of a drifting wind was suddenly gone.

The tension, most of it, went with him.

Well, some of it.

Kirk turned to his science staff. "Duty stations," he ordered.

The flood of blue uniforms toward the lift was as much a flood of relief. There was an uneasy pause as they waited for the tube to clear and another lift to appear there, enough for about half of them to leave; then another two minutes lagged as the remaining science staff huddled the hallway and Zennor by himself in the other half until a third lift was able to arrive.

Then they left, and Zennor was again alone up there.

He and Kirk looked at each other.

Without turning away, Kirk said, "All stop."

He was surveying Zennor as if scanning a sculpture and thinking about what he was going to say.

"I'm glad," he said at last, "that you found enough—or enough lack—of information to convince you we're not enemies."

Zennor's weighty head bowed slightly out of the shadow. "I am convinced not by *what* we found, but *who* we found." He offered Kirk a pause that was indeed heartwarming. "If I had found only the Kling, we would be occupying this space by now."

Feeling suddenly better, and supremely gratified, Kirk discovered after a few seconds that he was grinning. He hadn't felt that coming on.

"Captain," Chekov said, straightening sharply at the science station, "long-range sensors are reading a heavy surge in warp-field exhaust, sir! The Klingon fleet is coming in—a very large fleet—at high warp speed!"

Kirk nodded and motioned for the young officer to calm down, set a better example, and comprehend the vastness of space. They had time to move. Not much, but they had it.

He looked at Zennor. "We'd better wear ship and get out of here or they'll hem us in. Now that we know there's nothing here, there's no reason to stay."

Zennor—if that face could—offered what might've been on the other side of the galaxy a smile. "You go. Let me linger. I will happen to be here when they come. If they attack, I am no conqueror to destroy them."

"It's tempting," Kirk allowed, "but no."

The thick horns drew an imaginary pattern on the ceiling. "No matter, Vergokirk. Once we are among you and you have our technology, you will be able to take care of them yourselves." He lowered that drumbeat voice and added, "You know you will have to eventually."

"People change, Vergo," Kirk wagered. "We have to give them that chance."

He started to turn to the helm to usher Byers into a new course, but Zennor said, "No, they don't change. Good is good. Bad is bad."

Stifling any disappointment he might've been tempted to show, Kirk took the high road. Mildly he said, "I guess that's just another difference between us."

Every hospital has a morgue, and none wants one.

Leonard McCoy was in his, doing all those hundred things a doctor is obliged to do once he has saved all he can save and there is only clean-up work to do. Logging the names of the dead, matching physical attributes and body marks to the official file of each, to make sure there is no error, that no family gets the wrong letter from the captain, and so each family knows with absolute certainty that the body wrapped in silk and sent into the nearest sun was indeed the son they would never get back. No one should ever wonder. That was his job now, and he took it with supreme care.

Now, after the battle, after the ground assault, after the incident that asked of a serviceman the bottom-line sacrifice, came the time that came so rarely, and he realized in the midst of this sorry duty how lucky he really was to have Jim Kirk for a captain. Kirk had many reputations, saint or demon, depending on—what had he said?—whether or not somebody agreed with his work. And some who liked his work still didn't like him. Call it jealousy, call it impatience, call it just another method of doing business, some people just didn't like him. A lot of people, in fact.

But he was a leader, not a politician, and being liked was the last on his list. Some of his own crewmen didn't like him, but that didn't matter. This shooting star they were riding still had the lowest transfer rate of any ship in the Fleet. And the waiting list was the longest of all twelve starships.

Space was no fairyland and a charming captain did no one any good. They signed on because they knew he would fight for their lives. Down to the last man, he would fight for each of them.

What mattered was times like this, when hundreds of men had gone into battle and only nineteen failed to come out of it. More than any other starship captain, Kirk had a reputation for fundamentally despising the death of a crewman. It was his own tragic flaw. He took a shipmate's death personally. Sometimes too personally for his own well-being, McCoy felt.

In order to be a physician he had long ago learned to reconcile his bone-deep desire to preserve life and the quality thereof with the analytical callousness every doctor needed at times like this.

He placed the cool, rubbery hands of one of the Starfleet boys on the corpse's chest and covered him. That was ten done. Time for a break.

He looked up, and found himself gazing at the . . . whatever that poor individual was. It lay stark white and uncovered, headless and horrible on its bench. He'd been unable to go near it since the others left, timid about breaking any more taboos before the captain and the other captain decided what they wanted to do with it.

Yet it tugged at him. It was here, and though dead still under his care. He found himself reticent to ignore it. They all begged a few moments' final attention, and he ached to give.

A sound in the outer ward shook him hard and he fought to control himself. His nerves were on edge. Silly.

"Mr. Spock, if that's you getting up, I'll have your stripes," he called.

He wiped his hands, scooped up the medical tricorder he was using, and strode out of the morgue, gladly leaving behind the chilly room for the time being. After all, nobody in there was in any particular rush.

And he hungered now for a conversation, even a little lashing back and forth with Spock. He was in the mood for a semijovial insult, and didn't particularly care in which direction the barbs flew. Barbs could make him feel alive and he needed that.

The sight he met as he stepped out into the outer offices was not Spock leaning on a doorjamb proclaiming that he was perfectly well, thank you, but instead the elongated and cloud-woven form of Garamanus.

McCoy froze, drew a breath, then bolted back on a heel before he caught the edge of a desk and stopped himself. He chided himself for not being used to aliens by now, but *these* aliens . . .

Behind Garamanus was another of the horned beings, and behind that one was a tall bony creature with expanding membranes at rest between its arms and thighs. Probably some form of perspiration control, or mating consideration. Certainly locked in the appearance of otherworldliness, though, in the truest and most supernatural sense of the word.

He tried to be clinical as he gazed at the creatures crowding his door, blocking his way.

"May I help you?" he asked.

They said nothing, but moved a few steps into the room, so the doorway no longer cramped them.

"Oh," he murmured after a few seconds, "have you come for the remains? I haven't touched the body . . . I didn't want to make any more mistakes or insult you further in any way . . . if you'll come with me, I'll help you prepare the body."

Perhaps that was just another mistake. They probably wanted nothing to do with him, wanted him as far away from their dead as they could push him.

Scarcely had his hand left his side to gesture toward the morgue than the two beings behind Garamanus disappeared . . .

No, they hadn't disappeared, but had simply moved so fast that he didn't see, for they were on top of him.

He choked out half a word, half a cry for help or sense, but there would be none of either, and they had him. The horned being embraced him from behind in a grip like sculpture, and the being with the membranes raised its long thin arms. One of the membranes dropped over McCoy's head and formed itself to his face and shoulders as fitting as a fishnet. His lips pressed into the rubbery membrane, he felt it compress into the hollows of his eyes, bend his eyelashes, and cut off his breathing. He could see nothing now but the milky membrane and the outline of Garamanus moving toward him.

One feeble kick was the only motion of protest McCoy could manage as he was lifted clear of the floor and tipped sideways like a rolled rug on its way to the cleaner's. Balance went to the wind. They were carrying him—they were taking him away. They were *kidnapping* him.

They had to carry him through the main sickbay

entranceway in order to get out. Spock would be able to see from the other ward. Spock would call for help.

He heard the swish of the door panel, but there was no call from Spock, no demand that these brigands let the doctor go.

What had they done to Spock?

As he waited for common sense to descend, for them to come to their right minds and unroll him and apologize, McCoy's last conscious thought was of the hard pain caused by the medical tricorder as it gouged against his chest.

Chapter Fifteen

"SPOCK. SPOCK, say something."

"McCoy . . ."

"I think he's only stunned somehow, sir," Nurse Christine Chapel said as she and Kirk knelt beside Spock, whose narrow form lay sprawled on the deck a few steps from his bed. "That's what I'm getting on these readings. I've given him a muscle relaxant and a nerve stimulant. He should come around in a minute."

"With his nerves and muscles arguing, no doubt."

"No doubt. Sir," Chapel added, glancing up at the monitors and fingerpad desks set up at Spock's bedside, "Mr. Spock had a stack of computer files here . . . they're all missing. He might've had them put away, but there hasn't been anyone in here to do that except me, and I didn't do it. Do you think whoever did this could've taken them too?"

Kirk kept a grip on Spock's arm, but was careful not to push or pull, despite the urge to put his first officer back on the bed which had been doing him so much good. But he wasn't going to make that mistake again.

He was glad he had left Zennor on the bridge. Glad for now, at least. "Is it safe to move him?"

The nurse gave him a floorside medical nod. "I'm checking, sir."

"McCoy . . ."

"What about his other injuries?" Kirk asked the nurse. "Has his recuperation been compromised in any way?"

"I don't think so," the nurse said, her voice rough with concern. "They knocked him off the bed, but the anti-gravs held on to him long enough that he had a relatively soft landing. He might have some bruises."

"Spock." Kirk fixed a gaze on the narrow inkdrop eyes and demanded of the Vulcan that he meet the stimulant halfway and bring those thoughts out into the open. "We know they took McCoy. Who did it? Did you see?"

He knew, and the suspicion was a cold metal ball in his stomach. Garamanus.

Lying on his back, his knees supported by a pillow hastily shoved under there to assist blood flow, Spock blinked and struggled for consciousness. He looked like a man coming out of phaser stun.

Might be exactly that. Zennor's technology packed a punch, but there were explanations for that. Otherwise, their power consumption and energy ratios weren't all that unfamiliar. There was no notable reason their methods of stun would be much different either.

Unless they had some kind of Vulcan neck pinch of their own, which was a possibility too.

Spock fixed his eyes on Kirk and anchored there. He caught Kirk's arm and used it for leverage as he tried to raise his head.

His voice was a scratch.

"It was . . . the Furies . . ."

Furies.

What was that supposed to mean? Had Spock made up a word? No, that didn't make sense. It also had never happened before. Spock wasn't a making-up kind of man.

"Well?"

Kirk pressed up against the side of the diagnostic bed until the edge cut into his legs.

Nurse Chapel watched the readout panel, nodded, then sighed. "Much better now. Let's have a little more of the magic bullet—"

She checked her hypo, then pressed it to the hollow of Spock's shoulder and made it hiss.

Tense with effort, Spock suddenly relaxed and was finally able to quiet the interior struggle and look at Kirk with lucid eyes.

"Pardon me, Captain. . . ." He seemed greatly relieved to be able to make the connection between the complex racing of his mind and the articulation of his voice. "How did they get off the ship with the doctor?"

"They stunned the technician manning it the same way they did you. You're on to something, Spock. What is it? You said 'Furies.' What's that mean?"

"I was still dazed, sir."

"But you said it. What does it mean?"

Spock's expression told Kirk that whatever had been discovered was probably not scientific.

"A myth?" the captain pushed. "Some of that material McCoy found? You said you were going to follow that thread. Come, Spock, it's critical."

"Yes, of course . . . I was studying early civilizations in our quadrant and their mythological bases for fact.

Kirk gritted his teeth, then said, "And you *found* . . ."

"I found a striking, in fact quite disturbing, similarity between Zennor's people and a clutch of mythological figures called the Furies." His body tightening with strain, Spock reached for the fingerpads, then paused. "The files—did you take them, Captain?"

"No. The people who attacked you took them."

Spock's brows drew tight. "Why would they have taken my files?"

Kirk felt his hands go cold again. "They knew we were doing research into the past, to try to identify them. And they know you're the science officer. I told Zennor we were looking through our historical data, searching for correlations. He probably told Garamanus. I doubt he suspected Garamanus would do anything like this. What difference does it make? You didn't find anything conclusive, did you?"

Genuine alarm burst out of Spock's controlled expression, long enough for Kirk to get the gravity of the theft. "Captain . . . this is dangerous."

"What is? Can you show me?"

"Let me call it up."

The access to the fantastic log of information was eerily silent for long seconds, then came to life suddenly, as if pleased to show off what it had found.

Above, three of the screens popped full of pictures of horrendous fantasy beings, Medusa-types with snakes for hair and flamelike wings, nappy green skin, and pointed teeth.

Kirk hadn't paid attention to this stuff since he was ten years old. Fantasy. He was instantly ill at ease. Numbers, flight plans, light-years—he could deal with the concrete. But not this.

"The Furies," Spock said, "are images from Greco-Roman mythology. They were beings, generally portrayed as female, who pursued and punished crimes that had gone unavenged. Quite unpleasant. Ultimately they were associated with demonic behavior, but always with the element of reprisal."

"Reprisal . . . chasing down the 'conquerors' and kicking them out."

Spock moved his brows. "It certainly could be taken that way. The element of banishment or uncleanliness is deeply rooted in our cultures, Captain, and particularly in Earth culture. We would be quite remiss in our research if we failed to recognize the surprising similarity between these beings and images like the Furies, and witches and goblins as manifested in our own histories. These are images of which we are inherently afraid."

Lips cracking as he pressed them flat, Kirk asked, "Mr. Spock, are you trying to tell me that these people are witches?"

Pliantly Spock's dark eyes left the screens and moved to Kirk. "There are not true witches in the colloquial manifestation. I am saying they are archetypes. General representations, or they *look* like general representations found easily in our cultures."

"So Bones was right."

"Yes, the doctor was right. These people now have my files, and they will see themselves all over our culture, or at least things *like* themselves, and they may take those similarities as some form of gospel. And they'll also see that we are inherently frightened of them. They have built a civilization of very small clues, and thus will take these pictures quite seriously."

"If you're kicked out of your homeland," Kirk said, "any little bits you have left become valuable." He picked up the crescent etching from the table beside Spock and looked at it, feeling as if half the galaxy were about to bump up against the other half with himself in the middle. He put his other hand on the edge of Spock's bed as if to connect himself to the ship physically. "If all you have is your beliefs, you cling all the more tightly to them."

"Yes," the Vulcan said. "And—"

"Captain?"

Uhura. They hadn't even heard the gush of the corridor panel.

"In here," Kirk called.

"Sir?" She was there, but couldn't see them from the other side of the two diagnostic beds.

"On the deck," Kirk added.

"Oh, my!" She came plunging around the foot of Spock's bed, arms loaded with computer cartridges. "Sir! Mr. Spock, what happened?"

She knelt quickly beside Nurse Chapel.

"Just a friendly attack," Chapel reported sandily.

"Oh, Mr. Spock . . ." Uhura's lovely dark face, usually the essence of reserve, now became animated with concern.

"Don't worry," Chapel said. "He's in the best of hands."

Aware of her attention, which had proven in the past much less curable than a bad spinal injury, Spock looked past her to Uhura. "You have a report, Lieutenant?"

"Oh, yes, yes," the communications specialist said. She held up one of the cartridges. "Dr. McCoy's lead on old druid culture turned up a half-dozen matches right away. 'Vergo' could be 'vergobretos' or 'bretan,' which was a tribal chief. A captain of sorts, sir. The 'Dananns' were the priests, or those with special gifts."

"Those are too close for comfort," Kirk commented as he snatched another pillow from the bed and handed it to Chapel, who carefully put it under Spock's head so he would be more comfortable while she stabilized him.

"It certainly made me shiver," she agreed. "And I was bothered by the ship's name, so I tracked that in old Gaelic. It's not 'Wrath' as in 'anger.' It's 'Rath' without a 'w.' It's an Old English derivative of the word 'rathe,' meaning 'early.' "

"Early . . ."

"Yes, and it's also an ancient Irish word meaning 'earthwork' or 'hill.' I would say the most accurate translation would be 'fortress.' "

"An early fortress." With a thoughtful frown, Kirk looked at Spock. "A scout ship?"

"It fits," Spock confirmed as he lay there on the deck with Chapel working over him.

"This makes a big problem for us," Kirk said. "If they're anchored in their myths, then they're willing to act upon them. If their myth tells them to find their home space, and they want it back, that means they're prepared to take it back."

Spock tilted his head. "Meaning?"

"Meaning you don't send just one ship for that.

Zennor's not telling me something and I think I know what it is. I think there might be a fleet waiting for instruction from him. Him . . . or Garamanus."

"We have no proof of that."

"I can't afford to wait for proof. I have to act on my instincts. Now Garamanus has those files and he can show them to whoever sent them here."

"You believe they are communicating with someone on the other side of their portal somehow?"

"What good would it be if they couldn't?"

"Very little . . . Zennor says he cannot go back."

"That's what he *says.*"

Silence dropped between them for a few moments, long enough for them to hear the emptiness of sickbay, the passive twitter of the diagnostic panel above Spock, the whisper of some machine in the lab that had been left on to do whatever it was doing, the mournful presence of that sliced-up poppet beyond that door over there.

"I am sorry, Captain."

Kirk looked up. "For what?"

Spock's face was cast in regret and he didn't mind showing it. "I know you have forged a kind of synthesis with Captain Zennor . . . a friendship."

Bitter, Kirk gazed at the deck. How often had this happened to him in his life? To find synthesis, to have commonality, to make friends with someone, only to have that friendship blistered and ultimately sundered by some outside consideration. Competitors at Starfleet Academy, at Starfleet itself, in space, where his drive for the win had also driven a stake into the heart of any chance for amicable feelings when all was over.

And in deep space, there had been flat-out enemies he wished he could've known better.

But when the smoke cleared, he always stood alone. Some fences damned mending, and certainly climbing. He'd had to turn away time after time, leaving animosity where he had wished to have comradeship.

That was why, he realized in this moment particularly, he cherished and so unflinchingly defended and protected both Spock and McCoy. They had stood with him and never given in to the differences between themselves and him, as so many others had.

Differences. Differences.

Damned differences.

Suddenly he was mad again. "The friendship's about to be tested."

"How so?"

"I'll tell you how. I'm beaming over to that ship and get our doctor back. And while I'm there I'm going to see exactly what it is that we're up against."

He punched the nearest comm. "Kirk to bridge. Put Captain Zennor on."

The blade in his voice evidently came across for all it was worth, because Nordstrom didn't respond.

Very quietly, Spock asked, "Are you going to tell him, Captain?"

"I don't know. I promised I'd help him. . . ."

The Vulcan's face was limned with concern. "That could be most imprudent."

"I know."

"This is Zennor."

"We have a problem. Your Dana and others have attacked my first officer and kidnapped my doctor."

"Garamanus . . . kidnapped your McCoy?"

"He did and I'm not taking it well."

"I must go to my ship immediately."

"I'm going with you, and I'm bringing a Security team."

"They will be killed instantly. You must come with me alone, if you insist upon coming. We can only go there one time. I will give you the modulation to drop the block of your transporter beam, but as soon as we go, they will change it again. But we must go immediately. It is your McCoy's only chance."

Chapter Sixteen

"VERY DANGEROUS for you to be here now. If there is reaction, I cannot protect you."

"I'll take my chances. Where's my chief surgeon?"

"Come with me. Prepare yourself."

Not very reassuring, as phrases went.

The tour through Zennor's ship was skin-chilling. Like wandering through a cave behind a suddenly agile bat. Zennor, who had moved with such cautious reserve down the broad, bright, open corridors of the *Enterprise*, now skirted down shoulder-wide passages coated with dark velvety moss and overhung with some kind of web.

Kirk stumbled several times until his eyes adjusted, then stumbled a little less, but the deck was nearly invisible in the dimness. He felt he was stepping foot by foot through the chambers of a hornet's nest. Somehow they had beamed directly into these veins and now were moving through them.

There was something beneath his feet, not carpet or deck, but a litter of crunchy and mushy matter, all different sizes, different textures, as if he were treading over a dumping ground. Fungus gave under his weight and puffballs popped as he stepped on them. Other things cracked. The air was thick and musky with smells both plant and animal.

When he thought he couldn't stand another meter of the cloying dimness and moss that grasped at his hair and arms, Zennor led him out into a broader cavern, though still coated with growing plant life—and a sense, if not a visible presence, of other life, of eyes watching him. To all outward senses, he and Zennor were alone here.

But Kirk had spent his life being looked at. He knew when it was happening. There were beasts in the walls.

No, the walls didn't have eyes, but they did have punctures, dark recesses from which more of those skulls peered out, many skulls, but not humanlike skulls. There were many kinds, some belonging to creatures he hadn't seen yet but now assumed were here. Unless they were dragging along the skulls of aliens they met on their voyages, Zennor's amalgamated crew was even more amalgamated than Kirk had first guessed. These were most likely the skulls of fallen comrades.

So they kept the skulls of some, and the "souls" of others. And who could tell what else? Foreign cultures could be very complicated.

Suddenly he wanted the chance to get to know them better, and felt that chance slipping away as he dodged behind Zennor up their icy slope.

He forced himself to ignore the skull niches as he hurried behind Zennor, also forcing himself not to bellow an order to move even faster.

All at once they burst out into a blinding brightness, creased with the noise of hundreds of voices making disorganized, wild cheers and chants. Kirk shaded his eyes and paused until they adjusted, then tried to look.

The chamber was enormous, as big as a stadium and half again taller, lit with green and yellow artificial light, and twisting with a white haze created by vents clearly spewing the stuff near the ceiling. From the configuration of the *Rath*, he guessed they were near the aft end. So the propulsion units weren't back here, but somehow arranged elsewhere. He'd have to remember that—

But thoughts of hardware and strategy fled his mind as he looked up, and farther up.

In the center of the huge foggy chamber stood—yes, *stood*—a giant mannequin in humanoid form, with a head, two arms, two legs, like a vast version of one of those poppets, except that this mannequin was a good six stories tall and made entirely of slats of wood and raw tree branches, and veined with braided straw or some kind of thatch. Its arms stood straight out like a rag doll's, bound at the wrists with some kind of twine; its legs ended at the ankles, with only stumps of chopped matter for hands and feet.

Bisecting the hollow arms, legs, and torso of the wickerwork giant were narrow platforms—scarcely more than slats themselves, but enough to stand upon—and there, in the middle of the straw giant's see-through right thigh, Leonard McCoy hovered twenty-five feet above the deck.

The doctor clung pitifully to the twisted veins of thatch, looking down upon a gaggle of cavorting beings, all types of misshapen vagabond demons, from the snake-headed beings to the horned ones to those more squidlike than anything else, and the others who looked as if they had wings.

Evidently this was Zennor's crew, dancing around the straw legs of the monster, laying more straw and twigs in heaps around the giant's ankles, and chanting while they did this.

The Furies. Even if it wasn't them, it described them now.

Kirk stared, measuring the critical elements, consumed for a moment with astonishment and a bad chill. He knew a preparation for a bonfire when he saw one.

Stepping forward from the entranceway, he felt the green-tinted light reflect off the topaz fabric of his uniform shirt and sensed how bizarre his facial features must look with that light cast from below, like something boys would see playing with flashlights in a pup tent.

"Jim!" McCoy knelt on the slats and called down, pushing his face between the veins of thatch.

Kirk turned to Zennor. "What is *this?*"

Zennor gazed at him with ferrous eyes that held no apology. "Punishment."

The crew of the *Rath,* at least the off-duty crew presumably, jumped and rushed, chanting all the way, around the giant straw mannequin in a gangly kind of organization, each going his own way at his own pace, but all going in the same direction. They deposited bundles of straw, branches, and even whole trees at the ankles of the giant. Their metal wristbands, chains, medallions, bracelets, and belts bounced and rang, creating a fiendish jangling in the huge hall. On their metal belts, many of them had those linen poppets, each in the rough image of the wearer, doing another kind of dance.

As Zennor stood before him in his dominating and statuesque manner, Kirk was careful to stand still, not attract any more attention than necessary until he could size things up.

A sundry train of beings broke off from the dancing circle and hurried toward him and Zennor. It took all of Kirk's inner resolve to stand still and let Zennor handle his own crew.

The horrendous gaggle descended upon them in a rush until the last four feet, when they skidded to a stop and made Kirk glad he was still wearing his portable translator, because they were all speaking at once.

"We're home!" a winged thing said to Zennor.

"The Dana told us the news!" crowed an elongated creature that seemed to have no bodily mass other than bones thinly veiled with rubbery brown skin. It would've looked like a Halloween skeleton, appropriately enough, except that it had four arms.

A tentacle-head repeated, "The Dana told us the good news!"

"This is our place!" someone else trilled in a high voice, clearly meant to congratulate their leader.

"The Dana had no authority, Morien," Zennor said. His voice had a tenor of bottled rage. "You should be at your posts."

"But we have a criminal, Vergozen," the tentacled person said, and looked at Kirk. "Is this another one?"

The "it" gestured at Kirk.

"He is here for the final visitation," Zennor snarled, and Kirk couldn't tell whether it was sarcasm or not. Then Zennor motioned for Kirk to move past them. "Fetch me the Dana."

Morien quickly said "Yes, Vergozen!" and skittered off into the crowd.

Kirk took his cue and moved toward the wicker colossus. Other creatures seemed uninterested in him, though many glanced up in mild curiosity. They were involved in their work and looking forward to what they were about to do. They didn't seem to care about visitors who walked in with their captain.

He came to the bottom of one straw leg, as big around as a warp engine, close enough to speak to McCoy in a normalish voice, without attracting attention.

"Bones," he began tentatively, "you all right up there?"

"So far." The doctor gripped the reedy filaments of the colossus. "Did they hurt Spock?"

"They knocked him off his bunk. Chapel's taking care of him. I've never seen her so happy."

"Are the Klingons here yet?"

"Just popped onto our long-range. We were about to make a border run when you turned up missing. Now I'll settle for anything I can get away with."

Frustrated, McCoy glanced around, then reached down with a toe and found a lower slat, and climbed down through the wooden webbing until he could stand inside the giant's right leg, just above the knee. He could only make it about another seven feet down before the straw webbing stopped him.

"Jim . . . they're going to set fire to this."

Caught with empathy, Kirk nodded and tried to be clinical. "Yes, I know. I'm working on it."

"I broke their laws with that damn doll. You might not be able to do anything about it."

"Don't make any bets."

"I don't want to," the doctor said. "Jim, listen—when they put me in here, they shoved in a lot of other things. They put my medical tricorder in with me, and all this other stuff." He maneuvered with difficulty, having to stand on slats of bowing straw twisted to provide a foothold that was obviously temporary, and scoop up bits of material from around him. "There are thigh and hand bones here . . . and hanks of hair, skin scrapings . . . and this bony plate is the back part of a cranium."

"The place is full of skulls."

"Yes, I know. But this skull is Andorian!"

"That's not possible," Kirk said, but it came out with a terrible resignation that surprised even him.

McCoy raised a long gray bone, scored with cracks. "And this thighbone . . . it's human. From Earth. It's a perfect DNA match." He leaned on the slat with one knee and held up his medical tricorder with his other hand.

"Could they have acquired it here in the past twenty-four hours?"

"They could've. Except that they'd have had to raid an archeology lab for this. It's old as a bristlecone pine!"

"How old is that?"

"As nearly as I can estimate, it's over four thousand years old. A human bone!"

"Bones, are you sure about this?'

"I've had nothing else to do in here "

"They put those in there with you just now?"

"Just a half hour ago. I think they're raiding their own coffers and placing things in here that look physiologically like me. At least to their minds. Some kind of symbolic connection—who knows?"

"Can you explain the DNA link?"

The doctor scowled. "I'm not saying that humans or Klingons went out into space and met these people, but I'm wondering if somehow these people ended up on our planets a long time ago and affected our beliefs. If a shipload of Vulcans showed up on Earth in the fourteen-hundreds, they'd sure be taken for devils."

"And life has been around the galaxy for millions of years. Is it really any surprise if Earth, Vulcan, the Klingon homeworld, and a lot of other planets might've had visitations?"

"Given the numbers, I'd be surprised if they hadn't." McCoy squirmed for a better grip.

Kirk gripped the straw spokes too, as if to make a connection. "The dangerous bottom line is that it's beginning to look like this *was* their space."

"Then we'd all better get used to carrying pitchforks," McCoy said, "because I think that's the conclusion." He held up the human thighbone and shook it. "Unless they killed a human in the past twelve hours and somehow made this bone appear to my readouts as if it were four to six thousand years old. I think we got that mythological stuff from our Greeks and Egyptians and druids, but I think the Greeks and Egyptians and druids got it from *them.*"

He swept the medical tricorder to indicate the circle of aliens, then reached out between the wood and straw and tossed the tricorder to Kirk.

"If I don't make it, you've got to take that to Spock," he said urgently. "I don't mind being right, but this time I was even more right than I had the sense to know. It's not just a coincidence that these people look like our legends and myths of evil. They *are* our legends and myths of evil!"

A sight within a sight.

Furies and fire.

In the center of the great hall, twisted with manufactured fog and looming nearly to the ceiling, the straw giant had no face and no hands, only the bound strands of thatch to make up the most base form of intelligent life. On the walls, carved forms of animal heads and double-headed statues flared down in carnal images of the beings dancing below.

"Have you got your phaser with you?"

McCoy's question was subdued.

"Yes," Kirk said. "They didn't take it away. I don't know if that's courtesy or they're just not afraid of it. It's not because they're stupid, I'll bet."

Around them a drumbeat began, low and not very steady, timpani made of skin stretched over some kind of iron cauldron. Horned beings like Zennor were pounding them with thighbones the same as the one McCoy had shown him.

"Jim," the doctor began.

Kirk turned. "What?"

"If you can't get me out of here and they light this up," McCoy said with great struggle, "use the phaser on me."

Anguish pushed at the backs of Kirk's eyes as he looked up and saw McCoy for the fullness of his character at that instant. McCoy hadn't asked him to open up on these creatures in order to get him out of here, to incinerate them in order to spare him incineration, never mind that a single phaser could easily do that. Hundreds could be killed in a single sweep, much more painlessly than the death they were offering the doctor now.

McCoy didn't want that. He'd take the death, but he wanted to make sure that his life was the only sacrifice and that, if there was still a chance for peace, he should die to smooth that path of possibility.

"Understood," Kirk accepted. Sympathy tightened his throat. "I promise."

Each knew a heavy price was being asked here, and a terrible guilt to be risked. The space between them was a cursed thing.

He stepped back, through the chanting circle of aliens, to where Zennor stood waiting, colossal in his own way, perhaps vile in the same way.

"You know I won't let them do this to him," Kirk said.

"Nor would I, were he mine," Zennor said. "There are customs."

Abruptly petulant, Kirk squared off in front of him. "Where I come from we have laws instead of customs to rule us. We have trials before we have punishment. What about that?"

"He mutilated Manann's soul. He admitted it. He wished to atone. This is atonement."

"This is villainy. One crime doesn't absolve another. Are you going to stand there and let this occur?"

Zennor did not answer. In fact, he was no longer looking at Kirk.

"There are other crimes," Kirk pushed, not caring anymore if he was being rude. He all but shouted across the chasm of distrust that had cracked between them. "Theft, for one. Garamanus stole several computer records from my ship. That's Starfleet property. I want them back, untouched."

"What is upon them?"

"Give them back. Then we'll discuss it." In mortal panic of pressing the situation too far, too fast for McCoy's good, too fast to get back the records and the volatile information upon them, Kirk reined in his tone. He held out a supplicant hand. "There has to be some line of trust between us, or we have nothing and our cultures have nothing on which to build. I know you don't want that."

The entreaty burned in his throat, for it was a lie. He knew the tangled truth and dared not tell yet. If possible, he would introduce these people to the weird truth slowly to explain it, gradually enough to make them digest the distance in time from the common element, whatever that element turned out to be, and that whatever happened five thousand years ago, there was no one here to answer for it anymore. Slowly, he hoped, enough to explain that whoever the conquerors were, they couldn't have been Terrans, Vulcans, Romulans, Orions, or even Klingons. The years just weren't right.

That message had to be delivered with finesse, of which at the moment Kirk possessed not a drop.

Zennor looked past him, gazing instead at a new presence moving out of the greenish haze toward them.

Spinning quickly, out of instinct, Kirk found himself staring up at the imposing half-moon eyes of Garamanus.

Zennor stepped out and met him. "Why have you done this?"

"You know why," the Dana said. "This is our home space. The Danai are correct."

The galloping crew slowed down and few by few began to stop and watch the power struggle play out. None seemed surprised, though all were tense, and Kirk drew the sensation that this was an old struggle between the quest of the Danai and the hard science of machines and pilots, a struggle thousands of years old, today coming to a head.

"You have no proof," Zennor said when his crew dropped to a sizzling quiet and listened. He stepped closer to Garamanus. "You have told them a lie."

The reaction of the crew was bizarre—but somehow familiar to Kirk, who had seen many kinds of humanoids and aliens and had learned to read for clues. Color changes, changes in the shapes of eyes, altered posture. He saw all those now. Had anyone ever called a Dana a liar before?

Kirk entertained a particular shiver and kept his mouth shut.

"I know their secrets," the Dana told him. "I have seen their memories. They are the conquerors."

The priest indicated Kirk somehow without moving very much at all.

Relatively clear. Somehow he had managed to read the files even with mechanics from all the way across the galaxy.

While they were gone, power had shifted. How could they get it back?

"We are not conquerors," Kirk said. "I refuse to concede the point. The past you're talking about is all finished and all you have left is a festered memory. I'm urging you not to act on it."

"It is not festered," Garamanus said. "It is the Veil of Evermore and as real as you are. When we light the effigy and burn the one who cuts souls, it will be the beginning of our onslaught. We know who you are." He clasped the medallion hanging at his chest and turned it upward for the mirror side to show. Kirk saw the flickering reflection of his own face. "And we know who we are."

"What's that supposed to mean?" Kirk demanded.

Garamanus clasped his own medallion, but did not hold it up. "We each wear a mirror, to be sure we will never forget what the damned look like. Until now, we held them only to ourselves. But that is all changed. Now we are not the cast-out, the despised, the unclean anymore . . . *you* are."

The Dana kept the small mirror up, and in it Kirk continued to see his own flushed face.

He reached out and pushed the mirror down.

"We did what you asked," he went on persistently, unable to keep the desperation out of his voice. His words sped up. "We investigated your data and it turned out to be nothing. There's no scientific proof—"

"You have not disproven us," the Dana said.

"But not proven either," Zennor claimed.

In the full flower of his newly acquired mantle, Garamanus raised his opal horns. "Thousands of years ago the Danai decided you would not understand these things. There are millions of little clues."

"But we have not found *proof,"* Zennor said again, his voice echoing in the huge chamber now that the chanting had fallen away.

"It is proven to me," Garamanus said, "and to them." He made a long, confident gesture at the circle of Furies, while above it all McCoy huddled fearfully in his straw prison in the middle of the circle. The Dana was very different now from the way he had been when Zennor had embarrassed him on the *Enterprise.*

Zennor was different too. He was defending the future and Garamanus was defending the past. A pure, strange clash of two things which could never meet, but which today found embodiment in these two beings.

"Listen!" Zennor called to his crew. "You will decide between us! Come around us and listen."

His hands tingling and cold, Kirk slowly slipped the strap of the medical tricorder over his head and slipped one arm through. He reached around behind his back and drew his palm-sized phaser unit and brought it around front. It rested in his palm, warm with ready energy. If he opened up on all these beings, wide dispersal, he could betray the oaths both he and McCoy swore they would live by, slaughter them all in an instant.

Or he could aim at McCoy and do as he had sworn he would. The most duty-binding promise anyone could make to another—*I'll end your life before the pain comes.*

The desire to rush forward almost crushed his lungs. But what could he do? Pull that woven straw apart with his bare hands? It was as tight as steel cord.

Could he phaser it open with a narrow beam? Yes . . . *if* he could get close enough. But there were fifty strands of that stuff to cut apart before he could get McCoy out, and that would take time.

As the crew moved closer, uneasy, Garamanus faced Zennor. "The Klingon recognized us. They all know us. He knows who we are." Pointing at Kirk, the Dana narrowed his strange eyes. "This is our quadrant and you are colluding with the conquerors!"

"He led us here," Zennor accused, calling to the crew and pointing at Garamanus. "The planets to which he brought us are gone. I have seen the place. There are no planets, there is no proof, there is nothing. Now he wants us to kill these people and take what is theirs. We have squandered whole lifetimes in the Danai quest for power. Shall we crawl into the pit with them and their errors? I will not! The Danai are our inner conquerors! Which of you will come forward to defend this one?"

His voice drummed. He was fighting to get his crew back.

And they were vacillating, Kirk could see.

Garamanus raised one hand, scarcely a gesture at all, and dropped his medallion to fall again to the bottom of its chain; from the circle of beings there came a dozen or so breaking off from the others and charging toward them.

Kirk plunged backward against the nearest wall, but the charging Furies weren't coming for him—they were coming for Zennor. He tried to think of this happening on his ship, with his crew, but couldn't.

Perhaps here, with their odd rules, this wasn't considered mutiny at all. Garamanus was in charge, and he had made his order, unthinkable though it seemed.

"Zennor!" Kirk snapped. "Do something or I will!"

He raised his phaser. Abruptly he realized why Zennor let him keep the weapon. He was the living failsafe. If things went too far wrong, everything would be ended here and now.

But the other captain ignored him and even ignored the rushing creatures of his own crew. He countered the rush by plunging directly at Garamanus.

Instantly the two horned beings twisted in a bitter embrace, glowing with crackling electricity generated somehow by their bodies. Yellow lightning knitted their horns and ran up their arms and ringed their necks. Their eyes changed color as if boiling from within from some kind of biologically generated energy base.

Kirk shielded his face. All he could do was press his hip against the wall and fend off the sparks with his arms.

The Furies skidded to a halt and gave ground as Zennor and Garamanus whipped toward Kirk; then balance changed and the two grappling leaders plunged toward the wicker mannequin, falling against it and causing the straw to smoke and turn black.

McCoy huddled back, but there wasn't far for him to go, and there was nowhere for him to hide.

With the Dana's huge hands coiled around his throat, Zennor grimaced horribly and seemed to call up the determination given to him by his own secret hopes for his civilization. He freed one of his own hands from his own grip on Garamanus and reached out for a strand of the coiled straw.

Kirk craned to see. The coiled straw was stiff and firm as a dockline. How could it be moved?

But Zennor was moving it. Somehow he had the strength to bow out the strand, to pull it toward him. Roaring for a last surge of power, he thrust Garamanus's head under the strand, then let the straw snap back into place, taking the Dana with it.

Caught by the throat between two cords of straw rope, the Dana clutched at the thing strangling him, but Zennor cranked hard on the wicker and took hold of one of the horns in Garamanus's head, pushing him deeper into the deadly netting.

"Who is Vergobretos?" Zennor boomed at the undecided crew.

His voice filled the huge chamber, and echoed over and over. He swung his free arm violently and pushed Garamanus farther down with the other.

The Dana struggled. Not dead yet.

The Furies stared, waved their fists—or whatever—and bellowed some kind of chant that Kirk didn't understand.

Now Zennor took that free hand and grasped the straw vein nearest to Garamanus. He gripped it hard and it began to smoke. The energy that had flowed through the two angry, dangerous beings now flowed into the strand of straw and set it smoldering.

Sparks cracked, and the straw grew hotter, then popped into flame.

Zennor held on despite the heat. The snapping flame

crawled toward Garamanus, who was now bluish in the face and hands as his throat was crushed, though he continued to struggle.

"Bones, keep back!" Kirk called over the crackle as the flames ran up the straw form, drenching McCoy in smoke so that he could hardly be seen.

He came up behind Zennor, though he couldn't dare touch the body of the other captain while it was still charged with energy. "Zennor," he called. "Stop what you're doing. He's down. Back off."

But Zennor's hand remained tight on Garamanus. Flames crawled up the outer superstructure of the effigy's left leg and chewed at its torso, stretching out tall into the upper regions and rolling along the left arm.

Huddled in the thigh of the right leg, McCoy waved furiously at the smoke and counted seconds. "Jim!"

Kirk rushed to the right ankle of the giant. "Hang on!"

The creatures of the *Rath*'s crew began to howl a cheer and wave their arms, encouraging the climbing flames. Now the straw giant had no head, but only a rolling ball of fire. Kirk witnessed with a shiver the loyalty that a commander could possess as opposed to a secondary influence. Maybe this could only happen on a ship, but it was happening here.

"Zennor! Back off!" Kirk called, disappointed that a struggle and a quest that had gone on for millennia now apparently came down to a physical fight between leaders of two factions. He always wanted things to be loftier than that, and so often complex circumstances came down to shows of muscle, driven to victory or failure only by the intensity of belief driving them.

Grudgeful and clearly vexed, Zennor gave the Dana's convulsing form one last shove, then stepped away.

The creature called Morien and a dozen others plunged in to scoop up the choking Dana, who was too weak to struggle against them, and to Kirk's shock they shoved Garamanus through the burning slats of wood and strands of straw and into the burning leg of the colossus.

In a moment, the hall began to echo with the screams of the Dana as he was burned alive.

Zennor covered the space between the giant's legs in three strides, then grasped the unburned straw of the right leg. His hand began to shine and show its bones with that inner energy he could somehow generate when he was irreconcilable. There were apparently advantages to being hopping mad on the other side of the galaxy.

Propulsively Kirk hurried behind him, his own hand hot on his phaser.

Yanking hard on the straw line, Zennor snapped the straw cord at the place where he had burned it. He did this again, then again, gradually chewing his way upward as far as he could reach.

"Bones!" Kirk called. "Climb down! Can you hear me? Follow my voice!"

Through the curtain of boiling smoke he couldn't tell if McCoy were even still conscious.

Continuing to burn and yank, Zennor systematically opened a jagged gash in the straw giant's knee.

"Bones!" Kirk pawed at the smoke. It was hot—getting hotter. Sweat drained down his face and under his uniform shirt.

A hand, human, came out of the smoke, then a blue sleeve dusted with soot and smoldering matter.

Kirk grabbed it and pulled.

Scratched in the face by the rough burning edges that Zennor had broken away, McCoy tumbled out of the straw knee and drove Kirk to the ground. They sprawled into the smoldering twigs.

Feeling the heat burning through his resistant uniform, Kirk rolled to his feet, still holding McCoy's arm, and hauled away.

The doctor came flying out of the kindling and stumbled against the wall. Kirk hauled him up and held him away from the flames. McCoy blinked his watering eyes and grasped his right thigh as if it were hurt, but he was standing on his own. Together they turned and looked.

"Where's—"

"They threw him in there," Kirk said.

Astonishment rocketed across McCoy's face. "My God! He was innocent!"

Zennor followed them away from the straw giant. Now it was burning and the Furies were building to a shrieking frenzy. "Go back the way we came, through the Barrow and into the Ritual Shafts. That area is not shielded and you will be able to beam out. Go now, before they notice."

"I want our files," Kirk attempted corrosively.

For the first time, Zennor reached out and touched him. His hand was a shock of dry cold despite the temperature here and the moisture of the air. "There is no time. I will find them and destroy them. Go away . . . go now!"

Towering over them, the straw giant was now a giant of fire. Black and yellow flame rolled along its arms and coiled in its wide legs. The basic structure had apparently been built to survive until the last minute, so the thing would remain standing while the innards were consumed. Along with whoever they had decided to put in there. How many "criminals" had been disposed of in this way over the past five thousand years?

"My mama always warned me I'd end up here if I wasn't good," McCoy wheezed.

Kirk blinked into the stinging smoke. "Let's go."

"They'll burn their ship. . . ."

Glancing upward at the ceiling, where the smoke was separating into four distinct funnels and being sucked out before it could gather, Kirk told him, "It's venting. They've done this before."

Deeply troubled, he looked at the other leg of the straw man, and saw the outline of the Dana, sketched in flame, and knew he was watching the torture of an innocent person and that he had failed to stop it.

Though he took the doctor's arm, McCoy was unable to resist hovering briefly, just to take in the full sight of a sixty-foot man-shaped inferno, flames going on its arms like rolling pins, and the wild-eyed wraiths rallying and howling around it, thudding their drums. Together they watched the holocaust of the colossus.

McCoy's face glowed. "Captain, this may be the most poignant log entry of your career . . . 'Jim Kirk discovers Hell.' "

It's hard to dance with the Devil on your back.

—"Lord of the Dance,"
a folk song

Chapter Seventeen

"YELLOW ALERT. Mr. Donnier, lay in a direct course back to—Mr. Spock."

Donnier and Byers turned to gaze at him, caught briefly in the concept of laying in a course to the first officer, but that was what being on edge could do to concentration.

Jim Kirk paused on the middle step down toward his command chair, pulled himself back to the upper deck, and moved forward on the starboard side.

"Mr. Spock . . ."

"Captain."

Standing much too straight for comfort, Spock swiveled unevenly on a heel. He looked supremely in place here, living a life before the wind.

For the first time Kirk noticed a dull bruise shading the right side of Spock's face from the bad roll he'd taken on Capella IV. Somehow he hadn't seen that yet.

"Mr. Spock, you haven't been released from sickbay."

"Considering the circumstances, sir," Spock said with undertones, "when you left the ship, I invoked Special

Order Number Four Two Seven, Subsection J-Three, regarding the right of senior officers to override any departmental authority in a crisis."

"There's no such subsection."

"But Nurse Chapel did not know that. And since I am here already, I suggest we not embarrass her."

"As opposed to McCoy's reprimanding her when he finds you gone?"

"Is the doctor all right?"

"A little scorched, and don't change the subject."

Spock nodded, only once and with monkish reserve, being careful of his condition and trying not to move or twist, but he gazed at the deck for a moment, thoughtfully. "I am ineffective in sickbay, sir."

"But you're injured. Patients in sickbay aren't supposed to be effective, Spock. I want you back in recovery. I appreciate your dedication, but you're providing the wrong kind of example. The rest of the crew deserves to know that they're valuable too."

While nothing else would've gotten to Spock, that last bit did. There were some advantages to their knowing each other too well.

He lowered his eyes again and murmured, "Yes, sir, I understand." Then he looked up again as if just remembering. "Sir, did you retrieve the files?"

"No," Kirk sighed, and paced around to the other side of Spock. "It was all we could do to get out of there with our skins. Zennor killed Garamanus."

He felt the guilt rise on his face.

"Indeed," Spock murmured. "To free McCoy?"

"Partly. There was a power play going on. I think it had been going on a long time. Not just the two of them, but everything they both stand for. Now he's got command of the ship *and* possession of the files. I'll just have to trust him."

Almost as he said it, he realized how foolish that was. Wanting to trust someone and actually being able to were entirely different game boards.

He glanced at the helm. "Shields up, Mr. Donnier."

"Shields up, sir."

The turbolift slid open and McCoy hurried in, cranky and agitated, spotted them, and angled toward them, a sling on his right arm and a computer cartridge in his left hand.

"Subsection J, my backside, Mr. Spock," he scolded. "Nurse Chapel is a lot more upset than she deserves to be."

"I apologize for my deception, Doctor, and I will be returning to sickbay."

"Yes, you will be." McCoy handed him the cartridge. "That's all the information I collected on my medical tricorder over in that other ship. Jim, I confirmed everything. The ages of those bone fragments and hair, the biological roots and the planetary origins. There's no doubt about it. Those people had some contact with this quadrant on the order of four to seven thousand years ago."

Conveniently forgetting to remind them that he'd been ordered off the bridge by the only two people who could do that, Spock had turned stiffly to his library computer and inserted the cartridge, and was looking through his sensor hood at the readouts, probably running them through about five times faster than Kirk could've read them.

Kirk couldn't see inside the hood, but he heard the machine whir faintly, or imagined he did.

His movements hampered by pain, Spock slowly straightened and faced them again, his face expressive and heavy with import. He didn't like what he'd seen.

"This is unprecedented. Obviously the track we were on before is far more accurate than we guessed."

"Do you have a conclusion?" Kirk asked.

"I have a hypothesis."

"I'll take it."

"If there was some massive interstellar war roughly five thousand years ago and these people were the losers and they were banished, as Zennor insists, we might postulate that some survivors could have been stranded on Earth, Vulcan, and other planets that supported humanoid life. Beings with 'horns', or 'wings'—"

"Or snakes in their heads," McCoy filled in.

"If these were advanced beings who only wanted to survive," Spock went on, "among the nomadic Klingons, early Terrans, Vulcans, and Orions, and possessed powers unknown to these ancients—for instance, energy weapons, extreme speed, advanced healing techniques—"

Again McCoy interrupted. "Acts which in those days could only be taken as miracles."

"Or sorcery," Spock agreed. "Natural powers taken as supernatural. The 'Furies,' if you will. Trying to escape the mass relocation, they may have hidden on our worlds, and as they lived and died slowly, they floated into our mythos. These refugees may well have been the pathways along which legends have come down to us, and why we feel we 'recognize' them. Their physical traits could easily have been taken as animal parts, skull extensions as antlers or horns, feeding tendrils as snakes, stings for the power to turn people to stone, cooling skins for wings, bony feet for hooves."

"And in the changes of religion on these planets," Kirk uttered, thinking hard, trying to encompass millennia in his concrete mind, "they would have had to be considered. That druid Horned God . . . Zennor's race."

"The Hunter God was ultimately absorbed by Christianity, but they had no place for him in their pantheon. In order to turn the lay public to the new religion, the priests painted him as a devil. Satan."

The bell rang so loudly in Kirk's head that he almost glanced for the red-alert flash.

"This is not guesswork, Captain," Spock said, seeing Kirk's reaction. "We do know this happened." He gazed into his sensor hood briefly. "The woman's household tools were turned into elements of witchcraft when male physicians wanted to take over the healing arts. Now we have the image of the soot-darkened woman flying on a kitchen utensil and casting spells from a cooking pot. In the same way, the Horned God's pitchfork, a symbol of male toil, became associated with devils when Christianity moved him out of their way. These things are relatively easy to track."

McCoy's eyes were wide. "I'll bet the jewelry these people wear is the same kind of thing! All attached to something symbolic. Like those little mirrors."

"To look at the damned." Pacing past them, Kirk rubbed the dozen tiny burns on his knuckles. "Satan . . . wizards . . . witches, druid priests . . . all nothing more than remnants of a war in space during a superstitious time. It's mind-boggling."

Spock shifted his shoulders a little. "Before science and medicine upgraded the quality of daily life, there was little to turn to but superstition, Captain. Unfortunately, these innocent refugees fell victim to that."

Kirk looked at him. "You really believe this?"

"It is not a matter of belief. Long ago, Vulcan was indeed occupied, for a time, by beings we called Ok'San. They resembled the Furies in many ways, and their impact was keenly felt. Many Vulcans retain a distant memory of the turmoil they brought us."

Kirk nodded. "Yes . . . we've also run up on this kind of thing before. We know it's possible. According to Zennor, the losing civilization was banished, unceremoniously dumped on a handful of neighboring planets half the galaxy away. They fell into a dark age, crawled out of it, found each other, fought with each other, then found out they had similar backgrounds and that they'd all been kicked out at the same time. And during that time, we caught up with them technologically."

"And now they're back," McCoy said. "And we're all here together."

Kirk spun to him. "But it wasn't *them!*" He gestured as if to point through the bulkheads of the starship to the huge ship flanking them. "And it certainly wasn't us. The winning civilization is dead and gone, and all its war crimes are gone with it. I refuse to take responsibility for any action by anyone other than myself or my crew, and I only take on the crew's because I'm the commanding officer. We certainly don't owe them anything and they don't deserve to take what's ours. Times change, history moves along. No one is 'owed' by the children of others. This is as silly as if I went back to some corner of Roman Britain and claimed it as my own, because some ancestor of mine owned it a thousand years ago. I don't buy this collective-memory group-rights mind-set."

"We have to accept that Zennor's people do buy it," Spock said. "And that will be our stumbling block. The fixation on having been banished or punished is not a new one. Neither is the link to fire which you both encountered so intimately."

"How astute," McCoy drawled, and rubbed his sore arm.

"The concept of burning the guilty, or the 'damned,'" Spock went on, ignoring him, "has a logical source. 'Gehenna' was a pit outside of Jerusalem where refuse was burned. Parents frequently threatened children with 'sending them to Gehenna' if they failed to behave. Hence the images of flame in a place of punishment. Over the generations on Earth, that image took on names like Orcu, Styx, Aralu, Jahannan, Doom, Hades, Hell . . . and on other planets names such as Kagh'Tragh and Aralua. Even Vulcan had such a concept, though we dropped it generations ago. All involved banishment and punishment."

"If they'd had this on the mountain," McCoy grumbled, "there'd be eleven commandments."

"Captain," Spock cautioned, "although Zennor and his crew have the physical appearance of devils, of 'Furies,' they do not seem to have the inner makings of evil purpose. Legend was obviously written by the winners."

"Saints and demons can be the same," Kirk contemplated, "depending on whether you approve of their work."

He knew the bitterness was coming out in his voice,

but his feelings were boiling to the surface and he didn't feel inclined to push them down. He was beginning to get a picture of what his duty would be, and he didn't like looking at it.

"They're not demons, no matter what they look like. They're just people with a fixed purpose, no different from any others who get their minds stuck on something. Zennor's a decent, forthright captain on a mission and he wants to do the right thing. It's just what I would do if I had those beliefs. And I stood by and let him kill Garamanus, even though I knew Garamanus was on the right track. I should've stopped it."

Spock looked like a boy who'd broken a window with a rock, but wasn't sure whether the building had been condemned yet or not. He watched his captain. "Your devotion to Zennor is most unexpected, sir."

Gazing at the forward screen, Kirk sadly said, "I like him. We have a lot in common."

McCoy put one foot up on the stand of Spock's chair. "Figures you'd get on so well with the Devil."

Crooking that eyebrow, Spock almost smiled. His eyes smiled, at least, and Kirk was flooded with a sense of possibility that blunted the torment of the moment.

"What do I do now?" Kirk considered. "Escort a hostile power into Federation space? Abandon them here to stumble on the truth, then to attack the Klingons? Pretend they wouldn't find us eventually? I'll have to notify Starfleet. Have them standing by."

At this moment he hated his rank. He hated being the watchful renegade of Starfleet, who not only had trouble dropped at his door, but who went chasing when it appeared. He didn't feel as unshatterable as his reputation and now remembered Kellen's expression when the Klingon general had discovered that the great Kirk was as much cautious sentinel as sword swallower.

Kellen had been right about everything all along. So had Garamanus.

He moved between McCoy and Spock, running his hand along the red rail. "I have to talk to him. I have to make him understand, think past that tribal clubfoot he drags around."

"Captain . . ." Spock spoke, but he had no more to say, no way to bewitch logic so it could solve his captain's trouble.

"Come on, Mr. Spock," McCoy said, and took the Vulcan's arm. "It's that time. Back to sickbay. I want you to walk very slowly."

Spock lingered a moment longer, still watching Kirk, still searching for something to say.

In his periphery Kirk saw him, but this time didn't turn, didn't glance. He tucked his chin to bury a shudder. He would provide no excuses for Spock to stay. No more mistakes.

"Captain?"

"Mr. Chekov?" His voice was a croak.

"Reading the Klingon fleet coming into short-range, sir. ETA, thirty minutes, distance—"

The bridge went up on an edge as if it had been kicked from under the port side. Sirens blared; red alert came on automatically, changing the lights on all the panels for emergency readings in case the main power wobbled. Kirk slammed sideways and barely missed crushing Lieutenant Nordstrom at the communications station, where she was hanging over her console, pressed to the board by the impact.

He skidded past her and caught himself on the aft science board, bending his back painfully over the edge and holding himself by his fingernails on the rubberized edge. One foot came up off the floor. Around him the bridge flashed to black and white as the lighting blinked, searching for conduits that hadn't been ruptured. The surreal forms of Spock and McCoy were crushed up against the side of the turbolift doorway.

For a moment he couldn't turn his head. Artificial gravity was being compromised by impact or energy flush and he heard the systems yowl, but couldn't react. Any moment—

His arms and legs lightened abruptly and he shoved

himself off the console. He pushed Nordstrom back into her chair and told her, "All decks clear for action."

"Aye, sir!" she said on a rushing breath.

Stepping around her, he caught both Spock's arm and McCoy's good arm and provided leverage as McCoy got to his feet; then they both pulled Spock up and held him through the clutch of pain until he gained some control.

"Over here." Kirk drew them to the science station and brought Spock to his chair. "Sit down." As Spock valiantly reached for his sensor controls, Kirk dropped to the command deck and glanced at the helm. "Mr. Byers, visual checks."

Byers nodded and punched his controls, looked at them, then punched some more.

Several of the auxiliary monitors lining the upper bridge flickered on, snatching power from other systems long enough to do their jobs, to show scenes of open space around the starship, including, off the port beam, the enormous purple plates of the Fury ship.

"Put our forward shields to him, Mr. Byers."

Again Byers didn't manage to respond, but only complied.

The plates still glowed with expended energy. No need to ask what had happened.

"Hail him." Kirk braced himself.

"Channel open, sir," Nordstrom offered.

"Kirk to Zennor. Please come in."

He was as cold as a beached carp. His hands scarcely had any feeling. He knew what was coming and that there was no way to backpedal.

Nordstrom's wide Scandinavian features buckled as she touched her earpiece. "Channel's still open, sir. He's hearing you."

He took her at her word. Drawing closer to his command chair as if closer to Zennor, he spoke again. "You looked at the files."

Moments passed with not so much as a crackle on the comm. He waited. The bridge around him was dim now, some lights still flickering, trying to come back on. The whir of ventilators told him there was a gaseous leak somewhere and compensation systems had come on. The ship would take care of herself to some degree—

"I looked."

A glint of solid chance rang through with the sound of Zennor's deep voice.

"We have to talk about this," Kirk attempted. He almost winced. His sentence sounded hollow and pointless.

"There is no talk. I was wrong. The Danai were right all along. Garamanus was right. This is what he was trying to say when I ruined him. Now I must take on his purpose. He picked the right place, and I will reclaim it in his name."

The fabric of this tenuous peace was ancient and crumbling. Kirk felt it shred in his fingers.

"He wasn't right," he insisted. "You still believe the things you told me, don't you?"

"I was right only when I told you that people don't change. You are the conqueror."

"You know that's not true. The past doesn't matter."

"The past is all that matters."

Gazing at the slowly turning alien ship on the forward screen, Kirk gripped his chair. "We're friends. We're alike. Isn't that a better foundation than what you're talking about?"

He waited. Nothing came back.

No one on the bridge moved. The alarms and alerts seemed to get quieter in anticipation.

"You knew about this." Zennor's words were heavier even than the usual sound of his voice now, and the personal wounding came through. *"Is this how your people wrecked our civilization before? With trust as a weapon?"*

"No," Kirk said desperately. "Those mistakes were mine alone, not my culture's. Think . . . think! Be rational for one more moment. No one has any right to a particular piece of space. You have the right to live as free beings in our society. Our hand of friendship is still extended. Don't knock it away."

In the corner of his eye he saw McCoy step slowly down to the center deck and join him on the other side of the command chair, providing what moral support he could and trying nobly to join him in the responsibility for what had happened. Now the two of them had something more in common than they'd ever wanted.

McCoy moved forward a little and was about to say something when the comm boomed again.

"Go to your civilization and tell them to get out."

Kirk blinked at the screen.

Aggravated, he allowed himself a dirty expression. "You want me to tell a trillion and a quarter people . . . to pack up and move?"

"That is what you told us."

The statement burned, for it had its strange ring of truth, at least truth as Zennor saw things.

"It wasn't us," Kirk abridged. "No one alive had anything to do with what happened to your ancestors. My offer stands. Come with us and be welcome in the Federation. But you'll have to shed your attachment to the past."

He waited for the threadlike moment of communication to crack, but instead there was only another stretch of silence. This time he wasn't going to wait.

"Zennor."

When had this happened? At which moment had the career, the job, the duty become his veins and the blood flowing into them? When had the desire to drive a ship and do some good turned into responsibility for the whole Federation's well-being?

He'd crawled out of a rocky youth, or been kicked, gone into Starfleet, where everyone insisted on conformity yet gave him medals for fire eating. He'd innovated, he'd survived, he'd swallowed fire, and they'd pinned awards on him and handed him a few hundred other lives and a ship with which to execute his appetite upon the galaxy.

All for this?

Yes, exactly this.

"Zennor, answer me."

His answer came, but not in the form he desired.

"Captain—" Spock stared at his readouts, then turned his chair until he could look at the main screen without moving his head too much. "Something is happening in space. A fissure is opening. Reading a large solid object moving through. Coming toward us."

Kirk pushed forward, stepped up onto the platform and stood in front of his command chair. "Dimensions."

"Are . . . roughly seven hundred thousand metric tons. . . . Size . . . is . . . reading out at more than . . ."

Even Spock couldn't keep the astonishment out of his voice.

"Length overall is in excess of one thousand meters, sir."

Sweat broke out on Kirk's face. "On visual." Nothing happened, and he was forced to snap, "Mr. Byers, forward visual."

The big main screen dropped the image of Zennor's purple and black pinecone and caught a wide view of space in time to see a bizarre gash in the blackness of space, as if someone had come along with a giant cleaver and taken a random hack. Out of the gash spilled liquid blue light, and from within the light came a vessel.

More than half a mile long, a thousand feet tall, shaped like Zennor's ship, the enormous moving corkscrew twisted itself through the gash in space, and when it was through the gash sealed up with a snap that made everyone blink.

"Any drop in mass?" Kirk quickly asked.

"None," Spock said. "They must have solved that."

As they watched, the giant vessel screwed itself through open space toward Zennor's ship, and with skilled excellence the two came bow-to-stern and executed a flawless docking maneuver. Now Zennor's ship provided only the forward section of what had become a mammoth vessel.

Burning with the knowledge that his ugly guess had been right, Kirk looked upon the greatest assault vehicle he had ever seen. If its power matched its size, there would be disaster today.

McCoy backed off to the ship's rail, apparently sensing that this wasn't the time to be hanging on the captain's chair, disturbing the bubble that was the command sphere. Kirk sensed the change without looking. He'd noticed that since the beginning of his career—the more tense the situation, the more the crew tended to keep distance, giving the officers room to think. He'd come to use that as a jump-start for dangerous thinking, a kind of personal red alert. He wished his head weren't throbbing.

He didn't really care if the crew saw him wince. Maybe in a few minutes he would, if they lived.

"Emergency alert, all decks," he said. "We're about to do battle with the damned. And they have nothing to lose."

Your foes are determined, relentless, and nigh.

—"Lock the Door, Larrison,"
a folk song

Chapter Eighteen

"SOUND GENERAL QUARTERS."

He'd held off saying it, but the order was overdue. Hope had kept it back until now.

"Battle stations . . . all hands to battle stations. This is not a drill. . . . Secure all positions. . . . Damage-control parties on standby."

"Mr. Byers, veer us off to maximum phaser range. I don't want to take another of those hard punches at close range. Get me some room to maneuver."

"Yes, sir . . . maximum phaser range, sir."

"Mr. Spock, any other contacts from behind that fissure?"

"None, sir. They may regard their combined vessel as some kind of dreadnought. In fact, there is no sign of the fissure any longer at all."

"We know what kind of power it takes to open it," Kirk uttered, more to himself than anyone else. "Practically have to float a black hole in here just to open the door."

He should send Spock below while he had the chance, he knew. An inner alert stopped him. He noticed, though, that McCoy wasn't saying anything. Spock would be little better off being tossed about on the way down to sickbay than here at his post, where all people with spinal injuries should be, of course.

Kirk understood them both. He even understood himself this time.

He settled into his command chair and forced himself to steady down.

"Secure the ship. Shut down any nonemergency emissions. Short-range sensors on priority. Impulse engines prepare for tight maneuvering. Warp speed on standby. Arm phasers. And someone get me a cup of coffee."

"Nonemergency emissions, aye. Short-range sensors ready, sir."

"Impulse engines answering, sir."

"Phasers armed and ready, sir."

"Warp engines ready and standing by, sir."

"Cup of coffee, aye, sir."

The parroting back of his orders was reassuring and bolstered him. Underlying energy swung around the bridge from person to person, and through the ship like blood pumping.

"Photon guidance on standby," he added, and Chekov said it back almost immediately. Settling back in his chair, with the cool leather pressing to his lower back and reminding him of lingering aches from Capella IV, he surveyed the forward screen and the now-huge vessel that was at a notable distance now that the starship was moving back. "How close is the Klingon fleet now?"

"ETA fourteen minutes, Captain," Chekov reported. He'd been ready for that.

"Hail General Kellen."

"Go ahead, sir," Nordstrom said. "Channels open."

"General Kellen, this is Captain Kirk."

"I know what you think you are. I suggest you not attempt to stop us again. I have my fleet now. Ten battle cruisers. I am officially revoking your privilege to be in Klingon space. Go home. This is man's work."

"You also have my cooperation. And my apology. You were correct about these people's ancestry."

"Hah."

"I'm not saying you're right about the mythology and I don't believe in the thing you call Havoc. But there does seem to be an inescapable connection between them and this side of the galaxy."

"Thank you. Get out of my way."

"I will not get out of your way," Kirk blistered. "I *will* deal with this if you and your fleet will cooperate."

There was a pause, and he recognized it as the kind of pause a commander takes when he's weighing his options and trying not to give any away.

"What do you want?"

Respect for Kellen boosted a few degrees. He wasn't throwing the kettle out with the stew just because he had been disappointed before.

Kirk indulged in a pause of his own and let Kellen guess for a moment or two.

Then he said, "I want all of us to provide a united front and make them think twice about their intents."

"Against them? You're going to fight?"

"Only as a last resort. I want to back them down only enough to give me a chance to talk to Zennor."

"Talking again."

"Yes, talking. I want a chance to explain some historical data to him, without all this . . . fury."

How well the word fit.

Before him on the screen was a ship full of household spirits, glen nymphs, tikis, banshees and zombies, werewolves and medusas, none hellborn as legend had rattled down, but only a crew of Ishmaels. That wasn't hell over there, but another starship, crewed by expatriates with an ill-considered dream.

Still a dream, though. He didn't wish to wreck it, but only to redirect it. So much energy, a whole civilization and all its past for four thousand years, so much worth and resolve, if he could have the time to make them understand—

"No more talking," Kellen broadcast. *"This is Klingon space. You will stand aside."*

Gazing in unexpected longing at the purple scales of Zennor's now-vast ship, Kirk glanced at the upper starboard screens and noted the visual picture of the approach of ten full-sized Klingon battle cruisers, flanked by more than a dozen lighter-weight patrol cruisers. There weren't many overt differences between the two classes of ships—the difference was more one of hull weight and firepower—but to the trained eye, and Kirk had one, the difference demanded consideration.

"Hail Zennor again, Lieutenant," he crabbed.

Nordstrom's console beeped behind him, like pins going into his scalp. Went silent. Beeped again.

"No response, sir. He's closed his frequencies."

"Ship to ship."

"Go ahead, sir."

With a bitter hunch of his shoulders, Kirk leaned on his chair's arm, pursed his lips, and felt his eyes burn. "Very well, General. Both of you can have it your way. Be advised we're moving off. Mr. Byers, clear the way for the Klingon fleet to make their own maneuver against the Fury ship."

Byers glanced at him, emotions crashing across his round face. "Moving off, sir."

The Klingon fleet made no attempt to contact or warn off Zennor's invasion ship. They came in fast and firing, patrol cruisers rushing in first, with obvious intent simply to blast the invaders out of Klingon skies, or anybody else's sky. Kellen's determination had infected the fleet, and clearly they meant to be sure this threat would not exist after today, here or anywhere. They weren't going to leave enough of that vessel to limp into Federation sanctuary, only to come back at them later.

Kirk might've been reading too much into what he saw on the screen, but the sensations ran hot in his instincts and he didn't think he was misinterpreting much.

The patrollers led the way, strafing the closed purple

petals on the Fury ship, trying to punch weak points in the hull where the heavier goosenecked cruisers could then inflict deep wounds. The hematite blackness of space erupted into waves of disruptor fire, sheeting off the Fury ship's cornucopia hull as fluidly as water.

The resulting glow of released energy as it flooded into space made him glad he had moved off to observance range. Even from here he could see the quick, maneuverable Klingon patrollers rocking in the waves of backwash, wobbling like seagulls.

"Effectiveness?" His hands were clenching and unclenching.

"None readable." Spock bent forward, leaning on one hand and hanging on to the sensor hood with the other. He had stood up when Kirk wasn't looking. "I suspect Zennor's dreadnought is swallowing the power wash somehow. It is accepting the impact, then absorbing the energy as it attempts to dissipate. Possibly back into their own power wells."

"You mean Kellen's doing them a favor by firing on them?"

Spock nodded. "We may not have the capacity present to overload Zennor's ability to absorb the punishment."

"Could it do the same to phaser and photon energy?"

"No way to judge that." The Vulcan glanced at him. "Likely, though. To devise such an ability, they must have a remarkably resilient and adaptive culture."

"They had to be." Peering at the screen as if he were about to do surgery, Kirk mumbled, "Better do something else, then."

At the forward science station, Chekov straightened suddenly. "Sir, the general's heavy cruisers are moving in!"

"Which is the general's ship?"

The young man pointed at the main screen, lower starboard. "He was broadcasting from the ship with the yellow ensign, sir."

Kirk squinted.

On the screen, flooding past them at proximity range,

growing suddenly out of the edges of the screen, came the elegantly massive Klingon war cruisers, with their hulls of brushed silver, forms not so swanlike as the *Enterprise,* but instead mindful of the in-flight silhouettes of cranes on a dark horizon. Their necks outstretched with sensor bulbs chewing at space before them, they flowed past the starship on a rendezvous with General Kellen's version of foresight.

And there, on the right, was Kellen's own ship, banded with a yellow collar for identification over and above the other vessels, so everyone would know where the fleet leader was. Klingons didn't believe in protecting their leaders.

As soon as they reached short range they opened fire. There was no approach strategy—they simply plowed in, blasting away. The dozen patrollers vectored off, then swung around in circles, up, down, and at angles, buzzing about the attack scene and shooting whenever they had clearance.

Space lit up in a holiday light show, flash upon flash of bright blue-green energy, and there was so little damage on Zennor's dreadnought that the scene was nearly entertaining. Kirk felt detached, drugged with fascination and regret, as he watched the patrollers zag about the huge purple ship, having less effect than sparrows smashing into a brick wall.

He pushed out of his chair. Moving toward Spock, he hung an arm over the rail and kept his voice down. "Energy weapons seem to be about as useful as a waxed deck."

"Zennor's technology has found a way to negate enemy fire by absorbing it." Spock kept one hand on the sensor hood, bracing his weak back. "His claims were apparently not bravado. The ship is very strong. He has not even returned fire yet. . . .

"If, as I suspected, Zennor's ship has some way of not only funneling down the enemy fire, but drawing upon it . . . he may be taking the opportunity to build power while draining the Klingons'."

Kirk turned to Nordstrom. "Lieutenant, ship to ship with General Kellen."

"Yes, sir. Ready."

"General, this is Kirk. Be aware your shots are being absorbed somehow by Zennor's ship. We think you're providing him with energy to fight you."

"Mind your own business."

Shaking his head, Kirk pushed off the rail and went back to his chair, but didn't sit. "You're welcome. Lieutenant, keep the channels open."

"Channels open, sir."

McCoy joined him there. "One tribe fighting another tribe. And why? Because they're tribes. It's a sorry sight."

"Your civilization depends on how much you suppress the savage," Kirk told him. "They're giving in to it instead."

"We all have our inner demons. Just think of all the conflicts and stories and threats coming to a head today, right out there. All the childhood nightmares and confession-box repentances . . . it boggles the mind. Makes me want to study my history files a little more often. Just for the hell of it."

Kirk snapped him a fierce look. "Are you doing that on purpose?"

His pique pinned the conversation to the deck and the only thing that saved McCoy was Yeoman Tamamura appearing in the turbolift with the captain's tray and several cups of coffee.

"Sir," she greeted, but she was glancing at the action on the screen and almost dumped the tray onto the captain's chair. She recovered in mid-slosh, handed the captain his cup, then offered one to McCoy.

"Do we get popcorn too?" The doctor looked up, not at the yeoman, but at Kirk.

Over the open channels in the background, communication between Kellen and the other ship crackled as the captains and their helms coordinated an attack that was clumsy at best, but in essence the clumsiness didn't matter. They kept opening hard fire, but the disruption kept having no effect, just sheeting down the folded petals of the Fury ship and somehow being funneled away without cracking that scaly armor.

Petals . . . petals . . . scales . . .

He'd done and felt this many times before, yet each time the tapestry was different. The lives were the same, but not a thing else. No training scenario could anticipate the real thing, with dozens of minds working independently, and passions flying wild.

He flinched as an explosion on the upper left corner of the screen took him by surprise, and his mind was instantly back on the choreography of the battle.

The bridge crew flinched at the stabbing light and didn't even have time to shield their eyes. When the light faded, there was nothing left but tumbling hull plates, motes of smoke, and a forest fire of sparks. Gases and remnant plasma from the disseminated bowels of the cruiser spun through space, burning themselves away without purpose, with nothing left to push on.

A full-sized Klingon cruiser—gone!

"What happened?" Byers stammered.

Ensign Chekov gawked at the screen. "Sir, did they self-destruct?"

Realizing he too was staring like a struck midshipman, Kirk didn't bother to mask his surprise. "Mr. Spock?"

But even Spock frowned at the scene. "I . . . suppose they may have sacrificed shield power for disruptors. . . . Perhaps they did not have time, or forgot, to divert power back to their deflectors." He turned to his sensor hood, determined to depend on the witness of science instead of guessing. After a moment he reported, "Zennor apparently opened fire, Captain. Reading the same kind of energy flush signature as when we and Zennor engaged the Klingons earlier. Much stronger now, however. One Klingon battleship has exploded . . . a direct hit. Complete thermal compromise. They must have been hit squarely in the warp core. No survivors noted as yet."

"Pretty sore price for a mistake." Aware of his crew's glances, Kirk tried to be casual. He hadn't even seen the Fury ship fire. It must have happened while one of the other Klingon ships was masking the view. "Keep your eyes open, everyone. I don't want to miss another change. Keep the short-range sensors sweeping for life-pods, Mr. Chekov."

"Yes, sir," Chekov answered.

Spock's face was blue with sensor light, and he squinted as he spoke. "Residual energy is nominal . . . dissipating. No solid objects larger than point-five-three meters. No possible survivors."

Annoyed, Kirk peered from the corner of his eye. "Keep scanning anyway, Mr. Chekov."

"Aye, sir."

"There they go!" Donnier grasped the navigation console with both hands and held on.

The nine remaining Klingon battle cruisers moved in, using a dependable hourglass formation. Four ships came in, firing hard, then bore downward; then two more came in, separated, and strafed the flanks of the pinecone-shaped hull; then the last three, making a triangle around the enemy as they roared from the Fury ship bow to its stern, grazing the purple scales with full disruptor fire all the way.

Space before the *Enterprise* was no longer black, but made up of plumes of electric blue and sargasso green.

As the last wave of cruisers seared by, the Fury ship opened fire again. Lavender and yellow spirals of energy built along the half-mile-tall stern of the dreadnought, screwed down the body of the ship as pretty as anything, then went out from the ship like sound waves to engulf the passing Klingon fleet.

"Wow!" Donnier gasped. He rocked back in his chair and his hands fell onto his lap.

That pretty much summed up the expressions Kirk saw in his periphery.

The nearest three Klingon cruisers were knocked straight sideways—and no ship was ever meant to take that. They squalled off, spewing mare's tails of expelled gas and tumbling hot wreckage. Scorched bits of fragmented hull material rolled through space and splattered on the starship's shields.

Kirk and his bridge crew bit a collective lip at the sight. Those crews must be flying around inside there like so much trash in a tumbler. Artificial gravity would be screaming. Kirk could hear the bones breaking. Their propulsion systems were buckling. He could see it from here.

What a punch Zennor packed with that combined ship.

And not a word from him. Despite their dramatic manner and archaic speech patterns, Zennor and his people evidently hadn't come here to make speeches.

"Condition of the Klingon ships," he requested.

Spock studied his readouts. "Two ships veering off, both venting plasma. One is adrift . . . being tractored out of range by two patrol cruisers. Another is emitting spotty motive ratios, but is limping away under its own power. . . . The others are regrouping and coming back in." He paused again, then cleared his throat and added, "General Kellen's ship is shutting down partial life-support, but is not veering off."

"Thank you. Mr. Spock, sure you're all right?"

Spock looked at him as though threatened. "For the moment, Captain."

Might or might not be true. Spock was smart. He knew a hollow reassurance that he was just dandy would probably result in his being kicked below. Telling a hazy version of the truth, that he was suffering some, had a different effect and implied that he would speak up when he couldn't handle it anymore.

He probably wouldn't.

Feeling McCoy's dagger gaze from the port side of his command deck, Kirk deliberately didn't look over there. Gripping his chair as if holding himself to the concrete presence of the chair and the deck, he watched the Klingon fleet as it was casually smashed.

"Lieutenant Nordstrom, contact the flight deck and sickbay. Deploy four pilots and two interns in two shuttlecraft to retrieve lifepods and treat survivors. Instruct them to stay at safe distance until the engagement is over, and to make their reports to Mr. Chekov."

"Understood, sir," Nordstrom responded, and turned to her board.

"Sir!" Chekov bolted straight and looked at the screen, but there was no time for him to say anything more.

Turning its hornlike tip to meet the remaining Klingon ships, the Fury ship turned violent with yellow and thistle-purple electrical weapons that buzz-sawed through the Klingon approach. Amazing that such a knightly color as purple and all its florid shades could be made so bitterly deadly.

Before their eyes three more Klingon cruisers had their approach-side wings shorn off and were forced to drag themselves away, or be dragged, their structural balance sliced apart as if they had been caught in a bear trap. The ship from hell was a hell of a ship.

The main force of the Klingon battle fleet, crippled in minutes?

It was unthinkable.

"My God!" McCoy croaked. "All of them at once . . . Jim, Kellen's ship!"

The remaining Klingon vessel, the general's ship had turned up on a wingtip and was tilting drunkenly across space toward the midsection of the Fury vessel. The Klingon ships were very heavy, long-bodied, almost as heavy and long as the *Enterprise,* and a little better balanced. To see one skidding on an edge like this, rolling off its line of gravity and shrunken to toy proportions as it rolled nearer and nearer to the enormous modified *Rath,* shook the bridge crew for a few critical seconds.

Byers came halfway out of his seat. "It's going to collide!"

Chapter Nineteen

AS A MAN STEPS onto a guillotine ramp, Jim Kirk stepped onto the platform that held his command chair, slid onto the edge of the black leather seat, and spoke quickly so that his crew would move quickly.

"Mr. Spock, condition of the general's ship?"

"Impulse drive is off-line. They are helpless."

"How much of a pounding can we take?"

"Unknown." Spock swiveled his chair around to meet Kirk's eyes. "May I ask why, sir?"

"Because I'm going to move her in at close range."

At the helm, Byers turned and his eyes got big. "Sir?"

Kirk ignored the question. "Ahead one-quarter impulse, Mr. Byers. Mr. Donnier, ready with tractor beams."

"One-quarter impulse, aye."

"Tractor beams r-ready, sir."

"Full magnification on Kellen's ship."

The *Enterprise* leaped forward with breathtaking ferocity, as hungry to get into the cockfight as her captain was. The ship was different in battle mode than cruising mode, all systems warmed up, on-line, backed up, humming . . . maybe she actually did jump. Maybe it wasn't just imagination.

Patrol cruisers zigzagged in and out of the screen as the starship approached the scene of intensity. On the screen was a huge magnified picture of Kellen's cruiser sliding toward the sharp edges of the Fury ship's five-hundred-foot-wide scales. Kellen's disabled ship was still shooting, though it drifted at a nauseating pitch toward the *Rath,* making a last-ditch attempt to do the impossible.

The aft scales on the Fury ship were the largest ones, and Kellen's ship was sliding toward the big vessel's aft starboard quarter. Only now did Kirk get a full perspective of just how large Zennor's ship had become, with that vast new section added on.

What was in that section? Was that the power base?

"Mr. Spock, where's the emission center of those energy spirals? See if you can zero in on it."

Without answering, Spock lowered gingerly into his chair, ran his fingers over his controls.

Kirk waved over his shoulder for Nordstrom's attention. "Send Starfleet a recording of what we've seen so far. Do it right away."

"Deploying, sir." A crack came out in her voice. She was getting scared.

"Tractor proximity, Captain," Donnier struggled.

"Get it on, Mr. Donnier, don't wait for orders when you know what to do. Keep Kellen from colliding into that ship."

"Aye, s-s—" Donnier didn't get the response out, but he did get the tractor beam on.

The starship hauled back on the tractor beams and Kellen's drifting ship drew up sharply just as its sagging starboard wing grazed the edge of a purple scale that would've cleaved it in half.

"Power astern," Kirk ordered at the right instant.

"Astern." Byers was hypnotized.

Kirk leaned forward. "Let's go, move . . . don't baby her, Mr. Byers. Throttle up."

He wasn't watching the Klingon ship being drawn away from the *Rath*. He was watching the *Rath*.

Would Zennor fire on him?

"Position of the Klingon fleet."

The ensign shook himself and bent over his sensors. "Eight vessels . . . three completely disabled . . . one more moving at less than one-quarter power . . . four others regrouping."

"They actually retreated," McCoy observed. "After just a few minutes."

"How many patrollers left?" Kirk asked.

Chekov squinted into his screen. "Six . . . seven still functional, sir."

Looking blanched and strained, Spock pressed his wrist to the edge of his console and paused to look at the screen. "A great deal of damage with very few shots."

"Unless we find weakness, we can't deal with that ship under these conditions," Kirk agreed. "Bring her midships, Mr. Byers. Back straight off. I want my intentions clear."

"Aye aye, sir." Byers licked his lips as he worked to equalize the helm while hauling the Klingon vessel, whose damaged systems were still trying to propel it along its last ordered course.

If Kellen would shut down, this would be a lot easier.

"Pull, Byers. Faster."

"Trying, sir, but there's some kind of resistance."

"Yes, the cruiser's automatic drive—"

The petals of the *Rath,* filling the screen like huge theatrical flats, began to glow with that sickly yellow-lavender electrical presence.

Kirk drew a breath. "Uh-oh . . . double shields! Brace yourselves!"

He turned to say something to Nordstrom, but suddenly the ship heaved up as if in recoil and the night opened up with purple dragons, cutting a blazing wave across the primary hull and straight through the bridge, throwing the captain and the standing crew to the deck in a tangle.

"Overload!" Assistant Engineer Edwards shouted, the first time since coming on the bridge that he'd said anything at all.

Byers shielded his face from sparks launching from his console, then waved at the smoke and shouted at the screen.

"They fired on us! They fired on us right in the middle of a rescue maneuver!"

Smoke boiled across the bridge. Ventilators came on and sucked valiantly. Somehow the onrush of near-death had shaken Byers out of his timidity and made him mad.

Good.

Generally, those two, Byers and Donnier, would be nowhere near the bridge, yet they'd rallied here today, under adverse conditions. Ordinarily in battle Kirk preferred to have his senior crew there, Sulu and Chekov, or Sulu and another navigation specialist, but Sulu was down, Chekov was helping Spock, and Donnier had just caught the bad luck of the draw.

Donnier and Byers would be able to claim having served in the best crew in Starfleet—yes, they were the best, but they were the best at their own specific jobs. Nobody could be the "best" when thrown into somebody else's job. Almost anyone could fake it at the technicals of another position, but there would always be a loss of art. Kirk knew that he could bull and cackle his way around engineering, but that Scott would be a far better captain than Kirk would ever be an engineer. That was why people had specialties, and why the *Enterprise* was staffed with specialists. The *art* of the technology.

That was also what they needed today. A little creative art among the technical business. A little sorcery . . .

Kirk waved at the smoke, motioned McCoy back against the rail so he had something solid to hold on to, and spoke past him to the engineering station, though he couldn't see through the gushing smoke.

"Compensate," he authorized.

"There's a burnout on the crystal triodes, sir."

That was Nordstrom, but it came from the engineering

area. She was either helping Edwards or replacing him, if he was down. The curtain of smoke went from the ceiling to the upper deck carpet.

"Compensating," Donnier called from the starboard side, up where Chekov had been. Unable to cough up much volume, he spoke from the science subsystems station, leaving Byers to handle helm and weapons.

Was Chekov down?

Kirk flogged himself for not thinking to overstaff the bridge. With Sulu down, he should've called an all-hands, summoned the main watch, and just let it be a little crowded up here.

Violent lights, shadows, and sparks argued all around and hadn't settled when Zennor's ship turned loose another whipcrack of purple fire.

"Full astern! Byers! Byers!"

He plunged for the helm console, found the chair empty, poked through the smoke for the motive action menu and forced his fingers to tap the impulse generation up to full power.

"Power's wobbly, sir," Edwards reported innocently, as if he didn't notice the ship being pummeled around him.

"We've got to move off. Mr. Scott'll find the power."

The starship bolted again and his stomach went with her. The deck groaned as if in convulsion beneath his hands. A piece of the hull screamed past his face and he swore it grazed him, but it was gone before he could raise a hand to fend it off. The carpet and the deck beneath it slammed him hard and drove his knees into the side of his chair. The chair swiveled and he couldn't hang on. He sprawled to the deck.

Splinters whistled past his ears and speared his shoulders. He buried his head for an instant until the whistling bore off, then grabbed for the sky and caught part of the helm. He dragged himself to one knee, finally to both, and was about to cheer his accomplishment when he made the fatal error of looking up to scan the damage.

He saw Engineer Edwards' red and black form propelled sideways by a vicious eruption at the port console, slam into the bridge rail, and collapse to the deck.

The purple and sulfur twine of energy shined again on the main screen. Zennor's ship basted near-space with another razor of energy, and over Kirk's head—the ceiling exploded.

Chapter Twenty

JIM KIRK waved at the smoke as it piled before him and stung his eyes. Was the tractor beam holding? He couldn't see the forward screen.

He grabbed for the foggy shape of his chair and hit the comm. "Scotty, bridge!"

"Scott here."

"Trouble."

"See it, sir."

"Put everything to the shields and tractor beams. Reduce life-support if you have to, but keep those shields up."

"No priority to the weapons, sir?"

"We can't punch through those hull plates. Just keep the shields up."

"I like it, sir."

"I thought you would, Mr. Scott." He wheeled away, toward starboard. "Mr. Spock?"

From the anterior glow of emergency lights, the blue-blacks of Spock appeared out of the smoldering fabric of the bridge. "Here, Captain."

"Where's Mr. Chekov?"

"On the deck, sir."

"Hurt?" He squinted into the rolling smoke near the service trunks.

"No, sir," Chekov called, looking up from between his arms, which disappeared past the elbows inside one of the trunks. "Radiation wash in the bypass conduits, sir." He stumbled across the English syllables as though he believed he was speaking Russian.

Kirk turned, and realized the deck was at an angle. "Are the tractor beams still on? Mr. Donnier, where are you?"

"Here, sir!" Donnier dodged under a puff of sparks near the main screen trunk and landed on both feet.

"Take over assisting Mr. Spock while Mr. Chekov effects repairs. Lieutenant Nordstrom, take navigation and weapons. You're going to have to learn to shoot."

"Coming, sir!"

"Somebody have relief personnel sent to the bridge."

"I'll do it, Captain," McCoy called from the boiling gray mist. "Relief personnel to the bridge. Repeat, relief to the bridge, all stations!"

At once he realized they were all shouting. What was all this noise they were shouting over? The red-alert klaxon was howling, yes, and that god-awful whistle—must be a hull breach somewhere up in the damaged ceiling.

Somebody would pick up on it. Until it was sealed, atmosphere would pour out in a bitter silver funnel into the ice cold of space, and compensators would pump more and more into the bridge so they could keep breathing. The ship was exhaling herself to death to keep them alive and she'd go down to the last quarter centimeter of reserve oxygen before she gave up. She'd sacrifice deck after deck, hoping her crew heard the warnings and evacuated in time. If they didn't, they'd die there while she tried to save the rest of the crew, until failsafe made it all the way to the bridge. The bridge would be the last to be sacrificed. She'd steal from her own guts if that would work.

And it just might. It would buy them time. The bridge had to breathe if the ship was to be saved.

The turbolift wheezed two-thirds open, then jammed. Four bridge relief crewmen poured out, followed by three men in atmospheric suits. One of those carried a collapsible ladder. They went to work on the sparking ceiling while the relief crew dropped into appropriate positions.

Byers was back at the helm. Kirk had no idea what had happened to him, if he'd been knocked silly, if he'd frozen with fear, or what. He was back now.

Two medical orderlies dropped at Edwards' sides while relief personnel manned the engineering stations. Kirk hadn't seen the medics come out of the lift, but then he hadn't paid much attention.

The pair checked Edwards' vitals, then scooped him up and carried him to the lift. The lift wasn't happy about having to close that jammed door and protested with a metallic screech, but then that was done.

"Course, sir?" Byers asked.

"Away from the big ship any way you can do it, Mr. Byers. Ensign, how are you doing on that radiation wash?"

"I think I have a formula, sir," Chekov called as the ship bucked and whined again.

He cursed himself for his trust, his hope. Zennor had lashed out with no sign of regret or hesitation, and with a greater punch than Kirk would've bet on. He'd hoped to maneuver out of the trap, and now he had to fight his way out. He hunched his shoulders and glared at the screen.

"Magnification point five," he called over the whistle of the fans.

Ventilators had cleared the bridge of about sixty percent of the smoke, and he could see the action on the forward screen as it backed off its zoom view. He saw the tractor beams still holding Kellen's crippled ship, and he saw most of Zennor's huge *Rath*.

He also saw the Klingon fleet moving in again.

"Ship to ship, General Kellen," he said. But no one was at the communications console. He looked around and found McCoy hovering at the starboard steps. "Bones, get back up there and stay there."

"Oh—sorry." The doctor tucked his injured arm against his side and pulled himself back up the tilted deck to the communications station. "Ship to ship . . ." he muttered as he poked at the controls. "I think this is it. Try it."

"General," Kirk spoke up, "call off your ships."

"Fire! Fire, you coward! My weapons are down! Fire at them!"

"I'm telling you, the disruptor fire is providing power to Zennor and he's hitting us with it. Tell your ships to back off and save their energy. I need time to tow you out of here."

"Thank you for the tow. Now mind your own business."

"All right, but at least shut down your thrusters so we can get out of here. Your ship is providing resistance."

There was no response at all this time.

"General! Damn it." He motioned for McCoy to cut off the communication. Like the patrollers, he was knocking his head against the same kind of brick wall.

"Captain!" Byers called.

Kirk looked at the forward screen again in time to see four scorched patrollers soar past the *Enterprise* and viciously strafe the *Rath,* looking completely ridiculous in their total ineffectiveness. The energy they deployed simply washed down the cone-shaped hull and disappeared inside somehow. Damn it, damn it, damn it.

Zennor's ship glowed in retaliation, and Kirk braced to take another hit, but this one shot out in bright rings right where the patrollers were passing and selectively hit them. So the weapons were directional as well as area-wide—either that, or Zennor and his crew were learning as they fought.

"Shouldn't we return fire, Jim?" McCoy asked, sensing the starship would be next. "Isn't there some way?"

"It's a waste of effort. There has to be a weakness."

"I hope you find it."

"I hope so too."

He stepped to the bridge rail, and only now realized he was limping—his hip was hurting. He must've struck it on an edge when he fell. He reached up for McCoy to take his forearm and hoist him out of the center of the command deck, giving the repair crew more room to maneuver as they climbed about inside the ceiling like squirrels in an attic.

Byers ducked out of the way as much as he could, but somehow managed to do it without taking his hands off the helm, shuffling around in front of the console while repair work was done above him.

The repair crew went about their business with a zeal that suggested they were enjoying the terror, for it gave them something to do. Within a couple of minutes, the loud wheezing was reduced to a sorry whistle, then finally to nothing, and the hull breach was sealed.

The ship sighed with relief. Everything suddenly became quiet, as if to feign that nothing was happening.

Between Spock and McCoy, Kirk watched the Klingon patrollers being basted by the *Rath*'s selective hits. The patrollers shuddered and veered off, but one of them veered in the wrong direction.

"It's gonna hit!" Byers gulped, only an instant before impact.

The patroller decimated itself into the pleats of the *Rath*. The body of the ship exploded first, leaving for a terrible moment only the wings flying through space, unattached, before they too were caught by the points of the scales and the plasma inside them blew up.

"That's it!" Kirk said, and the sound was much softer than the thought. Only McCoy and Spock heard him.

Spock looked at him, but didn't have to ask.

"Look at the hull plates," Kirk said, pointing. "They're bent."

Seemingly impregnable moments ago, the fifty-foot plates of Zennor's ship were scored and misshapen where the patrollers had stricken them, but most important, they were peeled back several feet—several meters even.

And under there, he could see the faintest shimmer of bare hull.

Bare *unshielded* hull.

"That's it, that's our target . . . there it is—"

He started to step down to the command arena again, when, overhead, one of the repair crew fell out and landed on his back across the command chair, then rolled off, stunned.

Kirk picked him up roughly, then looked up. "Come down from there! Is that secure?"

"Yes, sir!" another repairman called as he and another one scurried down and folded the ladder.

"Then get out of here."

"Aye, sir!"

He stepped up to his chair, littered now with insulation crumbs and sharp bits of ceiling material that hadn't been cleaned off yet. Eventually somebody would come up here and vacuum it up. For now, he would sit on chips and fuzz.

"Sir, General Kellen's ship is no longer under thrust," Spock reported. "We are free to tow."

"I don't want to tow him anymore. Bring him out behind us and drop him."

"Sir?"

"And bring the tractor beams to bear on the forward points of those hull plates. Pick up as many as you can without reducing tractor capacity. Then I want to heel back and peel those plates up on whatever they have for hinges."

Spock thought about this for a moment, then said, "May I ask your intentions?"

"Yes, you can. We're going to fire straight down into the cracks."

The bridge crew blinked at him for a moment.

He glanced at each of them, waved his hands, and snapped, "Do you understand?"

"Yes, sir!" Byers said, and licked a bleeding lip.

"Aye aye, sir!" Donnier nodded furiously.

"Complying," Spock responded. He brushed crumbs of hull material off his console, then looked again at Kirk and waited for the order.

"Concentrate three-quarters from the aft end of the ship. I want to target the area of Zennor's original ship. That's where I think the command center still is."

"Aye aye, sir."

"I'm ready, sir."

"Ready also, sir."

Kirk settled into his chair, on top of the chips and the fuzz and the grit. "Haul away, Mr. Spock. Mr. Donnier . . . prepare to open fire."

"I'm ready, s-sir."

"Fire."

As the tractor beams strained and the impulse engines thrust furiously to pull back the scales of the *Rath,* one at a time, the ship's volleys of phaser fire opened up the bared hull between the sheared-back plates.

Cutting like a surgeon's lasers into the underskin of the *Rath,* the phasers immediately gave Kirk gratification. Sparks, hull matter, and atmospheric gases spewed past the starship and out into space.

"Shields are fluctuating, sir," Chekov reported. "The tractor beam is compromising deflector power consumption."

"We don't have any options, Mr. Chekov. Maintain."

Zennor's ship let loose another whip of glowing power, thudding the *Enterprise* viciously, but this wasn't the time to do anything but lie close and take the heat.

The tractor beams howled now, drawing power and arguing with the shields.

"Shut down aft shields," Kirk instructed. "Forward shields only. Keep pulling . . . full traction . . . good . . . maintain fire."

Would the inner hull on Zennor's ship give first, or

would the starship's shields go? There was no way to judge that. It was a night at the gambling tables.

Plate after plate, the *Enterprise* chewed her way across the *Rath*'s acres-wide hull, phaser fire burrowing between them and causing plumes of matter to erupt from in there. The big dark ship slid away and fell off its position, and he sensed that he knew where the havoc was right now. A dreadnought designed for invasion, vastly powerful, but untested in real battle, and a crew who had heard their whole lives about their destiny to invade but had never done any such thing, today were both finding out that plans and hopes alone do not serve. They had strength, delivered by the resources of a whole civilization, but they had no strategy, for they had never before needed one.

As the ruptures between the peeled-back scales began some serious billowing and gushing, Zennor's ship opened up again with another engulfing salvo of the burning power, and the *Enterprise* rocked hard to her starboard side, throwing everyone down hard. Not one of the bridge personnel was able to stay off the deck.

Kirk saw the bridge whirl around him, then blinked and found himself crushed into the crease between the upper and lower decks, under the rail on the starboard side. More smoke and sparks and putrid fluids and gases spewed all around him.

He reached up, caught the rail, hauled himself up, and instantly looked for Spock.

The Vulcan was on his hands and knees on the deck, slowly raising one hand and searching for the edge of his console.

"Spock, wait," Kirk said, and forced himself up there. "Slowly."

He got a good grip on Spock and took much of the Vulcan's weight as they both found their balance on a deck now tilted nearly forty degrees.

"Thank you, Captain," Spock wheezed, choked with pain again.

"Sit down and stay down. Don't get up again."

"Thank you." The first officer gladly settled into his now-dusty chair and closed his eyes for a moment, not caring that he had repeated himself.

"Stop thanking me," Kirk muttered.

"Captain, the weapons!" Donnier called, without a stammer. "We've lost weapons power! We can't shoot!"

"Confirm that, engineering." Whirling in the other direction, Kirk dropped again to the middle deck.

"Confirmed, sir!" Davis called over the surging howl of ruptured system.

"Not now . . . continue traction. Keep peeling those plates back. Bones, hail Kellen again."

"Kellen . . . yes, sir." McCoy swung around and almost lost his footing on the tipping deck, but waved away the smoke and found the same buttons he'd found before. "Ship to ship, Captain."

"General, do you have weapons power?"

"You were shooting. Keep shooting."

"I can't. My weapons are off-line. How are yours?"

"Mine are on, but I have no engine thrust."

"You don't need thrust for what I have in mind."

"You want me to do what you say? You want Klingon commanders to do your bidding?"

Kirk glared at the main screen as if at Kellen's face and imagined the general standing before him and expecting something spectacular.

All right. Fine.

"Yes, I want you all to do my bidding. I will take care of this problem for you, but I want senior authority, clearance to act on my own judgment, and absolution from any breakage of treaty until the *Enterprise* is safely on the other side of the Federation Neutral Zone, or I veer off right now and leave you to the Havoc. It's your turn to cooperate, General. I want you to make me Commodore of the Klingon Fleet."

Chapter Twenty-one

He refused to ask again. He let Kellen hang out there, without engine power, staring at the monolithic threat of the invasion dreadnought, and he bided his time.

"I concur."

Kirk gave his command chair a victorious pounding on the arm. "I accept. Inform your commanders."

"They know."

"Good. My first order to them is that they cease random fire and prepare for coordinated strafing with specific targets, on my orders only. I want you to divert all your power to weapons and stand by while I attempt one last time to talk to Zennor."

"Talk? You're going to talk again?"

"Yes, I'm going to talk," Kirk roiled indignantly, "I'm going to talk and you're not going to question me anymore. You have your orders. McCoy, hail Zennor and hail him good."

McCoy didn't respond, but jabbed at the communications board in what seemed childlike confusion, then looked up and shrugged with his eyes. "Channel's open, Captain."

He didn't add the implied *I think.*

Gnashing his teeth, Kirk felt his brows go down as he glowered at the *Rath,* the early fortress.

"Zennor, this is Commodore Kirk of the combined forces of the United Federation of Planets and the Klingon Imperial Fleet. I know you can hear me. We've discovered a weakness in your armaments and I'm about to launch an assault against it. I give you one more chance to stand down and let me try to explain to you exactly what it is that you're acting upon. Legends and folklore over five thousand years old, stories told to children to frighten them into behavior . . . the stuff that ignorant people allow themselves to believe because they haven't learned any better. We've learned better . . . and now we have a chance to mend the wrong done to your civilization by people who are strangers to all of us."

His words rang, and tension set in. The *Rath* hung out there, several of its hull petals torn backward, bent up out of place, rupturing the floral symmetry of the huge conical hull.

"I'm offering you one last chance to build instead of wreck. Isn't that what you've wanted all along?"

Over the open channel came only the faint clicking and crackle of distant damage, of voices barely more than echoes calling out to each other in frantic desperation. So it was only bare hull in there after all and he had been right. There was a chink in the armor of the damned.

Changing the timber of his voice to something he reserved for other captains, he simply requested, "State your intentions."

Then all would know, and all duties would be clear.

He waited.

Under his skin he sensed Zennor's eyes, watching the *Enterprise* just as now he watched the *Rath,* peering at each other over the short gap of space, the long gap of time, wondering if the weaknesses they saw in each other were real, and if the time to crow was over.

"We will build."

Hope flared and Kirk leaned forward. Zennor's voice was underlaid by the groan of damage over there, the whoop of alarms, and the frantic voices of the alien crew.

"Upon the ruined cities of the conquerors' children, we will build our rightful place. There is no giving up. History renews itself and breathes life into the doomed. This is the Battle of Garamanus. This is our place and we will defend it. First we will smash the Klingon civilization, and then we will come for yours."

The flare guttered and sank away. Kirk sighed, shook his head, pressed his lips flat, but there wasn't anything else to say.

"I regret . . . it has to be you," Zennor added then. *"I did not expect to like the conqueror."*

The station-sized ship began to hum and glow again in a now-recognizable process of building to open fire.

Kirk nodded as if Zennor could actually see him. "I'm sorry too."

He motioned for McCoy to close channels.

"Kirk to Kellen. Brace yourselves and prepare to open fire."

"Ready."

"Mr. Donnier, tractor beams. Mr. Byers, full power to thrust. Let's pull that ship apart. General, open fire."

The starship whined and dug in its heels, pit-bulling the hull plates of the *Rath* up two by two. The Klingon ship blasted photon salvos with accuracy down into the grooves left exposed as each plate was squalled backward. The blue balls of energy plowed straight down inside, to detonate deep in the grooves, pounding the inner hull of the *Rath* to bits and sending destructive explosions ricocheting around in there.

Kirk crimped his eyes in empathy. He knew what was happening to the interior of the *Rath*. But there was also a naughty I-told-you-so swelling in his chest, and that was the feeling he grabbed on to for stability.

Zennor's ship glowed and vaulted another heavy attack at the *Enterprise* and Kellen's ship.

The bridge lights flashed, then went out completely for

a moment, leaving only the bright glow of the main screen and the scene on it. A moment later, small emergency lights came on along the deck and about halfway around the ceiling area, just enough to work by. Around him the crew's faces were sculpted to the bones by hellish red lights from below and creamy yellow lights from above, the hollows of their eyes made deep by shadows and their noses and chins turned to sickles.

"Captain, shields just fell!" the relief engineer called. "We've got no protection anymore."

"Spock, confirm that."

"Confirmed, sir. No shield power left at all."

"Perfect. If they hit us again, it's all over."

"Sir," the engineer called again, "Mr. Scott says we've lost the conduits to the warp drive. The engines are good, but we can't engage them. We'll need twenty minutes to reestablish."

"We've still got impulse, correct?"

"Yes, sir, we've got that."

"Understood. General Kellen, maintain fire. Attention, Klingon fleet. All available ships begin strafing maneuvers now. Come in at full impulse speed. Target specified areas of weakness between the abutting ends of the plates."

Zennor's ships built to fire again and tried to pick off the Klingon ships as they rushed in like streaks of light, but at high speed they were better able to avoid the washing yellow-purple energy blasts, or at least to take only glancing blows. Two Klingon cruisers were slammed out of the way in the first attack, but others made it through and hammered the exposed inner skin of the *Rath* with blunt photons.

The Fury ship started to move, to fall away, trying to gain some room, but the *Enterprise* stayed with it, and Kellen's ship continued to fire down into the fissures caused as the starship pulled up petal after petal.

The bridge crackled and fumed with new damage, but the starship kept working. Kirk imagined the flurry belowdecks to keep the systems on-line long enough to succeed. Engineers would be tripping over damage-control parties, who would be stepping between clean-up crews. Everybody was hustling today.

"Sir, they're starting to pitch," Byers called out over the whistle of a leak on the port side.

Before them Zennor's huge vessel began to tip downward and to roll sideways, bucking and twisting like an elk trying to throw off a clinging bobcat, but Kirk wouldn't call off. Zennor didn't have tractor beams and his technology hadn't anticipated them. That was why this could work.

"Look!" Donnier choked, and pointed.

"Flux emanations are off the scale, sir!" Chekov sang out, and also looked at the main screen.

Zennor's ship, the whole vast length and breadth of it, was beginning to glow, but not like before. This glow came from inside, shining out of the edges of all the petals in the wide midsection, bright neon yellowish white, and it was expanding through the ship, spilling forward under the plates. Several of the plates were blown completely off as the violence traveled.

"Building up to overload," Spock concluded as he looked at his sensor screen. Sharply he looked up. "Detonation any moment now."

Nobody had to tell Kirk that. Halfway across the galaxy or not, he knew a main power core meltdown when he saw one.

"Mr. Byers, full about! Ship to ship—General, we're evacuating. Notify your fleet to clear the area at high warp. Broadcast long-range warnings—"

"We have no thruster power. You go, Captain Kirk, and we will continue firing until we all are a ball of fire. We will personally take that demon ship to its own prophecy!"

"They don't need an escort. Donnier, shift tractor beams to the general's ship."

"Shifting beams, sir."

"We'll tow you out of the immediate impact range, General. With full shields you should be able to survive the blast."

"Use your warp speed to get away, Kirk. All warriors die."

"Yes," Kirk said. "But it's my turn today, not yours. Our shields are down and we've lost warp maneuvering power. We can't get far enough away from here to survive without shields."

The crew tried to keep their faces still, but their postures were revealing. Kirk was careful not to turn his head, so none would feel lessened in his captain's eyes, even as he spoke of their impending deaths.

The best crew in Starfleet. Didn't mean they were icicles. He regretted not coming up with a word or two of shallow comfort. They needed to hear that in his voice, but he had none. The only gift he could give them was that they would die while saving others.

"We can tow you to safe range and your shields will protect you." He glanced around at the sweaty faces of his crew and noted how young they all were. "Everybody has to die sometime. At least we're dying for a good reason."

"Idiot." Kellen's insult was almost warm. *"Do you think you're dying today? Shields on extension mode."*

As the two ships drew away from the *Rath* at painfully slow speed, the Fury ship glowed brighter and rolled in space furiously now. More and more hull plates blew off as explosions tore through the inner core. A moment later, the point of the horn-shaped bow blew off, leaving a shorn stump through which plasma and radiation boiled freely into space.

"Captain," Spock began, "General Kellen's ship has extended their shields around us."

"That stretches him too thin," Kirk commented, but didn't bother to call Kellen.

As he looked from Spock to the main screen again, the *Rath* reached its critical mass. The hull plates blew off all over it.

Then, an explosion the size of a continent erupted across open space, devouring the purple structure until nothing could be seen but tumbling plates, spraying matter and energy, and bright incendiary destruction.

Shock waves rocked the starship and the battle cruiser, shoving them bodily backward through space. Kirk clung to his chair as pressure hit him hard and artificial gravity on the ship crushed him toward the deck as it tried to compensate.

The *Enterprise* went up on a side, almost ninety degrees. The crew tumbled, but they knew what to grab for and managed to pull themselves into place as the deck began to right.

The Klingon shields crackled and sparked around both ships, but held. Wave upon wave of energy plied space across them in a vast sphere.

Kirk waved at the electrical smoke and blinked as it burned his eyes. On the screen, the Fury ship was gone.

Hell had gone to hell.

What is death but parting breath?

—"MacPherson's Rant,"
a folk song

Epilogue

"SECURE FROM RED ALERT. Establish contact with the shuttlecraft and have them report on any rescues and return to the ship as soon as possible. We need a damage-control party on the bridge."

The bridge gasped and spat around them, but there was a sense of control again. Pausing to cough out the acrid smoke that was tickling his lungs, James Kirk prowled his bridge and checked on his people one by one. In their sweat-streaked faces he saw the charity they offered him for the decision he had been forced to make, their willingness to do it all again if necessary, and a respect he found somehow saddening.

One by one they assured him they were all right and would now begin the slow process of piecing together the damaged systems that had brought them through all this alive.

There wasn't one of them who would jump ship at the next dock after all this. These were the kind of people who discovered themselves better for having fielded mortal danger. No matter the fright, they hadn't crouched scared or shrunk from the face of it or let it petrify them out of doing their jobs. Not even Donnier and Byers, who had found themselves in the wrong place at the wrong time, doing things they'd never imagined they would have to do. But if the ship had been wrecked under them, they'd have died with their hands on the halyards. That was something to write home about.

One by one he congratulated them, and finally made it around to Spock.

"Mr. Spock."

"Captain."

"Final analysis?"

"Zennor's ship has been completely decimated. Their dreadnought attachment was apparently a massive power factory, and once unshielded and ignited . . ."

Spock paused and shook his head, communicating silently the ferocity of such a chain reaction.

"I am certain it was very quick," he added.

Gratefully, Kirk made a small, inadequate nod. "Thank you. But Zennor made his own choice. I'm sorry it had to happen, but I won't blame myself."

Spock seemed relieved by that. "Both the shuttlecraft *Columbia* and *Galileo* are on final approach, and both report having picked up survivors from several Klingon lifepods. *Galileo* reports she's towing what may be a lifepod from Zennor's ship, but there are no life signs aboard."

"I want to have a look at that. Tell them not to open it until I get there."

"Yes, sir."

"Captain," McCoy interrupted, using his good hand to hold the communications earpiece to his ear. "General Kellen's requesting permission to come aboard."

Kirk glanced at him. "Fine. But tell him to come unarmed this time and expect to be under armed escort at all times."

McCoy paled at having to tell that to a Klingon general, but turned back to the board.

"Captain," Spock went on, "I have also picked up telemetry broadcast by Zennor just prior to the final explosion, but it has not been sorted out yet. The signals were scrambled and quite complex."

"Telemetry? Meant for us?"

"No, sir. I believe he meant it for broadcast back to his own people."

"Do you think the message got through?"

Spock canted his head to the side, then winced and straightened it again. "No way to tell. I know it was successfully broadcast, but there was no evidence that the fissure opened to receive it. Still, their technology is largely an unknown."

"See if you can make any sense of it. I'll be on the flight deck. Have the general brought there when he comes aboard. McCoy, with me. And, Spock . . . thank you again."

Spock clasped his hands behind his back, a casual motion considering his condition. "My pleasure to serve, Captain. As always."

The flight deck was organized chaos. Well, havoc, to keep in the spirit of the occasion. The two newly returned shuttlecraft lay in the open rather than in their docking stalls, having just come in with their various acquired rescues and tows. Several Klingon lifepods littered the deck, in various conditions from pristine to burned and dented, unable even to sit on the deck without tilting.

Wounded Klingon soldiers, also in various conditions, sat or lay against every bulkhead. At first glance as he and McCoy entered, Kirk guessed there were over three hundred of them.

McCoy broke off immediately to collect reports from the dashing interns, nurses, and medics. Orderlies and ensigns moved about everywhere, passing out drinks and something to eat that made most of the Klingons sneer, but they were all eating whatever it was and trying to be polite.

Those who were conscious looked up at him suspiciously as he surveyed them and received reports from the shuttlecraft lieutenants. He saw in their eyes their fears, relying on rumors of the savagery inflicted by Starfleet on any prisoners of war. They didn't seem to have quite absorbed the fact that they were in fact allies for the moment and were in the care of their commodore.

"Lieutenant," Kirk greeted as the commander of the *Galileo* approached him with a manifest.

"Staaltenburg, sir."

"Yes, I remember. Eric."

"That's correct, sir."

"You're the one who reported picking up a pod from the big ship?"

"Yes, sir." Staaltenburg brushed his blond hair out of his eyes and led the way around to the other side of *Galileo,* where there lay a solid black pod without so much as a running light upon it. In the blackness of space, it would've been completely invisible if they hadn't been scanning for things about that size.

"We practically slammed into it, sir, before we realized it was there and wasn't an asteroid. I never heard of a lifepod that didn't want to be found. No life signs at all in there, by the way, sir. We've scanned it . . . no harmful rays or leaks, and there is an atmosphere in there, so it's properly pressurized. We can open it anytime you like."

"Do so."

Staaltenburg waved up two men who had been standing by, anticipating the order, who came in with phaser torches and went to work on the locking mechanism of the pod.

"Captain," Staaltenburg said then, and nodded toward the port side entryway.

Kirk turned.

General Kellen trundled toward him, flanked by two Starfleet Security guards.

"General," Kirk greeted, not particularly warmed up.

"Commodore. My men are being taken care of, I see," the wide Klingon said, glancing about at the rows of rescued soldiers. "I shall expect them to be completely cooperative."

"So far, so good," Kirk said.

Kellen faced him and looked over the tops of his glasses. "I congratulate you. You saved what is left of my fleet. You are the Kirk."

Unable to muster any mirth, the captain—commodore—bobbed his brows in response. He got a little jolt of satisfaction at being reinstalled as the resident buzzard of Starfleet.

"Thank you. You still have charges to face regarding the murder of a Starfleet serviceman and a guest of the Federation. Counsel will be provided if you require it."

Kellen made a small conciliatory bow. "I know. I shall face those charges boldly. I accept your offer of counsel, as it will go in my favor to have Federation lawyers speaking to a Federation court."

"Very wise, and probably true, General. There are considerable mitigating circumstances. Be forewarned that I take the death of my crewman very seriously and I intend to testify against you. However, I'll also testify that you stopped the assault on Capella Four and by doing that probably forestalled many other deaths. It'll be an interesting few months for us both, I think."

"I am ready. I confess that I do not understand what makes you humans fight. You did destroy them after all, but even though I told you what these people were, it took you a very long time to decide to act."

"On the contrary," Kirk pointed out, "I decided not to act rashly. That too is a decision. You were right about who they were, but you were wrong about *what* they were. No one is inherently evil. That comes only from the choices we make and the actions we take."

"Perhaps." Kellen's small eyes twinkled. "I wish you people would fight against us. What a grand war we could have!"

Kirk leered at him, now somewhat amused in spite of everything. He felt an unbidden grin pull at his cheeks. "Maybe someday, General."

"Sir!" Staaltenburg called. "It's open."

Kirk glanced around the vast, high-halled flight deck. "McCoy! Over here."

He waited for the doctor to join them, then nodded to Staaltenburg. "Go ahead, Lieutenant."

Together, Staaltenburg and the two other crewmen hauled open a very thick hatch on the black pod. There was no light inside, but only a slight gush of atmosphere as the pod equalized.

"Get a light," Staaltenburg ordered, and one of the crewmen passed him a handheld utility light.

The crewmen, the general, the doctor, and the commodore pressed into a half-circle and huddled up before the open hatch.

"Well, I'll be damned," McCoy spouted.

The light cast a bright blue-white glow inside the pod. There, with tiny faces in many shapes, their bodies stuffed with memories, lay carefully stacked what must have been over a thousand linen poppets.

Kirk looked at McCoy.

"Rag dolls?" Staaltenburg blurted. "They bothered to save a bunch of rag dolls?"

They stood back from the hatch, contemplating what they saw there.

"You want me to have these disposed of, sir?" the lieutenant offered, clearly aggravated that he'd gone to the trouble of capturing and towing in a pod that turned out to be stuffed with stuffed dolls.

Kirk gazed into the bubble of tiny sojourners and remembered a moment, a conversation, that might have flowered into something very good, had the past not thrown out its tripwire.

"No, Lieutenant. I want these carefully catalogued, then permanently stored in airtight containers. It's a trust I owe to a friend."

Staaltenburg frowned, then shrugged. "As you wish, sir."

The lieutenant and his men moved off to follow their assignment, and McCoy was watching Kirk. He was the only one who understood the strange order, and Kirk found comfort in that.

"Very nice, Captain," the doctor offered. "I don't know what else we can do."

"If that door ever opens again," Kirk said, "we may need a peace offering. And their families will want to . . . have those."

McCoy nodded. "Zennor would be glad to know you picked them up, Jim. In spite of everything, I believe that."

"Captain," Staaltenburg called from the bulkhead, and motioned at the comm unit. "Mr. Spock, sir."

McCoy followed as Kirk headed over to the port side, both of them a little too aware of that pod back there.

"Kirk here."

"Spock, sir," the baritone voice came through. *"I have translated the telemetry. The message was launched at nearly warp twenty-five. I had believed such speed impossible, but they have somehow overcome that. I remind you there is still no way to know whether or not the message went through the fissure or will travel on its own to the other side of the galaxy."*

"Go ahead, Mr. Spock. I think I'm beyond surprises."

"I hope so, sir. The message is from Zennor himself. It states, 'The Battle of Garamanus is lost. We have not survived, but this is our rightful place. Try again.'"

The

Invasion

Continues

in

BOOK TWO

The Soldiers of Fear

The message from Starfleet had been curt. Assemble the senior officers. Prepare for a Security One message at 0900. Picard hadn't heard a Security One message since the Borg were headed for Earth. The highest level code. Extreme emergency. Override all other protocols. Abandon all previous orders.

Something serious had happened.

He leaned over the replicator. He had only a moment until the senior officers arrived.

"Earl Grey, hot," he said, and the empty space on the replicator shimmered before a clear glass mug filled with steaming tea appeared. He gripped the mug by its warm body, slipping his thumb through the handle, and took a sip, allowing the liquid to calm him.

He had no clue what this might be about and that worried him. He always kept abreast of activity in the quadrant. He knew the subtlest changes in the political breeze. The Romulans had been quiet of late; the Cardassians had been cooperating with Bajor. No new ships had been sighted in any sector, and no small rebel groups were taking their rebellions into space. Maybe it was the Klingons?

He should have had an inkling.

His door hissed open and Beverly Crusher came in. Geordi La Forge was beside her. Data followed. The doctor and Geordi looked worried. Data had his usual look of expectant curiosity.

The door hadn't even had a chance to close before Deanna Troi came in. She was in uniform, a habit she had started just recently. Worf saw her and left his post on the bridge, following her to his position in the meeting room.

Only Commander Riker was missing and he was needed. Picard waited anxiously.

It was 0859.

Then the door hissed a final time and Will Riker entered. His workout clothes were sweat streaked, his hair damp. Over his shoulder he had draped a towel, which he instantly took off and wadded in a ball in his hand.

"Sorry, sir," he said, "but from your voice, I figured I wouldn't have time to change."

"You were right, Will," Picard said. "We're about to get a message from Starfleet Command. They requested that all senior officers be in attendance—"

The viewer on the captain's desk snapped on with the Federation's symbol, indicating a scrambled communiqué.

"Message sent to Picard, Captain, *U.S.S. Enterprise V,*" said the generic female computer voice. "Please confirm identity and status."

Picard placed a hand on the screen on his desk. "Picard, Jean-Luc, Captain, *U.S.S. Enterprise.* Security Code 1-B58A."

The computer beeped.

Picard's palms were damp. He grabbed his cup of tea, but the tea was growing cold. Still, he drank the rest, barely tasting the tea's bouquet.

When the security protocol ended, the Federation symbol disappeared from the screen, replaced by the battle-scarred face of Admiral Kirschbaum. His features had tightened in that emotionless yet urgent expression the oldest—and best—commanders had in times of emergency.

"Jean-Luc. We have no time for discussion. A sensor array at the Furies Point has been destroyed. Five ships of unknown origin are there now, along with what seems to be a small black hole. Two of the ships attacked the Brundage Station and we're awaiting word on the outcome. I'm ordering all available ships to the area at top speed."

The Furies Point. Picard needed no more explanation than that. From the serious expressions all around him, he could tell that his staff understood as well.

Picard's hand tightened on the empty glass mug. He set it down before he shattered it with his grip. "We're on our way, Admiral."

"Good." The admiral's mouth tightened. "I hope I don't have to explain—"

"I understand the urgency, Admiral."

"If those ships are what we believe them to be, we're at war, Jean-Luc."

How quickly it had happened. One moment he was on the bridge, preparing for the day's duties. The next, this.

"I will act accordingly, Admiral."

The admiral nodded. "You don't have much time, Jean-Luc. I will contact you in one hour with transmissions from the attack on the Brundage outpost. It will give you and your officers some idea of what you are facing."

"Thank you, Admiral," Picard said.

"Godspeed, Jean-Luc."

"And to you," Picard said, but by the time the words were out, the admiral's image had winked away.

Picard felt as if someone had punched him in the stomach.

The Furies.

The rest of the staff looked as stunned as he felt.

Except for Data. When Picard met his gaze, Data said quietly, "It will take us two point three-eight hours at warp nine to reach Brundage Station."

"Then lay in a course, Mr. Data, and engage. We don't have time to waste."

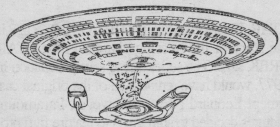